JULIANA SMITH

"Hilarious and heartwarming, Baggage Claim is rom-com gold."
– Lynn Painter, NYT Bestselling author.

"Baggage Claim is the perfect holiday romance. I really enjoyed this novel, it had it all: fake dating, some Christmas fun, a little bit of grumpy x sunshine, and some incredible healing and growth." – Abigail, Goodreads reviewer.

"This book showcases everything Juliana has to offer us as an indie author, and it's so exciting to see the love that's been given this story already! The depth of the characters, the cuteness, the banter, and the scenic setting are enough to keep any romance lover deeply invested in this story from beginning to end. " - Emma, Goodreads reviewer.

To my mom,
who loved to read but never got to see me become an author.

Copyright © 2022 by Juliana Smith

All rights reserved. No portion of this book may be reproduced in any form without written permission from the publisher or author, except as permitted by U.S. copyright law.

For permissions, contact authorjulianasmith@gmail.com

Cover by Sam Palencia at Ink and Laurel.

Editing by Alex Whitmarsh.

Proofread by Amanda Chaperon.

CONTENT WARNINGS: The main character of this book suffers from body dysmorphia and there are many manifestations of such throughout the story. Readers please be advised. We deserve to love our bodies, no matter what they look like, and Olive is a representation of that.

Contents

1. One   1
2. Two   10
3. Three   20
4. Four   25
5. Five   29
6. Six   39
7. Seven   45
8. Eight   55
9. Nine   63
10. Ten   70
11. Eleven   76
12. Twelve   82
13. Thirteen   95
14. Fourteen   102
15. Fifteen   111
16. Sixteen   121

17.	Seventeen	127
18.	Eighteen	133
19.	Nineteen	139
20.	Twenty	149
21.	Twenty-One	156
22.	Twenty-Two	165
23.	Twenty-Three	168
24.	Twenty-Four	182
25.	Twenty-Five	186
26.	Twenty-Six	191
27.	Twenty-Seven	201
28.	Twenty-Eight	205
29.	Twenty-Nine	215
30.	Thirty	219
31.	Thirty-One	224
32.	Thirty-Two	229
33.	Thirty-three	233
34.	Thirty-Four	236
35.	Thirty-Five	242
36.	Thirty-Six	246
37.	Thirty-Seven	255
38.	Thirty-Eight	260

39.	Thirty-Nine	264
40.	Forty	269
41.	Forty-One	273
42.	Forty-Two	276
43.	Forty-three	283
44.	Epilogue	288
Afterword		291
Also by		293
Acknowledgments		294
About Author		296

ONE
OLIVE

I used to say I didn't believe in fate. I always thought, ultimately, your choices—good or bad—controlled your destiny.

As it turned out, fate was tangible, and it was a bitch.

Currently, I was sitting in seat 15A, en route to see some of my least favorite people in my least favorite place. I could have picked any flight; there were a multitude of options when I booked the ticket. But fate led me here, to this particular one, squished in an uncomfortably tiny seat aboard an equally tiny plane that was most definitely going to fall apart seconds after takeoff.

Every November for the last three years when my mother called and gently asked, "*Don't you want to spend the holidays here? You don't want to be all alone on Christmas,*" I couldn't help but laugh. On the contrary, I absolutely *did* want to be alone on Christmas. In fact, all I wanted was to snuggle up on my couch in a sea of giant, fuzzy blankets, binge true crime documentaries, and devour an entire Costco rotisserie chicken by myself, sides and all.

My oversized tote bag was proving to be a poor choice on this budget airline. As I tried to shove it between my legs, it got stuck halfway. I gave it one more push, groaning as it snagged against the rough fabric of the chair and probably smashed the contents in the process. I hoped my YSL lipstick wasn't smushed or someone on this plane would feel my wrath.

"Just. Get. In. There," I spoke to myself, more aggravated the harder I pushed it. When it finally slid into place, I let out a deep breath and leaned back into my seat.

Ah, the joys of flying on the cheapest airline possible.

Between the musky smell of this plane and my nausea-inducing apprehension about going home, I felt the need to keep the barf bag in close vicinity—just in case. A dull ache formed between my brows from the overstimulation of noisy passengers and crying children. My fingers trembled in my lap, and a bead of sweat rolled between my shoulder blades at the thought of being trapped on this plane. Everything inside me screamed to get out of this seat *right now*.

Only a four-hour flight. Four hours. That's like watching eight episodes of The Office, *which is a typical binge session for me, no sweat.*

I took in my surroundings; there were pamphlets and brochures about the airline, along with some tiny orange earplugs and a prepackaged black eye mask shoved in the seatback in front of me. The tablet screen above it displayed a map with lines showing our flight path from Point A to Point B.

West Palm Beach, Florida to Aspen, Colorado.

What a dumb flight. What were you even supposed to wear? If you wore pants here, you would sweat so much that you'd have to wring your socks out. Judging by the smell of the plane, someone had already done so. If you wore shorts, you'd be freezing cold and have permanent goosebumps when you landed. With all of that in mind, I'd settled on athletic shorts and a tank top with many, many layers packed in my unreasonably large handbag.

My flight anxiety was creeping up on me, and I suddenly wished I had bought some of those *relaxing* gummies that everyone says to take before flying. The kind at gas stations that look like peach rings but would make you feel like you're in a circle with the *That '70s Show* crew.

If it was only the flight that I was concerned about, I wouldn't be this high-strung. But it was *who* I was headed to see that had my stomach in seized knots. I hadn't been in my right mind when my mom called me three weeks ago. She made it very clear she was worried about my *social calendar* when she texted me a screenshot of the WebMD page on scurvy, and then proceeded to tell me to eat an orange and open my blinds. So, I called her to confirm that I did, indeed, get enough vitamin c and my daily nutrients.

It was the day after Black Friday, and I had my phone on speaker as I sifted through my insurmountable pile of clothes and random household items that I certainly didn't have room for.

"Did I tell you that your dad just got a new grill? As if he is going to be out in 30-degree weather with a pack of steaks," Mom scoffed.

I folded a new top from Saks 5th Ave and set it aside. "No you didn't," *I mumbled, hardly paying attention as I sorted through the mounds of business attire I didn't even need since I worked from home.*

"Olive, dear...I'm worried about you down there. When's the last time you left the apartment?"

I looked at the shopping bags sprawled across the floor. Sephora, Urban Outfitters, and Nordstrom all stared back at me with judging eyes.

"I will have you know I was out all day yest—"

"Other than shopping."

I quickly snapped my lips closed. She knew me too well. "Well..."

"Honey, you need to get back out there. Have you heard of this app called Tender? Taylor was telling me you should go on there. Some very nice men would be glad to go out with you." I rolled my eyes and bit my lip, because *of* course *my sister-in-law told my mom I should be on a dating app.*

"First of all—it's Tinder. *Second of all—I don't need a stupid dating app."*

Her turn signal blinked in the background, filling the silence before she answered. "And why is that?"

Before I could think, before I could filter my words or stop my mouth from moving, I blurted, "Because I have a boyfriend."

I reached into the seatback compartment and grabbed the black eye mask, which was still wrapped. I fumbled with the plastic then placed the flimsy fabric over my head, surrounding myself with darkness in an attempt to drown out all other distractions.

You're on a sandy beach, drinking cosmos. There is no plane in sight, and you are certainly not about to see a sibling you haven't spoken to in years. You are a waterfall. A calm, ever-flowing, beautiful waterfall.

It turned out that, contrary to what Perry Como says, there is a place better than home for the holidays—and it's in West Palm Beach under a cabana with a blue frozen drink in my hand.

As my nerves slowly drifted away, there was a jolt in the seat next to me. *So much for being a waterfall.* A duffel bag hitting the hard seat on my right side shook me. Without lifting my mask, I slowly breathed in and out, not wanting to know who I would be stuck with as a seat partner. With my luck, it would be a large man who hadn't showered in days or an obnoxious teenager who wanted to cry on my shoulder about her first heartbreak. Maybe even someone who would try to show me their sleight of hand magic for four hours.

A low, masculine groan sounded beside me as the man attempted to shove his bag in the tiny overhead bin. While he struggled, jostling the seat and making an obscene amount of noise, my patience wore thin.

By the time he finally sat down, his shoulder bumping against mine in the process, any composure I had left was gone. My leg bounced rhythmically, and I picked at the fraying hem of my shorts.

"Anxious flier?"

The deep voice resonated beside me, and as someone who listened to podcasts regularly, I could appreciate a good rich voice.

"Yup."

My tone was clipped, no doubt seeming rude. But, I needed this guy to know he did not have permission to talk my ear off for the next four hours. I had to let him know upfront that I had no interest in conversations that went further than, "Hello, how are you?" Like when you dig in your purse in Target to avoid speaking to your OB-GYN.

"You should have pregamed in the airport bar. You could be riding a nice buzz right now instead of thinking of everything wrong with the plane."

Oh God, was there something wrong with the plane?

"Mhm, sure."

I leaned my head back into the seat, probably ruining my perfectly styled blonde hair. I had a blowout yesterday and should've known this would happen. Rookie mistake. My fists were tightly bound on the small armrests, blood rising to my face.

"Or you could have smoked a little right before."

My ears felt hot, and I bounced my leg faster. *Who did this guy think he was?*

He continued. "Maybe eat a little pot brownie or something?"

I abruptly lifted my mask in frustration. "Look, dude, I—" Oh. *Oh.*

My complaints died on the tip of my tongue when I caught sight of the man sitting next to me.

He was gorgeous; the thick waves of his dark brown hair were perfectly placed, and his full lips were tilted in a mischievous smirk. His eyes reminded me of rich, dark chocolate on the outer circle and warm caramel in the center. Like a Ghirardelli square calling my name in the middle of a Keto diet. His long legs, which looked uncomfortably squished in these Smurf-sized seats, were clad in black sweatpants. My eyes surveyed his lean body, cataloging his big hands and the way his chest filled out his army green tee with just the right amount of muscle.

If this were a few years ago, I may have taken the opportunity to charm a man like this and possibly try to join the mile-high club. However, I was long past those admittedly wild days, so for now I admired him from afar. Or I guess, not so far given the tiny size of these seats.

"I am doing just fine, thank you," I said, my voice hushed and gruff.

He huffed out an amused breath, nodding his head, and looked down at his phone. A cute, barely five-foot-tall flight attendant made her way by our row, stopping directly next to us.

"Can I get you anything?" Her voice was suggestive to the man beside me, and I couldn't help but roll my eyes. I couldn't blame her though; I'd never met a J-Crew model look alike either. Besides, I was pretty sure flight attendants weren't supposed to be doing any services until we're in the air.

"Actually, yes, Ms…" He leaned forward to take a look at her name tag. "Victoria. Can you get me and my new friend a couple of the strongest drinks we can legally purchase?"

She murmurs, low enough to be considered suggestive instead of professional. With a small frame and wide eyes, she reminded me of Bambi. "Of course, we can do a sample bottle of Jack Daniels and bring you a couple of Coke cans?"

I grumbled, "Aren't you supposed to do that *after* we're in flight?"

Bambi took her eyes from the man over to me, "I can always make an exception." She glanced back at him and smiled. Gross.

"Ahh. Perfect, thank you, honey." He winked her way and made a clicking noise in his cheek.

Ugh, flirt. And a shameless one, judging by how quickly he jumped from me to her.

He settled back in his seat and lifted his muscular arms behind his head. When he did so, his scent wafted my way. He smelled of clean laundry with a hint of mint coming from whatever brand of gum he was chewing between his gorgeous teeth.

"So, what's bringing you to Aspen?"

I was certainly not in the mood to talk, but I doubt this guy cared. It seemed like whether I was chatty or not, he would keep going. Maybe I'd be better holding a mirror and he could keep the conversation to himself.

"I'm staying there for the holidays." I purposefully did not ask him why he was going; judging by his looks, he was probably there for some kind of model ski shoot or to star in one of those Hallmark Christmas movies. I turned my head to the tiny window to see the lights from the airport shining down on the workers loading different pieces of luggage and preparing us for takeoff.

"Well, I've lived there for years, so I can tell you all the best places to go to."

I let out a rough chuckle. "Yeah, I'm good." The man's facial expression was amusing, both shocked and confused that I was not interested in whatever he had to say. It was clear he wasn't used to being told *no.*

"Come on, flying isn't that bad. And you're going to a pretty cool place; you'll want to know all the fun things to do."

His smile was warm and charming, inviting me in like a warm heater on a cold, rainy day. I shook my head, snapping myself from the trance his handsome face had put me in, and said, "I've been there plenty of times. Trust me, I will be fine."

He raised his eyebrow curiously but didn't respond. When the flight attendant returned with our drinks, the stranger happily took them from her and pulled down both of our trays.

"I didn't get to introduce myself. I'm Finn."

He extended his hand, and I reluctantly shook it. The warmth of his firm grip spread through my palm.

"Olive," I quietly introduced myself, more anxious about talking to him and less about the flight and my destination.

Finn poured our drinks into the tiny Styrofoam cups and held one out to me. I grabbed mine, but before I could chug it in a hopeful buzz, he lifted his cup in a toast.

"To the red-eye."

TWO
FINN

I was always blessed with good luck, which is how I ended up sitting next to a pretty girl on a long flight with a Jack and Coke in hand. I was also blessed with good looks (plenty of thanks to my personal trainer Josh at Workout 24/7 on that part), but I couldn't help but notice that Olive was seemingly immune to my flirtation. It was disappointing but also refreshing, no point in wasting my time trying to charm the pants off this one—she was making it completely obvious she was not interested. Shame for her, I was what some of my mom's friends considered a "catch," according to her Facebook posts.

I relaxed in my snug seat and took a sip of the rather strong drink brought to me by the tiny flight attendant. Meanwhile, it was obvious that Olive didn't want to talk, but her bouncing leg and shaky hands picking at her shorts told me she needed a distraction.

"So, you said you've been to Aspen a good bit?"

She puffed out a breath. "I grew up there. Haven't been in a while." Her tone was brief, signaling me to not ask further questions. A hint I clearly did not care about.

"I see. So, you're going to visit family? They're probably excited to see you."

Olive sipped on her drink and looked out the window before answering. "I guess so."

I wanted to chuckle at the girl's poor spirit. I couldn't remember the last time a woman had been so annoyed to be in my presence. Maybe never?

The familiar *ding* came over the speakers in the plane, signaling everyone to take their seats and buckle up. After a few minutes, the plane slowly pushed back from the gate.

I had not taken this specific flight before, but I had flown quite often, and I was used to the familiar movement of takeoff. Flying to see my parents for the holidays extra early this year had not been ideal. Taking off work this close to Christmas was a menace, but they decided to go on a two-week cruise during the holidays, so it was either see them early or don't see them at all. I spent a week with them in West Palm at their short-term rental. We ate homemade pizza and charcuterie boards for "Christmas dinner," but I didn't mind. For the real holiday, I'd be back home in Aspen. Snowy mountains, steep slopes, and hot chocolate so good you would think Buddy the Elf made it.

The plane taxied out to the airstrip and sped up, the wheels lifting off the runway. The weightless sensation settled along my bones as the plane shot into the sky. Next to me, Olive had her head down, her straight hair covering her eyes. As we reached higher altitudes, my ears familiarly popped as they did on every flight, the chewing gum helping to alleviate the pain. With the way Olive's hands aggressively gripped the armrests, I could tell she didn't expect it.

I pointed my finger out the window where we were rising above the city lights in hopes of distracting her.

"It's crazy how fast this plane can go." Olive turned her head slightly to the window and then immediately back in front of her.

I continued, "It's like a city full of ants now. Man, we're getting up here pretty quick. I bet we're already at ten thousand feet, huh?" When she didn't respond, I kept talking. I pointed out big landmarks that now seemed like tiny pins on a map. "It's like the city lights are stars. I didn't expect a plane this size to take off so fast. I hope they've got some good engines for this thing. You know what they say about plane crash—"

"*Please* stop talking," Olive interrupted me. Her anxiety toward flying was amusing, and I couldn't help but push her buttons a little more. I didn't bring any entertainment for the flight and watching her squirm next to me was kind of cute.

"Think about it this way, if we crash, there's that cool evacuation slide we could go down."

"Are you going to be like this the whole way?" she asked. "Because if so, I'm going to need about four more of these." She gave the drink in her hand another swirl then brought it to her lips and took a large gulp. How high we were didn't seem to be the only thing bothering her. She kept checking her phone every few minutes like she was waiting for communication from someone, even though we had no service. An airline this cheap had no in-flight wi-fi so I wasn't sure why she kept reaching to check it.

"It's not just this flight that's got you anxious, is it?"

Olive turned to me, and I got a closer look at her. As her deep green, doe eyes met mine, I took notice of her bright blonde hair framing her heart-shaped face. Her freckled cheeks were flushed, presumably from the alcohol missing from her half-empty cup. She wore very little makeup, and the fresh-faced look was definitely something I liked on this girl.

"Is it that obvious?" The quiet words slipped from her full, rosebud lips.

I wasn't sure what exactly was bothering her but there was no way this was her first flight, judging by her fancy luggage and the fact that she was familiar with the code on when we were allowed to drink in flight.

"So, what is it that's got you so high-strung?" I typically wasn't nosy, but this girl brought out a curiosity in me that I didn't know I possessed.

"It's just..." she started reluctantly. "It's been a few years since I've been home. The thought of being in the same town as some of my family is terrifying, let alone the same house."

I nod my head in understanding, although it wasn't like I could relate. I saw my parents every chance I could. Both my mom and dad are incredible. While I was growing up, they attended every sports event and awards banquet. Since I'm an only child, they made sure they cheered the loudest everywhere we went. After they both retired, they moved to Florida while I stayed in Colorado and moved to a bigger city. They spent all their time on the beach or traveling, so we usually didn't get to see each other on holidays.

"Well, let's get you another drink and we can watch something to distract you. I bet they've got all kinds of Christmas movies."

I tapped on the screen in front of me in an attempt to find a holiday film. Olive groaned next to me. "Ugh. No Christmas movies, please." *What?* This chick was crazy.

"It's two weeks before Christmas and you don't want to watch *The Grinch*?"

"Nope."

"*Christmas Vacation?*"

"Ew."

"*Home Alone?*"

"No, thanks. Child services needed to intervene on that one."

"*Elf?*"

"Ugh, absolutely not. The cotton ball scene alone makes me sick."

"You are insane. I don't think I'm going to last this plane ride. How can you not like any Christmas movies?"

Olive shrugged her shoulders and tilted her head to look at the list of movies.

"Fine. We can watch this one." Her hand moved to the screen and began tapping away, pulling up the *Harry Potter* series. She pressed play on *Sorcerer's Stone,* and I rolled my eyes.

"This is *not* a Christmas movie."

She gave me a look of disgust and handed me a pair of headphones from the below compartment. "It definitely is, and if you don't like it, you can sit somewhere else." She turned her nose up like a brat.

"That's not how airplanes work. You're stuck with me."

She scoffed and pushed the headphones into my lap. I ignored the way her soft hands spread warmth down my body as she brushed against my arm in the process.

"Well, you're stuck watching *Harry Potter*."

Olive was as stubborn as she was pretty, and I couldn't decide if it pissed me off or turned me on. Maybe both. She had this attitude that told me she got everything she wanted, exactly the way she wanted. That, or at least she'd put up a good fight before giving in.

We each ordered another drink and put on our headphones. Every now and then I would tap her shoulder and ask a question about the scarred wizard on the screen. Each time she would roll her eyes, but always answered. Eventually, she'd tell me things before I even had the chance to ask, pulling back my headphones to whisper in my ear as the rest of the plane slept.

Halfway through, we ordered another drink, our third of the evening. Three turned into four, and although I was pretty sure it was illegal to be drunk on a plane, Olive and I were definitely tipsy.

"Do you think you'd catch the golden snitch?" She hiccupped in a cute squeak, and I nodded my head. The cabin seemed to be very floaty.

"Heck yeah! I'd catch that thing midair with nothing but my bare hands." I hadn't watched this movie in years, and I didn't recognize most of the scenes, but it was adorable listening to her tell me all the details. In her alcohol-ridden state, Olive was an open book. She was sharing things with me that she no doubt wouldn't have dreamed of saying only a couple of hours before. It was like a kid confessing their deepest secret after getting their wisdom teeth pulled. Meanwhile, I was just the local dentist who enjoyed the town drama.

"So, what are you all worried about seeing your family for, anyway? Are they in a cult or something?"

"Um, no."

"Did they leave a sibling for the circus?"

"Why would—"

"Maybe a cousin who eats whole sticks of butter?"

"What—no. Are you okay? What kind of people do you hang out with?"

I shrugged, and the movement made the plane...swirly. "I watched a lot of *My Strange Addiction* growing up."

Olive's lips tucked in like she was holding in a laugh, and I smiled down at her. "But really, what could be *so* bad for you to be this nervous to see them?"

Her cheeks flushed and her pupils dilated like she sobered up for a second. "It's just been so long at this point it's weird. Everyone there has another half and it's like each time I talk to them, they have this pity for me. For being alone. It's not a great time for me, so I'm not thrilled at the idea for the next two weeks."

I nodded my head and put my eyes back on the movie, although I couldn't quite pay enough attention to comprehend the scenes. Olive's answer didn't sit right with me, and I felt the need to push her buttons just a little more.

"andimighthavemadeupafakeboyfriend..."

Apparently, I had more to drink than I thought. I must have misheard her. "You what?"

"I may have told them that my boyfriend is coming..." I quickly decided I didn't like the word *boyfriend* leaving her lips. "But I don't have a boyfriend," she muttered, and this time I couldn't hold in my cackle. I was pretty sure I snorted somewhere in my laughter. I also knew our entire plane hated us.

"Why would you make up a fake boyfriend?" Surely it would've been easy for her to get a guy to come with her.

"My mom has convinced herself I'm a hermit crab and that I will die an old cat lady. And something in me just clicked and I let it slip out. I didn't mean to, but I just bought a new Kate Spade wallet at thirty percent off, and I was on a high from it."

She was absolutely crazy, and as much as she tried to seem put together when I first sat down on this flight...home girl was a hot mess. "So, you couldn't get a guy friend or someone to help you?"

She looked down and something told me that the answer to that question was better left alone.

"You must have a pretty relaxed job if you can leave for Colorado for two whole weeks."

Good. Distractions were good. Olive shrugged and tried to take a sip of her drink before she realized it was empty. She grabbed mine instead and finished it off. "I edit podcasts from my laptop. It's freelance so I work wherever I need to." I waited for her to ask me what I did for a living, but being the brat that this chick was, I was sure she wasn't going to. Considering how thrilling my job was, I couldn't understand the appeal of a desk job, much less sitting around editing podcasts. Listening to the same voices over and over sounded miserable.

"Well, I am a kid's ski instructor." That was usually the line. The one that caught women by surprise and always had them climbing all over me. Working with kids and having professional snowboarding and skiing skills had certainly never given me trouble with women in the past. But Olive's reaction was a huge disappointment. She looked up and crooked her brow as if to say "Okay...and?" At this point, I was desperate to find out what *did* impress this little scrooge.

Olive drained my drink and after watching her guzzle down drinks like water, she had to be full-on wasted. She increasingly got louder, but it was clear she was a "friendly drunk," which was a nice alternative from the rude stranger I had first sat with. She would whisper jokes in my ear that didn't make sense and mess with the volume on my headset for fun. Her version of a whisper after a few drinks was a sober person's version of talking normally. She would also tell me I smelled nice when she leaned too far in my direction and would eye my dimpled cheeks when I smiled. It did wonders for my ego.

Olive pointed down to the snacks I ordered, which had yet to be eaten.

"Pssssttt, Finn. Hand me the thing of penis. Peanus. Peanuts."

I let out a loud laugh, my deep chuckle filling the aircraft. *Maybe we're both loud drunks.*

"Shhh!" The older woman seated diagonally from us whisper-yelled in our direction. I turned my head to reply but Olive beat me to it. She leaned over my lap and obnoxiously pushed a finger to her lips. "You shh!"

I snorted at her brazen attitude, and I wondered if she was going to get us in trouble with the tiny flight attendant. I turned my head back to her a little too fast and my eyes seemed to lag from my brain.

"You're gonna get us in trouble." I scolded my newly found friend.

"Shh. You're being too loud, Finland."

Maybe I should have taken a different flight.

THREE
OLIVE

The closer we were to Colorado, the bigger the ball of nerves in my stomach grew. I felt like I was at the top of a rollercoaster, but instead of a fun descent, I had a drop straight down into a fiery pit of briar patches. The alcohol helped. Until it didn't. I had four of my own drinks and finished one of Finn's, and my empty stomach did the rest. The handsome stranger didn't seem to mind; he was almost as buzzed as I was anyway. Soon enough, the turbulence was getting to me, and I kept the motion sickness bags close by.

The distraction of *Harry Potter* was now over, and I didn't want to watch a cheesy Christmas movie like Finn. I leaned my head back in my seat and groaned.

"What is it?" Finn turned to me.

"I feel like I'm going to be sick, and I no longer have a distraction." My shaky hands attempted to brush through my tangled hair.

"Let's play twenty questions." He said in a quiet tone, careful not to upset the cranky lady asleep catty-corner to us. I rolled my eyes and didn't look his way.

"Ugh, no. I know how that goes."

"What do you mean?"

"I've done this before. *What's your favorite color? Do you have any siblings? What's your favorite sex position?* I'm familiar with this move."

He chuckled deeply at my response. "Well since you're asking. Red, only child, and—"

"Nope. Don't tell me." The last temptation I needed right now was this gorgeous man next to me talking about exactly how he wanted it in bed. He smiled over at me with his straight white teeth shining obnoxiously under his Cupid's bow.

"How about we just talk?" He suggested quietly.

"Or we could just sleep like everyone else," I countered and grabbed the opened eye mask in my compartment.

"Now what's the fun in that?" He took the silk mask out of my grip, leaving warmth to spread through my palms where his touch lingered. "What are your plans for when you land?"

I hadn't let myself think of plans yet; I was just trying to get past the fact that I was seeing my sister, and everyone else, for the first time in three years.

"Probably work. Go to the family dinners they're making me attend. Avoid all the Christmas things they're going to do."

"What is it with you and Christmas? Did someone give you a used candle or something? Maybe a bad meet-the-Santa experience?" He questioned with a laugh.

If only he knew.

"Just not a fan. The lights give me headaches, the cold is unbearable, the music is too loud, and everyone expects something from you. No thanks."

He looked at me as if I had grown a third eye. "You are such a...curmudgeon. A little Grinch."

"I am not a *curmudgeon*...but I will accept *Grinch*. I just think it's all a little overrated."

Finn had slowly inched his way closer to me in our conversation and with the armrest between us lifted, it felt like he was right on top of me. I was trying, and failing, to ignore the way his arm brushed against mine, sending shockwaves up and through my chest.

"Maybe you just haven't had someone show you all the best things about Christmas." His husky voice trailed through my ears and straight to my chest.

Or I just had someone show me all the worst *things.*

"Maybe. Or maybe you just follow all the other little elf sheep blindly."

He straightened his back quickly, as if an idea popped into his mind. "You should let me be your boyfriend."

"*What?*" I don't always make the best decisions, but I knew good and well that was not the right route to go.

"I mean your fake boyfriend. I can come to family stuff to keep them off your back, take them skiing where I work, and show you Christmas is certainly *not* overrated. Win-win."

I laughed at the idea. I hadn't brought a boyfriend home in years, and I was not going to let the first one be fake. The plan was simply to tell my family that my boyfriend moved to Russia to test different soils there and he would never be back due to radiation. "What's your win?" I asked him.

He squinted his eyes like he was searching for one. "I can show off my favorite town, and it gives me something to do since I don't have any plans for the holidays." His shrug was nonchalant, as if this was a regular occurrence for him.

I didn't even consider it. No way. It was comical: meeting a stranger on a plane and then taking him home to my parents and siblings, who have enough ammunition on me already.

"Absolutely not. You are a *stranger*. I don't even know your middle name."

"It's Danger."

I let out a loud laugh and quickly forced myself to be quiet again, on account of the other passengers who slept under the dim yellow lights of the plane.

"Well, I am certainly not going to now." I grabbed the eye mask back from him, ready to shut down any more drunken ideas he would come up with, but he slapped it out of my hands.

"Did you just—"

"Listen. I am going to give you the best Christmas you have ever had, and in two weeks, you're going to fall to your knees and apologize for how wrong you are."

The nerve of this guy. I wondered how often someone told him no; it was obvious he thought he could use that charming smile and sweet-as-candy accent to get anything he wanted.

Well, *almost* anything. Me being on my knees for him would *not* be one of those things.

"Excuse me? You are a stranger, and I will do no such thing," I scoffed at him and leaned toward the window, away from his cozy warmth—even as I mourned the contact.

"We will see about that." *Yes, we will.* Finn was cocky, and I knew the remainder of this flight would be filled with his persuasion methods. What he didn't know was that his attempts would be futile, because I am *always* in charge. I reached for my headphones and went to play the next movie in the series, needing to block out his babbling.

I clicked on the next movie in the series and leaned back in my seat. I kept my eyes straight ahead and pretended not to notice Finn picking up his own headset and tuning into my screen. He leaned closer to me, and I put all my focus into the movie and none on the clean laundry scent he was sending my way.

Soon enough, my eyelids grew heavy, and I relaxed into my chair. I drifted to sleep, falling into a slumber filled with dreams of my days far before I stepped on this plane.

FOUR
FINN

I planned on falling asleep soon after Olive. I was exhausted and had drank too much. Plus, it was three in the morning, and I was running on half a bag of peanuts.

But, shortly after Olive drifted off to sleep, her head shifted onto my shoulder. I started to move and let her lie on the armrest, but I was frozen. Looking down at her pretty blonde hair splayed across my shoulder, her mouth slightly parted as her breath evened out…it was like a snowflake had landed on my shoulder, a crazy, grouchy, beautiful snowflake. I certainly wasn't going to be the one to wake her. I already had enough of her attitude when she was awake and sober; I didn't want to see what that looked like when you woke her up from sleeping off a buzz.

So, I stayed awake. I could easily catch up on sleep since I had tomorrow off from work. I watched the rest of the wizard movie because I was too scared to reach over and change it to anything else.

A familiar *ding* came over the speakers followed by a woman's hushed voice, "Ladies and gentlemen, we will be landing in about thirty minutes," she said, then proceeded to advise us on landing procedures.

Olive slept through the announcements and nuzzled into my shoulder more; her tiny arms wrapped around mine, and she squeezed my bicep with one hand. I bit back a big grin. I didn't have huge muscles, but I got plenty of exercise from working out in my spare time, and I certainly did not hear many complaints from women.

When I first boarded this plane, I had no intentions of offering to be Olive's pretend date while she was in town; quite frankly, I had no plans on seeing her after we landed. But hearing her go on and on about how overrated Christmas was, I felt compelled to change her mind.

Of course, someone living in Florida would hate Christmas. Maybe she just forgot what holidays were like in Colorado. With the lights shining everywhere and snow falling, Aspen was North Pole status. With no plans for the next couple of weeks, the opportunity to charm a stubborn and beautiful girl sounded like a good time. She would be gone by the new year, and I would return to my regular schedule, which seemed like a good idea to me. But, there was the fact that she seemed almost...disgusted at the thought of spending time with me. That was new, and I was not a fan. This left me no choice but to pull out the big guns—if she was going to be stubborn, so was I.

The airplane was about to land, and the petite flight attendant walked by and tapped me on the shoulder. "You'll need to put your seatbelts on, sir." I flashed my bright grin and nodded my head.

Straightening my back, I slightly moved my shoulder to wake Olive up. She raised her head slowly; her once perfectly brushed golden hair was now more of a bird's nest, and she had a combo of smeared mascara and a tiny amount of drool on her cheeks. She looked adorable, like a puppy who just woke up from a food coma.

Olive realized her hands were still on my arm and pulled them away. She yawned and groaned what sounded like "sorry," but it came out more like "sooahhheee" in her deep exhaling tone. I smirked over at her, and she looked out the window. It was still dark outside, but with the few lights sprinkled around, you could see the blanket of snow that sat on top of Colorado.

"Are we almost there?" She rubbed her eyes and looked innocent as can be. I wanted to remember how sweet she was when she woke up compared to the cranky girl I first boarded with.

"Yeah, they're telling us to put our seatbelts on."

She stretched out her arms with a low rumble in her throat but placed the seatbelt over her lap.

As she woke more, her body tensed. It was comical, like seeing a cat back away into their corner of the room.

"So, where are you staying?" I questioned, hoping to have a conversation with her before our separate departures.

She must have taken my question the wrong way because she cut me a sideways glance like I was some nosy pervert.

"Why would I tell you that?"

"So, I can meet my fake future in-laws, of course." She pinched the bridge of her nose and shook her head.

"You will *never* be meeting my family." I was the best with parents actually; usually when I broke up with a girl, her parents were as upset as she was.

"Ahh, you *say* that but who will save you from the nagging of making up an imaginary boyfriend and also give you the best vacation of your life?"

Olive rolled her eyes and crossed her arms. "I can handle all of it just fine." Her voice wavered like she didn't believe what was coming out of her. What she didn't know is that I don't let up easily.

After a moment of silence, she continued. "But...if I were to agree to this, what would the catch be?" She was considering it, I could tell. I didn't know a thing about her family, but it must have been pretty bad for her to consider pretending with me.

Questioning the willful blonde beside me, I said, "Does there have to be a catch?"

"In my experience, there's *always* a catch."

Interesting. The more I learned about Olive, the more curious I became about her.

"Well, maybe just this once there isn't one." She scoffed a laugh at my response, as if she could never imagine such a possibility.

"Right. Well, either way, it doesn't matter." She turned her head to the window and scooted away from me.

This girl...she has no idea what's about to hit her.

FIVE
OLIVE

Between the peanuts and a granola bar that Finn had, I mostly sobered up during the time that it took for us to land. I wasn't sure what possessed the not-so-stranger, Finn, to be so adamant about helping me but I was weary.

As we landed and waited for the all-clear to get up and grab our carry-ons, I turned my phone off airplane mode. When I did so, my screen was overwhelmed with messages. Among the notifications from work, emails, and social media, my most recent texts stood out to me the most.

Matt: Excited to see you, don't think too much.

Mom: Call me when you land! So excited to meet your man friend. Love you!!

Dad: See you soon kiddo, we ALL are ready to have you.

I noted that I had messages from everyone in my family, except my sister Sarah. I doubted she had my new phone number, anyway. My nerves came back full-force, and I wished I had faked the flu and stayed home. There was no way I could survive the next two weeks like this. I'd have to see a cardiologist if my heart kept racing this way.

I had purposefully planned around holidays for the last three years. I would schedule meetings, vacations, pretend illnesses, and anything I could to get out of flying home. Unfortunately, they all knew it too. My brother, Matt, would call me out on it, but he knew it was never his fault. He and my parents had visited me a couple of times here and there since I moved to Florida. They would come in the summer; Matt, his wife Taylor, and my parents would all pack up for a week and enjoy the beach while I worked. They would convince me to go to dinner or make me take them to a tourist spot some days. But eventually, they would all go back home to Aspen. Back to Sarah.

The sound of people standing and grabbing their bags out of the overhead bins shook me back to the present.

"You good over there, Olive?" Finn's rich voice gave me comfort for a millisecond. It wasn't much but I definitely felt it.

"Yeah, yeah. I'm fine. Sorry, just zoning out." I reached between my legs for my large carry-on and began layering up my jackets to prepare for the frigid air.

I don't know exactly how long I slept on the plane, but it was not enough. My eyelids were heavy, and my muscles were sore from the tightly cramped seats.

Finn stood, and his tall stature took up the aisle. He stretched his lean arms over his head, his shirt lifting with the movement, flashing me his perfectly sculpted stomach. *Ugh, of course, his body is beautiful.* I fought not to roll my eyes around in aggravation.

When he was done stretching, he reached by my feet and grabbed my carry-on bag. I tried to pull it back, but he insisted.

"I'll get it for you. Just till we're off."

It was annoying how sweet he was being, no matter how much I tried to shut him down. I let go of my bag, simply because of pure exhaustion, and let him take the lead off the plane. We walked by the flight attendant, who wished everyone goodbye. She made eye contact with me and looked back and forth between Finn and me.

"Have a good day, sir." She said to him. *Only* to him. This eye roll was not going to be contained.

"Thanks, doll." He smiled brightly at her, his beautiful teeth shining through.

Finn and I walked down the ramp and entered the Aspen airport. I checked the time on my phone, noting it was half-past six in the morning. I followed him to the baggage claim, and we quietly waited in a line for our luggage to pop through. He must be as tired as I am. On the plane he wouldn't shut up, but now he was radio silent. We would yawn here and there and make small comments, but mostly just swayed mindlessly like zombies. When my familiar white suitcase popped on the running belt, I sluggishly reached out to grab it. My bones were already sore from the cold, and I was more than ready to snuggle in my childhood bed with a warm blanket and ignore the world.

I turned back to Finn, whose luggage had yet to pop through. He was still holding my carry-on; I reached out to grab it, but he didn't move.

"Come on, after everything we've been through. Let's at least get a coffee or something."

I was too tired for any comebacks. "Sorry, bud. I am exhausted, and I have to get home before everyone wakes up." Thankfully, my house was a short thirty-minute drive from the airport. But it was going to be a drive I had been dreading for so long.

"Can't I get your number or something?"

I considered it for a second. Finn seemed like a good guy: sweet, comical, handsome, charming. But, I had too many walls up for a man like that, and I wasn't going to hook up for two weeks then fly home like nothing happened.

"Probably not a good idea. But it was nice meeting you. Maybe I'll see you around."

His shoulders sank, and he looked like a sad puppy denied a bowl of treats. I felt bad, but he was a big enough flirt that he would find a new toy by tomorrow. I grabbed my bag from him and placed it atop my rolling suitcase.

"Maybe. Bye, Olive." His morning voice was deep and raspy, and I needed to get out ASAP, before my body overtook my mind. I quaked a quick bye and with no hug, handshake, or any physical touch as I walked away from my handsome new acquaintance.

Once I was comfortable in the cab with my sleepy driver and his multiple cups of coffee, I texted my mother that I had landed. Shortly after, my phone began to ring.

"Good morning." My voice was monotone and cold, a mistake on my part for greeting my precious mom that way.

"Good morning, my sweet Olive! Are you so excited to be home?"

I looked out the window at the streets covered in string lights for Christmas and a blanket of snow on the ground. The road was recently scraped, but my driver was still slowly making his way through the streets I once called home. Memories came flooding back: sledding through the snow, drinking hot chocolate, watching the Christmas shows in the theater, and fireworks over Aspen Mountain. I used to love this town dearly; I was so proud of it and said I would never leave. But that was before I was forced to grow up and see the real world for what it is. It was easiest to leave and not look back.

"I am excited to see you." I purposefully avoid calling this place *home*. But I haven't seen my mom in months and even though we spoke on the phone regularly, I missed her and Dad greatly. "And the others. I'm surprised you're up this early." Mom always liked to sleep in on account of her needing 'beauty rest.'

"Well, you are only in town for so long! I have to soak up every minute. How was the plane ride? Is your little friend with you?"

I reminisced on my time with Finn. Watching *Harry Potter*, drinking a little too much, laughing loudly at strangers. It definitely wasn't the worst plane ride I've had, and the memory brought a slight twitch of my lips. Watching him see how many peanuts he could catch in his mouth and him telling me conspiracy theories about aliens was a little more than I expected, but fine, nevertheless.

"Plane ride was pretty good. And he had to work." Not necessarily a lie. I'm sure my imaginary boyfriend worked all the time. How else would he support his addiction to buying me things and donating money to animal shelters?

"Oh. Well, I wish you would've told me, I made arrangements just for him."

Oh gosh. *Arrangements* probably meant mom was fully prepared to lock us in a dark room lit by candles as Marvin Gaye played over the speakers.

"Sorry, Mom. I'll try to bring him another time." I felt ridiculous saying it out loud because we both knew there wouldn't be another time.

"Okay, well I at least expect some pictures or something. Did you get plenty of rest?" Pictures I could do. Shout out to Google and Photoshop.

"Not really, I just couldn't relax." I danced around what she knew were my nerves keeping me from sleeping.

"She isn't here yet. They won't be coming till tonight. I thought you would need a break before you saw her." Of course, she knew my worries. That was the hardest thing about leaving: my selfless, kind-hearted, caring mother always looked out for me, even when I broke her heart by leaving them all in the dust.

"Thank you," I said, my voice cracking, and I forced myself to finish. "I will be there in about twenty, but I'll probably just go straight to bed."

"Okay, dear. Be careful and I'll see you soon." She tried to hide her disappointment, but it weaved its way in between her words. Mom knew I was different from the last time I was here; the old Olive wouldn't be able to pick me out of a line up.

My cab driver stayed quiet as we carefully rolled down the icy streets. My chin rested on my hand as I looked out the frosted window. The trees had icicle lights dangling from them, and the streetlights were faded underneath the thick layers of snow that coated them. The town was quiet, as it was too early for any shopping or restaurants to be open. It looked like it was right out of the magazines in the dentist office, with a cover of the streetlights and mountains in the background, the caption reading: "Walking in a Winter Wonderland." Snow flurried down the town's beloved streets like it was made specifically for Christmas day. The early morning sky peeking through the mountain oasis was still sprinkled with bright stars, occasionally dimmed by a streetlamp. This place was once a paradise to me. It had been the purest form of comfort, like a cup of warm cider, thick socks in front of a roaring fire, and Christmas lights twinkling. Now the cider has gone cold, and the lights have burned out.

The car ride wasn't as quick as I hoped. When I arrived at the house, all the lights were on, illuminating familiar cars in the driveway and the still slightly crooked mailbox. I grabbed my luggage out of the cab and tipped the driver. As he slowly creeped back down the slick driveway, I made my way toward the cozy log cabin I once called home.

The tall cabin was made of cedar with floor-to-ceiling windows that allowed you to view straight to the kitchen. Thankfully our street was private, so we never cared about the openness. I could see Mom's wreath on the front door and lights strung inside but noticed there was no Christmas tree in the window yet. As I adjusted my bags and walked down the snowy drive, the lights inside mysteriously turned off. My suitcase rolled over the slick ice, and I had to walk slowly so as not to fall on my butt and ruin my perfectly styled travel wear. When I reached the front door, I found it unlocked. I inched the door open, calling out, "Mom?"

She knew I was on my way here, so she must still be awake, but why would the lights randomly go out? I made my way around the corner, through the living room and into the kitchen. The dark was disturbed by whispering and shuffling behind the bar counter. Suddenly, a bright flash of the kitchen lights blinded me.

"Surprise!" Across the counter, Mom, Dad, Matt, and Taylor jumped up. My mom was holding a plate stacked with chocolate chip pancakes, which she knew were my favorite. Her hair was curled, and she was dressed for her day like she had been anxiously waiting for me even though it was only six in the morning. She had to have been up for hours already. The rest of the crew was beside her, still in their pajamas, looking like they rolled out of bed five minutes previously.

"Oh...Thanks, guys." I hadn't wanted to come, but I was thankful to be here with this sweet group. They were there through every bit of grief after my sister's betrayal, and they're the only reason I'm here now, not sipping tropical drinks in Florida, yelling at tourists to stop taking selfies in my backyard.

"I told you she wouldn't be surprised, Mom. She knew we would be here," Matt groaned and his wife, Taylor, elbowed him. He wasn't wrong; I did expect that they would be here. Still, it was refreshing seeing them up to their usual shenanigans. Mom was always dragging them along to different dinners, events, movies, games, and things of that nature. Dad gladly followed because he was utterly in love with her. Even after twenty-seven years of marriage, he was still obsessed with his wife. It set some unrealistic expectations of love; I thought that's how everyone was supposed to be. Unfortunately for me, I learned the hard way that wasn't always the case.

"Welcome home, sweet pea." Dad walked around the bar and hugged me. I wrapped my arms around his large frame and breathed in his familiar scent. My hug didn't last long, as Mom pushed him out of the way and took me in her tiny arms. "Oh, my baby is home." She squished my cheeks against her chest and shifted side to side.

"I think you're gonna suffocate her, Mom." Matt tapped her shoulder, and I gave him and Taylor quick hugs. We caught up on the basic plans for the day, ignoring the elephant that was *not* in the room.

"Well, I'm going to settle in and sleep for a little bit. I'll eat when I get back up?" Chocolate pancakes sounded amazing, but I didn't get this hourglass figure by slipping up on my diet, and I refused to take a step back in my progress while I was here. I reached for my suitcase and dragged it down the hall.

"We're going to get some rest and then we can all get ready and head to town so you can catch up on sleep. Don't forget to be ready for dinner tonight at Ellina's." I nodded my head and stepped into my childhood bedroom. Mom had left it the same as it was when I last came here. It was bittersweet, like stepping back in time and seeing my high school self all over again. Part of me felt like I wanted to go back and tell myself all the things that would come, but another part loved the innocence that this room held. The light pink walls filled with pictures of me and my friends from middle and high school. My desk in the corner with my old laptop and files still placed there as if I never left. I could have used this desk back at my place in West Palm, but the last time I was here I left so abruptly that I didn't stop to think of such things.

Without unpacking anything or changing out of my dirty travel clothes, I climbed into my bed, which my mom had topped with clean sheets and my favorite comforter. I felt like I was floating on a cloud, the comforting scent of Mom's signature laundry detergent surrounding me. It was the one piece of comfort I needed now to forget the dinner coming shortly. I drifted off to sleep quickly, not at all thinking of what Finn was doing at this moment.

SIX
OLIVE

My stomach was in knots as I dressed for dinner. I slipped on my short black dress along with a pair of heels. I put on my armor of nude lipstick, which fortunately was not ruined on the plane ride, and minimal jewelry.

It's just dinner, I reminded myself repeatedly until my hands stopped shaking enough for me to put my earrings in. Just a dinner with people you've been avoiding since the worst day of your life. It was all going to be fine. Maybe I should have gotten Finn's number. He would probably say something sweet that was exactly what I needed to hear, or he would hit on me in this dress and make me blush. In the long run, it would be a good thing I didn't have the chance to call him. A man, especially one like Finn, was an accessory I couldn't afford currently. Unlike my Kendra Scott earrings.

"Olive! You ready, honey?" Dad hollered down the hall. I took a deep breath and mentally prepared myself for the night ahead. I clomped in my tall shoes down the long hallway into the living room. Almost everyone was ready and sitting around on their phones. Mom was looking in the big wall mirror, adjusting her pink lipstick. When she dressed up, most people would assume she was my sister and not my mom, to which she replied, *"Oh, stop it."* But we all knew she loved it.

"They should be here soon," Matt said, and I could feel his eyes on me, but I avoided eye contact. I refused to break tonight. I spent years building these walls up for a reason, and Sarah was not going to tear them down. I was unmovable. I was the '70s wallpaper that refused to leave your grandmother's bathroom. Good luck getting me to crack.

Soon the door creaked open. "We're here! We're here! Sorry, we were running a bit late. Logan is parking the car." Sarah's beautiful voice echoed through the house, but it sounded like nails on a chalkboard to me. Her voice matched her looks: alluring. I couldn't even turn around to see her. I could hear her shuffle in the door, greeting everyone one by one. I soon heard another, deeper voice follow behind her.

"Hey, I just parked on the road so we can all ride togeth—" A pause in the voice told me they both were aware of my presence.

"Olive?"

I slowly turned on my heel and faced Sarah and her husband, Logan.

Sarah was stunning, as usual. She was always the pretty sister, with a tiny nose and thick brown hair that she got from my dad's side. She had the perfect hourglass body that I worked for years to imitate when I was younger. Her heels made her legs look a mile long, and I felt put to shame in my tight black dress. It didn't matter how much weight I lost or how expensive my makeup products were—I was never going to be Sarah.

Logan was the same as always, with a bit more beard. He was tall and lean, dressed in a nice suit, looking like he stepped out of an Armani commercial. Together, they were *perfect*. It was like watching the stars of a modeling reality tv show enter the room. Once Sarah's shining looks stepped foot in the door, everyone else's dimmed around her.

I was instantly thrown into a pool of melancholy and uncertainty. I looked back and forth between Sarah and Logan, unsure of how to answer my name being called into the room. *Hi, yes. I am Olive. I have not seen you in a while.* Maybe I wasn't the stubborn glued-on wallpaper. Maybe I was the waterlogged popcorn ceiling threatening to crack at any moment.

"I—I thought you were coming to town later in the week," Sarah, who hadn't moved since she caught sight of me, said. She was probably shocked by my looks. She hadn't seen me in three years, and since I deleted all social media, I doubt she saw pictures of me. I looked over to my mother, and she was playing with the leaves on a plant like it was the most exciting thing she had ever seen.

"No, I um. I got in this morning," I said to Sarah, though I wanted to scold Mom for playing her little tricks.

She eyed my dress and replied, "Wow, you look..." I imagined how she'd finish that sentence. Skinny? Tan? Blonde? Everything I never was before I left? "...amazing," she finally said. "It's great to see you." She walked my way and circled me in the most uncomfortable hug the world had ever known.

Last time Sarah and Logan saw me, I was on the heavier side with short brown hair, and I was paler than a ghost. I didn't mind it in those days; I was more of me back then than I am now. I was authentic, raw, real. I liked my body, I didn't care what random strangers thought, and I felt beautiful on my own without all the extra. Wearing only leggings and an old high school t-shirt never bothered me back then, but now I feel like if I'm not dressed to the nines, then I'm being gawked at.

After the day that shook me to my core, I moved away. Dropped over 70 pounds, dyed my hair, and being a Florida resident, I got a tan pretty quickly. I'm surprised any of them recognized me.

With an awkward silence in the air, Matt cleared his throat. "Let's go ahead and head out so we're not late." Big Brother to the rescue!

We all piled in two cars, purposefully avoiding any uncomfortable situations by carpooling with the sister I hadn't seen in years. When we got to the restaurant, they seated us at a long rectangular table and my nerves rose higher. I chose a seat randomly and ended up between Matt and Logan. I pretended to be engrossed by something on my phone to avoid any conversations.

While Matt, Sarah, and my parents talked amongst themselves, Logan quietly cleared his throat next to me.

"Hey, Olive."

My cheeks flared red, and a whirlwind of emotions swept through me: anger, confusion, sorrow, you name it. Because the last time I saw Sarah and Logan was the last time we even had any contact whatsoever.

"Hello." I didn't look at him, instead staring down at my phone resting shakily in my palms. I aimlessly swiped through apps on my phone, pretending as if I had someone to talk to on it or something that needed my attention.

Open the notes app, type random letters, close app. Swipe, open another meaningless app, type a little, close app. Repeat.

The black glass mirrored me, showing a coward and a liar in the reflection. The face of a girl I no longer knew. I couldn't let anyone know how unbearable I was right then. I needed to be calm, neutral.

"So...what have you been up to?" Sarah asked from the next seat over. I couldn't even look up from my small device. I began doing my square breaths: in for four, out for four. *Oh gosh. I can't do this. I've got to leave.*

My cheeks burned red hot, and I put my phone down and placed my hands on the table to prepare myself to leave.

As I was about to stand, a familiar voice echoed through our section of the restaurant.

"Hey, babe!"

I turned sharply in my seat to see none other than Finn walking toward me.

It was official: I was living a nightmare.

He was gorgeous, with navy suit pants and a white button down. His brown hair was more tamed than it had been on the plane. He seemed well-rested, and until that moment, I had no idea how handsome he truly was. On the flight, he was tired and wore sweats and a T-shirt, but when he was put together and cleaned up—he was downright delicious. Everyone in the restaurant seemed to turn to him.

Finn made his way to my side of the table, put both of his strong hands on my shoulders, and leaned down to kiss my cheek. His full lips smacked against my round cheek, and I hadn't moved an inch. My face had to be the same shade of red as my dad's tie.

What did he think he was doing here?

SEVEN
FINN

Olive was pissed. I could tell. But, in her drunken state on the plane, she told me about their plans for dinner tonight, and it was too tempting not to show up. She was dressed in a tight black dress, and I was having a hard time keeping my eyes to myself. On the plane, I couldn't see an outline of her body because she kept layering up more and more. But now she was on display in front of me, and my tongue felt numb.

"What are you doing here...honey bunches..." *Oh Lord, how long has it been since this girl's dated?* She looked up at me and we held a conversation with our eyes.

What are you doing here?

Hush and act normal.

I could tell she wanted to roll her eyes but stopped herself, refusing to make a scene in front of her family.

"Sorry I'm running a bit late. Work was crazy and then my mom was on the phone with me talking my ear off. She says hi by the way." A lie, really. But possibly a believable one?

A woman who looked a lot like Olive spoke up across the table. "Oh, you must be Olive's..."

"...boyfriend." With a hand still on her shoulder, I knew Olive tensed under me at the word. "It's nice to finally meet you guys." As I was about to introduce myself, Olive turned back to the table and said to no one in particular, "Excuse us for a minute." She stood and I got a better view of her in the dress. I would have to work extra hard to not check her out all night in front of her family. Definitely not a great first impression if I'm undressing her with my eyes during dinner.

Olive grabbed my hand and pulled me toward the front of the restaurant. As we strode by different tables, all eyes were on us, probably because they all wondered how I snagged a Sports Illustrated model.

I happily followed wherever she was going, which was probably to beat me up in the parking lot. When we reached the exit, she pulled me into the frigid air outside. We stood in the snow without our jackets, but the sight of her had enough heat coursing through me to keep me warm.

"What do you think you're doing?" Venom dripped from her words.

I forced myself to focus on her face, but it didn't help much. She had on more makeup than she did on the plane and her once-straight blonde hair was now curly and pulled back with little braids. She looked beautiful, and I found myself having a hard time speaking, which was especially odd considering I had an extensive vocabulary. I liked seeing this Grinch all dressed up.

"You told me you were coming to dinner here tonight. Thought you could use some company."

She crossed her arms and scrunched up her nose. "Um. No, I did not."

Unable to contain my smile at her reaction, I shook my head. I knew she wouldn't remember our previous conversations on the plane, but I didn't know how she would act when I would show up.

"Yes, you did, you told me everyone would be here and that you would try to fake food poisoning so you could go home early."

She twisted her lip in a way that told me she suddenly remembered telling me their plans while she was drinking.

"I haven't dated someone in years, so they're probably all freaking out right now. The plan was just to tell everyone that my imaginary boyfriend couldn't make it and now you show up looking all..." her cheeks turned rosy as she eyed my suit, "...*you*. I had all of this handled and now they're going to dissect you like a frog in eighth grade science class."

Years?? This girl...Years? Yeah right, she's probably had a hundred men message her since she landed. "Come on, it'll be fun. Like we have a secret that no one else knows. I'll talk you up the whole time and they'll love me." I was known as the guy that parents love, but unfortunately for them, I didn't stick around long. Usually, their daughter said she wanted something casual, but the second her family met me, she started picking out wedding flowers. Therefore, I was the perfect *fun guy*. The guy you have one good night with, then never see again. Or the one you pass at a grocery store and think *hey, he looks familiar.*

A group of people walking in the busy restaurant came close to us and Olive looked between the restaurant and an alley next to it. She put her tiny hand on my broad chest as she moved me back toward the alley. She pushed me against the brick wall and spoke quietly as if the alley was filled with reporters waiting to find us. "No one would ever believe us, Finn. You don't understand. This is more complicated than you know."

I wasn't sure what she thought was so complicated about us acting like we're going out for a couple of weeks, but she had no idea how good I was at acting.

"We'll be totally believable! I was a tree in my high school play, and I nailed it. I've got this."

She groaned and ran her fingers through her curled hair. "Ugh. Here's what we're gonna do. You will sit for five minutes, you'll eat a couple bites of food, and then say your house is flooding. You'll excuse yourself and then in a few days I'll say we broke up." It was cute that she thought she was in charge. She stood firm but she was no match for me. I was Obi-Wan, and she was Anakin; I had the high ground on this one.

"Alright, blondie. Let's go."

She eyed me up and down, curious. "Why did you agree so easily?"

Shrugging my shoulders, I walked away in hopes she would follow. Her steep heels clicked against the frozen concrete behind me, and I slowed my stride so she could catch up. We made our way back to the table with all eyes on us. Olive's mother spoke first.

"Olive, are you going to introduce us?"

She cleared her throat and straightened her dress. "Yes, um. This is Finn. Finn, this is my mom, dad, Matt, and his wife Taylor." There was a pause for a second. "And that's Sarah and her husband, Logan." Her sister looked between me and Olive like something was off.

"Well, it's lovely to meet you, Finn. Olive said you had to work." Her mom was all smiles and blushes; it was adorable. On the other hand, Olive's dad did not seem pleased at all by my presence. *Just give me until the end of the night, I'll have them all wanting me over on Christmas morning.*

"I think she was planning on surprising you. You know her—always up to something." *Was she?* Heck if I knew. I only said it to make it sound like I knew her the best.

Olive let out an awkward chuckle. "Ha. Ha. Oh, yes." She was so bad at this. She was going to blow our cover quicker than I expected. Her stiff voice and movements made it seem like I was holding her captive, and I feared her family would catch on. Her mom was going to write on a napkin and slide it across the table, *"Olive, blink twice if you're in danger."*

Olive moved to sit and with no other free chairs at the table, she scooched hers toward Matt so I could fit in. I grabbed a chair from an empty table behind me and pushed it between her and the other man, Logan.

The whole family together looked like a group of models. Matt and Taylor looked like a couple straight out of a movie; their confidence was clear but not obnoxious. Sarah and Logan both seemed more shy and timid but still were dressed up for the evening. Even her parents had young features and could pass as Olive's siblings. But Olive was the most gorgeous one there; she was a knockout. Bright, silky blonde hair, deep green eyes, her tan skin such a contrast to the usual paleness in this town. Freckles sprinkled across her cheeks like stars in a night sky, and I wanted to trace my fingers over those constellations. And in that dress, even as nervous as she clearly was, she owned the table. She was the best-looking one in the restaurant. Probably the best-looking one in the state.

"So, Finn. When did you and Olive meet?" Her dad eyed me across the table when he asked the question. This felt like a test, like a state-your-intentions-with-my-daughter kind of conversation. Olive opened her mouth to answer, but I put a hand over hers under the table to stop her.

I looked in her eyes, hoping to send calming wavelengths to her. If I tried hard enough maybe it would work.

"Gosh... I can't even remember how long it's been." *13 hours ago.* "I actually ran into her at the coffee shop down the street in Florida." I was a little concerned at how easily the lie slipped out. "Her blonde hair was covering her eyes so I couldn't see her well, but man..." I turned to look Olive straight in her eyes. "...I was a goner when I saw those green eyes." Her cheeks flushed, and I continued. "Turns out she was actually quite the grump, and after finding out she was from Colorado too, I just couldn't leave without her."

No lies there. Olive had my interest piqued, and I couldn't stand us being in the same town for two weeks with no communication. I turned to look at her in a way that I hoped was lovingly. "Seems just like yesterday." It technically *was* yesterday.

Olive smirked a little at my last comment, and I couldn't help but smile back at her at our little secret.

"Wow, what are the chances that you're both from Colorado? It must have been fate." Olive's mom had her hand over her chest.

Without breaking eye contact with Olive, I said, "Yeah...definitely fate."

"Oh! That is so sweet, isn't it Tom?" Olive's mom touched her husband's bicep. "We actually met on a cruise when we were young. Fell in love in just a few days!" Olive's dad, Tom, cracked a smile but quickly sealed it away.

Her mom moved to the next couple. "Matt and Taylor used to work together when they were in high school. They've been married for almost five years." Matt smiled dearly at his wife, and you could tell he was as smitten as Tom.

When Olive's mom didn't say anything about Sarah and Logan at the end of the table I asked, "How did you two meet?"

The waiter came up right before anyone could answer my question. "What would you like to—"

"Drink! Yes, Long Island iced tea please," Olive loudly interrupted, and everyone at the table turned to her. Her cheeks were flushed, and she looked ready to crawl under the table. Concern flooded my veins as her face turned bright red. I made a mental note to ask her what that was about later.

While everyone ordered their drinks, Tom looked at Olive and lowered a brow, his eyes suggesting something, but I wasn't sure what. I took notice of his tie, patterned in a deep red and light blue I would know anywhere.

"You a fan of the Colorado Avalanche, sir?" I pointed to the tie with my team colors and hoped it wasn't a coincidence. Thankfully, I was correct.

He nodded his head and seemed a bit more interested in me now. "You're a hockey fan?"

"Oh yeah, I have been since I was a kid. I always loved the NHL." Tom lifted his chin and gave me a grin.

While the rest of the table settled into their own conversations, I was buttering Tom up. I warned Olive I was the master at wooing parents and this time I was not holding back.

Although I was talking with Tom, I couldn't help but notice Olive sinking into her seat in discomfort. She placed a soft hand on my bicep, which I might have flexed a little for her.

"Hey, didn't you have a missed call from your landlord or something?" She looked back and forth between me and my phone lying in my lap. Her eyes widened and I knew what she was suggesting.

Get out of here before it gets out of hand.

"Nope. Not a single call or text." I winked at her, and Olive's spine stiffened as she narrowed her eyes at me, silently fuming. I could pick up on every hint her body language threw my way, and I knew the car ride back to her house was *not* going to be good.

When the food was served, the conversations lowered in volume as everyone dug in, but Olive was barely eating. She was picking at her salad, and I wondered if my presence truly bothered her that much. My stomach clenched in guilt. If her foul mood was due to me, I gladly would have left. Well, not *gladly* but I still would have. When no one was looking, I leaned into her ear and whispered, "Are you okay?"

Olive nodded her head but didn't answer me. I still hadn't quite figured her out yet, so I wasn't sure how to take it.

"So, Olive, how's business been?" Sarah asked from a few seats down, but she seemed shy. Or nervous?

"Fine," Olive said, her tone clipped, as twirling her fork around her salad but not picking anything up.

"Mom said you're editing podcasts. That sounds fun." Sarah leaned forward and stared at Olive, hoping for a reaction. You could practically feel a chill radiating from her. She was a female version of Mr. Snow Miser.

Olive let out a bitter chuckle. "Ha. Yup."

It was clear I was missing something big here. On the plane Olive said her family was a lot to deal with and she was anxious the whole way to see them. But, now we're here and they all seem perfectly normal. Maybe too normal? It was a mystery I couldn't unravel, and I would definitely be asking for more details later. That is, if she let me see her again.

Dinner finished quickly and during dessert Olive's mom asked me more questions. "What is it that you do, Finn?"

I loved talking about my job, and I couldn't help but grin. "I'm a children's ski instructor down at the resort off Mountain Street."

She perked up. "Oh, how fun! We love that resort, but haven't been there in years."

An idea popped in my mind and instantly shot from my mouth. "If you'd like, I can take you guys up there. It's free for me of course. I could teach you to ski." I turned to Olive and if looks could kill...I would be a puddle on the floor. She was trying her hardest to shoot me with laser beams or to use her telekinetic powers to throw me out of the restaurant windows.

Matt spoke up next to Olive. "That actually sounds like fun. Taylor's never been skiing, and Olive hasn't done it since we were kids."

I decided to push a *little* further. "You guys should come tomorrow. Tuesdays are the slowest and I don't think I have any classes in the morning."

A sudden jolt of pain shot up my leg, and I groaned.

"Oh, I'm sorry, *babe*. Did I kick you?"

"It's fine." I croaked out.

Two could play that game.

EIGHT
OLIVE

You know what's worse than an awkward first date? A first date that's fake. Oh, and your entire family is there.

Admittedly, my family was falling more for Finn by the second. He complimented my mother's necklace, talked hockey with my dad, told Matt about his future business plans, and still managed to find time to flirt with me in between. The guy had to have a play-by-play manual on fake dating. Or maybe he had someone in his ear whispering which move to pull out next. Either way, Finn knew *exactly* what he was doing. And it infuriated me.

What was his game? What did he get out of this? There's always a reason. I'm not naive; people are selfish, and they'll take what they want and leave you in the dust. But Finn was over here, wooing my entire family into him being *their* boyfriends, and I was losing more control by the minute. However, although I'd never admit it to him, Finn was somewhat...helpful tonight. The last time I saw Sarah had undoubtedly been an utter disaster, and I had been dreading this eventual meet-up ever since. But Finn distracted me from all the anxiety by forcing me to focus on him. It worked better than I expected. But it still didn't mean he was right to just show up here tonight, uninvited.

We were all stuffed, bloated, and possibly needing to be rolled right out of the restaurant when Finn reminded us about skiing with him. "I'll text Olive the details about how to get to me and what times. It'll be fun seeing this one ski." He patted my leg, and I resisted the urge to pinch him.

"Oh, that sounds wonderful!" Mom answered for the table.

I hadn't been skiing since I was a kid, and the thought of going for the first time with Finn was not pleasurable. *A last-minute colonoscopy doesn't sound too bad right now.*

When we got up to leave, Finn hugged my mom and shook my dad's hand. He politely said goodbye to my brother, sister, and their spouses.

"I'll have Finn take me home so we can catch up." *And so I don't have to ride with a certain sister.*

"Be careful, dear." Mom kissed the top of my head. "Finn, it was lovely to meet you! Looking forward to tomorrow. Don't hurry home now." She winked at me, and I blushed a bright red.

"Okayyy. On that note, we are headed out. Bye." I grabbed Finn's hand and pulled us out of the restaurant as fast as possible with him chuckling beside me the whole time.

"I'm parked over here." He dug his keys out of his pants pocket to unlock his vehicle, a blacked out Chevy Tahoe that he must have remote-started from inside, as it was already running when we reached it.

"You have a mom car," I said, unsure if that was a question or a statement. Either way, I was surprised; I expected a sports car or maybe a big diesel truck.

"Sometimes I have to carry ski equipment back and forth between the two resorts, so I need the room." *Makes sense.* "But eventually it'll be a hot dad car," he said with a wink. Ugh. He would be such a DILF.

I climbed in the passenger seat, and once settled behind the wheel, he turned the heat up all the way and turned the butt warmers on. I leaned into the warming leather and became one with the car. Exhaustion hit me all at once. I didn't realize how tired I was until I let my body relax. We waited for the windshield to defrost, and he looked over at me. "Told you I'm pretty good with parents." He winked again, and I pushed away the desire it stirred up in my stomach.

"Yeah, *too* good. Now they're going to be all upset when we break up and I'm gonna have to tell them something terrible about you to make it even." I leaned my head back and groaned. "Did you have to know so much about hockey? Or talk to Matt about his business strategies? Where did you even pull this stuff from?"

He chuckled at me and leaned back, mimicking my stance. "I warned you on the plane, Little Grinch. I've got the magic touch when it comes to wooing people." He wiggled his long fingers.

The nickname made my lips twitch briefly, but I sealed them. "Well, I don't know what I'm supposed to say to get us out of going tomorrow."

He cocked a brow. "Oh. No, no, no. You're going tomorrow and you're going to have the time of your life. Don't forget that I told you I'm going to give you the best Christmas you've ever had. Can't have the best Christmas if you don't go skiing." His grin was like a mischievous cat, and I didn't trust it—no matter how attractive it was.

I groaned. "Finn. We can't seriously do this. I haven't even known you a full 24 hours and we cannot pull this off. Did you not notice how bad I was at that? I'm a *terrible* actress." Finn put the car in reverse and headed to the highway.

"I think you're underestimating my skills. I'll take care of everything and all you have to do is sit around and get Christmas-y."

I pointed my finger left when we got to a stop light to signal him to turn.

"I think you're insane," I told him. This guy needed to see a psychiatrist.

He simply chuckled and continued driving. He followed my directions and we argued back and forth about our reasoning with the soft music in the background. Soon, Finn pulled into the driveway of my parents' home.

"Wow, nice place. You grew up here?" He took in the view of the two-story cabin.

I muttered quietly, "Mhm."

I often forget how nice the cabin is sometimes. With tall floor-to-ceiling windows and wooden shiplap covering the walls, Mom always had the place immaculate. She would go all out for Christmas especially, stringing lights across every surface and buying the tallest Christmas tree she could find. Cozy blankets could be found in every corner of the house, and an apple cinnamon candle was lit at all times. It used to be my safe haven. Now I looked at the beautiful cabin like it was a haunted house full of the ghosts of my past.

"Man, I would've killed for this. I grew up in a tiny house in Carbondale. This would have been my dream." I held back the frown that threatened to poke through my neutral face.

"It was a good first home," is all I can manage to let slip. He doesn't need to know any other details of what went down in this house.

"Well, I guess I'll see you tomorrow. Be warned, I haven't skied since I was a kid, and I can't guarantee I won't topple over people." I pointed a finger his way. He pushed my finger down in my lap, sparks lighting up my palm at his touch.

"How about you worry about getting there, and I'll worry about everything else?" I almost grinned at his excitement.

"So, you really want to do this?" The rhetorical question slipped from my mouth. Finn clearly already had our fake dating plans stapled in an itinerary labeled "Raise Olive's Chronic Stress."

"Oh yeah, Grinchy. Hop aboard the Finland Train. Whoo whoo." He mimed pulling a train whistle, and I rolled my eyes.

"I'm still going to be staying up all night thinking of an excuse for us to 'break up.'"

"And I'll sleep like a baby knowing tomorrow I'm showing my fake future in-laws how to become Olympic skiers." I couldn't hold in the embarrassing snort that left my mouth.

"I should get inside before my mom accuses me of making babies in her driveway." He chuckled and I reached for the door handle.

"Wait," he said, stopping me. "Let me see your phone."

I looked down to the device in my hand and eyed him skeptically. "Why?"

"So I can text you how to find me. Come on, I gotta make sure my girl's got my number."

"Still not your girl," I reminded him as I shoved my phone in his hand.

He didn't argue this time, too busy typing away. Soon I heard his phone buzz and assumed he sent himself my number. I retrieved my phone and opened the door of the car.

"Goodnight, Li'l Grinch." I couldn't help but grin at my newest nickname from him; it was nicer than usual 'babe' or 'doll.'

"Goodnight, Finnegan." That got a chuckle out of him.

When I got down the driveway, I noticed Sarah's car was gone and breathed out a sigh of relief. That was one more thing I could put off. I opened the front door and slipped my heels off, sighing at the oddly pleasurable ache of being back on flat feet.

I didn't start wearing heels until the last few years. My style always tended more toward comfort over fashion. But as the rest of me changed, so did my priorities. No one was in the living room, so I planned on going right to bed. As I turned the corner toward my room, I found a figure standing there.

"Hey. I'm glad I caught you." Sarah stood against my door frame, sheepish as she rubbed her palms together. If any of us had the right to be uncomfortable right now, it was me.

"Hey. Can I help you?" My tone was insensitive, but I didn't have it in me to pretend anymore.

"You know we're going to have to talk about it sometime."

And there it was. The dreaded conversation that I repeatedly prayed wouldn't happen. I was unsure how to answer. *Did* I know we had to talk about it eventually? Sure. Was I ready to tackle a past that I shoved deep, deep down *right now*? Not at all.

"I'm exhausted from my flight, Sarah. Can we do this another night?"

I need more time. Three years isn't enough.

She sighed and pulled away from the door frame, letting me in my room.

"Yeah, okay. I'm sure you need to rest. Just know I'm here whenever you're ready." She tapped the doorframe with her knuckle and left with a sigh.

Part of me wanted to hash it out; I wanted to yell and scream for the whole house to hear. I wanted to tell her every single thing I've thought about for the last three years. Or tell her how she's the reason I'm this shell of my former self. But the part of me that was reserved, shy, and timid knew that no matter how much I kicked, screamed, and yelled, the past is the past. It was unfortunate that this piece of it would always affect my future.

I opened my suitcase and pulled out my clothes for the night. I went through my rigid nighttime skincare routine with products that cost the majority of one paycheck. I used to not care so much about it; I was as low maintenance as you could get while still maintaining good hygiene. But, since I'd left Aspen, I took everything more seriously, including my skincare. Once I was oiled up and feeling like a wet seal in flannel pajamas, I climbed into bed. As I was drifting off, my phone buzzed. I opened it to see a new text along with another one that I definitely did not send.

Me: Hey, Handsome. Had a great first date. Let's do it again soon!

Hottie in Seat 15B: Me too, babe. See you in the morning ;)

NINE
FINN

I'd be lying if I said I didn't spend my morning making sure everything was perfect for Olive and her family at the resort. I went through the locker room and found some skiwear that *should* fit Olive; we recently had a female instructor quit after being here for two days. She bought all this fancy gear and never so much as left a bunny slope in it. Once she was gone, we were stuck with me and my best friend, Cooper.

Coop started here a couple of years ago, around the same time I did. We hit it off immediately over our love for hockey, cars, and women. He has been my bromance soulmate ever since.

I got to work an hour early in an attempt to set everything up correctly and possibly stretch and warm up before Olive got here. I may or may not feel like flexing a little bit in front of her; she is not easily shaken it seems, and I want to see that pretty little jaw drop to the floor.

"Hey, what are you doing here so early?" I hear Coop holler from across the giant locker room.

"I've got a girl coming by later and just thought I'd, uh, get ready."

We both brought girls here all the time; it wasn't like this was my first rodeo. But it may be the first time that I've been *anxious* about a girl coming here.

"Two hours before your shift begins?" His grin broadcasted every one of his thoughts.

I shrugged my shoulders as if it was nothing. "Yeah. You know…" I drag my sentence out, unsure how to end it. It's not like I could pull out anything extra for Olive, but I was too excited to wait it out at home.

His stupid grin grew even wider, and he crossed his arms and leaned against the lockers. "Oh, I get it. You've got it bad for some girl and now you're looking to impress her even more."

I don't have it *bad* for Olive. No way. I simply wanted this to work out for her and her family. And I wouldn't mind impressing her a little since, up to this point, she had been so unaffected by my natural charm. "Nahhh," I said, but didn't meet his eyes.

"So, who is it? Someone local?" Knowing Coop, he's going to keep digging until he finds what he's looking for.

"No. Well yes. Kind of. She is from here but moved away and hasn't been back in a while. I met her on the plane."

His chuckles bounced off the locker walls. "You met her on the plane? Damn, that's pretty cool. So, when's she coming?"

I looked down at my phone for the time. 8:03. "Two hours." Coop pointed to my bag and said, "Go ahead and suit up, I'll get everything else ready." I nodded as a quick thank you and put on my layers. With a low of eleven degrees and the sun barely peeking over the snow-covered mountains, I pulled on my moisture-wicking long-sleeve athletic top and long underwear as my base. I layered from there to end with a top look of all black from head to toe, except for my silver reflective Oakley snow goggles. My short dark hair was loose and wild before I placed a matte black helmet on top of it. With my ski gear all together, I looked like the Grim Reaper only, instead of bringing death to everyone's doorstep, I brought snow and flirty winks.

Coop and I made our way onto the resort bus that took us to our section of the slopes. We always had to reserve a spot off the side for kids coming in to avoid any of the adults coming down too fast.

Sitting side by side with our equipment between both legs, Cooper turned to me. "So, what's your plan with this one?"

I took women to the slopes, or met them at the slopes, on the regular. Sometimes Coop and I would be a hype man for the other during those times. But, I had a feeling my regular tricks weren't going to pass Olive's standards.

"I don't know for sure. She's...complicated. It's kind of a long story, but I basically told her I would pretend to be her boyfriend while she's in town so her family wouldn't be on her case the whole time. I thought she would be excited or at least grateful but instead she acted like she was disgusted by me or something."

For some reason, Coop thought this was the funniest thing he's heard in weeks. His loud laugh barked through the bus, and I was grateful it wasn't very full. "So, she's playing hard to get?"

"Not even hard to get. She's unattainable. It's driving me insane."

Even after buttering up her parents and wearing my best-looking suit, she still told me no. It knocked me down a few pegs, but thankfully I have ego to spare.

"Well, maybe today will change her mind. I got mad hype skills going to waste since you've been out of town." He flexed his arm, as if I could see anything under his ski gear.

I looked out the window at the snowy slopes we were nearing. "I dunno, maybe. She's really not interested in anything it seems like."

Coop pushed my shoulder. "I think you're underestimating yourself, Finny. And my ability to talk you up."

We hopped off the bus loaded down with ski gear and tiny orange caution cones. I placed the cones in our designated section as Cooper took our bags and equipment to the row of bar height seats behind us. Our flags were placed, and our normal spot was reserved when we were done. I still had an hour before Olive's family was supposed to arrive, so I grabbed my phone from my jacket pocket and sent her a quick text.

Me: Text me when you get here, and I'll meet you at the bus entrance.

Shortly after, I received a text that made me smile to myself—I had forgotten about Olive's contact in my phone.

Lil Grinch: Still can't believe you are making me do this. I hope an avalanche comes for us.

I couldn't help but laugh at Olive's poor attitude about bringing her family up here. At dinner last night, it seemed like everyone but her was excited to come..

So, what would it take to get her excited?

My mind wandered to a private place with Olive facing away from me in that heart-stopping dress from last night. She would look back at me with those pretty green eyes and her perfect lips slightly turned up. Her long blonde hair trailed down her fit, but feminine, back. My eyes would slide down to her perfect backside and—Cooper's voice shook me back to the present. "You good, man?" I must have been staring off in space.

"Yeah, yeah. I'm fine." I had to get my mind out of the gutter. But it was such a nice gutter.

"So, you just have no clue what to do when they get here?" Cooper asked and I wasn't sure how to answer. I didn't have plans. I wasn't a *plan* kind of guy. I was the *show up last minute to a random girl's family dinner and pretend you're her boyfriend* kind of guy. Should I have made a plan for this? I didn't even think about it.

"Um…" I trailed off, making it obvious I had nothing on the itinerary for today.

"You gotta get some clue of what to do. You like this girl, right?"

Did I? I mean, was I attracted to her? Absolutely. Could she be a great distraction from being alone for the holidays? Sure. Did I possibly want to sleep with her? Certainly. *Wait. What was his question?*

"Judging by your face I'll take it as a yes," Coop continued. "So you need to get a few moves ready."

"Moves? I don't need moves." I flashed him my normal cocky grin only for him to knock me down a peg.

"You just said she was 'unattainable.' You need moves." Maybe he was right. My usual tricks of throwing her a flirty smile and telling her I work with kids didn't even strike her. How do you impress the girl who seems unimpressed by everything?

"So, what am I supposed to do?"

He sat down on the bench and tapped the empty seat next to him, like a creepy Santa in the mall asking me to sit in his lap. I hesitated, but relented after a handful of seconds, trudging over and plopping down next to him.

"You gotta do a little more than usual, but not too much because her parents are there. If she hasn't done this in a while, show her how to ski. You can put your hands on her hips or hold her hands if she's wobbly."

I pictured trying to help Olive ski. I think if I dared to put my hands on her waist, I'd probably sprout a semi in front of her whole family. Her dad likes me, but that didn't mean he wouldn't push me down a mountain.

"I don't know. Got anything more subtle?"

He looked off in the distance like he was searching for more tips. "Maybe adjust her goggles. Put her skis on for her. Tell her she looks cute. You know, the essentials."

I nodded quickly. "That's more like it."

Cooper and I suited up and did a few practice runs, gliding down the slopes effortlessly. He might've been faster than me, but I was more skilled. Together, we were a team known as "the Kings of the Hills"—a nickname we did not approve of but unfortunately got stuck with months ago. Cooper flew by me, laughing as he passed me, but then I would do a mute grab on a steep decline, and he would immediately shut up.

I was a kid when I first started skiing. My parents would take me to different slopes and let me loose. Soon I became addicted to the freedom it gave me. With wind in my face and my legs in control of every move I made, it was where I felt I naturally belonged. It was my comfort place, the best one I had. And although I had to give up on my dreams of being a professional, I loved my job, and I knew I wouldn't trade it for anything.

When we got back to our bench, I saw a text from Olive.

Lil Grinch: We'll be there soon. Please no more surprises.

Me: I make no promises.

Lil Grinch: I am fully prepared to push you down a hill.

I smiled down at my phone and waited to see her again.

TEN
OLIVE

I had two goals for today:

1. Survive being with Sarah longer than an hour.
2. Don't kill Finn.

It seemed simple enough, except being with my sister and her husband made my skin crawl. And it doesn't help that Finn tended to make spur-of-the-moment decisions involving me and my dating life, a fact that's become glaringly obvious on the last forty-eight hours

Thankfully, I packed well enough for the cold weather this trip, and I layered on my winter gear as best I could. Finn said he had some ski gear for me to borrow, since I had no clue where I could find any this late in the season—unless I wanted to pay an arm and a leg for them. But I needed that arm and leg to beat Finn when he inevitably embarrassed me.

"Olive, you ready to go, darling?" Mom shouted from the living room as I prepared myself to deal with this morning. I walked out into the main area where everyone stood ready to go.

"Olive and I can ride together, and you all can fit in Matt's SUV," Mom stated, which made no logical sense. Her car was as big as Matt's. I was instantly skeptical of why she wanted to get me alone.

Everyone else piled in Matt's car while mom and I got in hers. She bombarded me immediately. "So, tell me more about this Finn." The problem was at this point she probably knew as much as I did.

"I—I mean he works with kids, loves all things Christmas, travels a lot." That should be enough.

"But what is your relationship like? You tell us you're seeing someone last minute and that he's not coming but then he just pops up at dinner?" *This* was why I didn't want to go along with Finn's plans. They didn't match me. Ever since I moved, I was the furthest thing from spontaneous. I loved my routines.

"Yeah, sorry about that. I didn't know he was going to show up last night. But he is a good guy..." *From what I can tell so far.* "...and our relationship is good." I didn't offer up any other details for fear of her seeing right through me.

"He seems very sweet, and he works with kids." Her brows wiggled suggestively, Mom was always going on about grandkids, and I could almost see the cogs in her brain turning. "I think he's good for you. You need to get out of this...funk." *Funk* was a sweeter way to say *downward spiral*, and I appreciated the sugarcoated version from her.

"Yeah, I mean he's fun."

Mom stopped at a redlight and looked over at me. "Don't do this."

"Do what?"

She tapped her finger on the steering wheel. "Don't try to downplay what this is. He's the first guy you've brought home since—" She stopped abruptly. "Just don't waste a perfectly good relationship because of your past."

We must have put on a good show for Mom to think we were *that* serious. Maybe Finn's acting skills paid off.

When we got to the resort, I texted Finn our location. He told me which bus to take and dropped me a pin where his section was. The resort was decked out in Christmas trees, colorful string lights, and wreaths. There was holiday music playing around us with lyrics of 'snow' and 'cheer.' It was annoying but expected in a ski resort in Colorado twelve days before Christmas. Even when I was a kid, I remembered the town going all out for the holidays. Everyone would put giant, tacky decorations in their yard and the town lit up like a clear night sky. It was basically Whoville over here—minus the weird lips, bingle balls, and whofoo fluff.

My mom stood on the tips of her toes to wave down the rest of our family when she saw them coming our way. A heavy silence hung in the air around us, and I wondered if they had these awkward silences when I wasn't around.

I doubted it.

When we reached the bus, we all piled in, everyone holding their ski gear except for me. Finn supposedly had some for me from another girl, which didn't surprise me at all. I was sure taking women to the resort was something he did regularly. I made a point to sit far away from Sarah to avoid any unnecessary conflict. The last thing I needed today was her trying to have a come-to-Jesus meeting with me.

Taylor sat next to me and played with the ends of my blonde hair. She and Matt had been coworkers for a long time and when they finally started dating, she became a dear friend of mine. I had overwhelming guilt for not being able to see her and Matt as much as before, but traveling back and forth from Florida to Colorado took time and energy that I didn't have to spare.

"Are you excited?" Her voice shook, like there was another question lying underneath the one she had spewed out.

"Yeah, I haven't been skiing in a long time." Even when I did go as a kid, I was horribly uncoordinated, so I had no idea how this was going to turn out. Probably with me skiing right into a child, dragging us both downhill and creating an avalanche. Maybe that would give me an excuse to leave.

"No, I mean are you excited for us to hang out with Finn? He seems like a good guy," Taylor said, and I did my best to portray some form of excitement.

I smiled softly. "Yeah, I think it'll be fun." *And temporary.*

Matt's deep voice rose from the aisle opposite us. "I can't believe you didn't even tell me you were dating someone."

Matt was always protective of me. Every boyfriend I ever had, he would make me give him all their information before I even went on a first date. He always said they had to go through him first, and if they passed his tests, then I could continue. Like he was a secret detective instead of an accountant.

"I didn't really plan on him showing up at dinner, I was hoping to let you guys meet a few days after I settled in." My stomach twirled as the lie slipped out. How was I supposed to pretend all day long?

Matt opened his mouth to protest but Taylor spoke before him. "He's very cute. You lucked out on that one."

Ugh, he *was* cute. Actually, cute didn't do the man justice. Finn was one of the most gorgeous men I had ever seen; his smile alone could make me melt, even in this below-freezing weather.

"Oh yeah, he is," I said as my cheeks flushed.

When I snuck a glance at Sarah and Logan, I found Logan already staring at me. Rage rushed through my veins at the sight of him, and turned my head to look out the window, and away from his prying eyes.

Taylor continued to brush my hair with her fingers, providing comfort like a big sister *should*. Even when we were states away, Taylor was always there for me. She would periodically give me updates on Sarah because she knew I was too stubborn to ask. I didn't ever have to tell Taylor what I was thinking because she always just *knew*.

So only the two of us could hear, she whispered, "Have you spoken to her yet?"

My eyes stayed glued on the snow-covered mountains as I responded. "No. She tried yesterday, and I deflected. I'm just not ready to tackle that yet. I need some time."

Taylor nodded as she split my hair into two sections and began braiding them, like I was a little doll.

"Well, maybe you can get some closure while you're here. I'm not saying you have to become best friends with her, but it may be good for you."

I didn't respond, only turned enough so she could see my face but wouldn't mess up the Dutch braid she was weaving. I smiled softly at her, and her honey-brown eyes flickered with a mix of sympathy and love.

The bus ride wasn't long, but it gave Taylor enough time to give me two Dutch braids that settled down to my chest. Ever since I dyed my hair blonde, I had created a strict hair care regimen. I took vitamins like crazy, soaked my hair in rice water once a week—thank you, TikTok—and applied oils that cost me more than I was willing to admit. It was the complete opposite of when I was here last. My old just-past-shoulder-length brown hair was always a mess; it was unkempt and free. Much like I was.

The bus slowed to a stop once we got to the slopes. My heart beat faster, and I felt sick to my stomach. I hoped Finn knew what he was doing.

ELEVEN
FINN

I had no idea what I was doing.

Olive stepped off that bus, looking like an angel bundled-up in her winter clothes. She had that pretty blonde hair pulled back into two braids, and her tan skin popped in contrast to the snow behind her. She gave me a quick wide-eyed look that said something along the lines of *don't screw this up*.

I shook my head and put on my usual smile. "Good morning! You guys ready?" Olive's mom, Denise, looked as excited as ever in her bright yellow gear and next to her, Tom looked like he recently fell out of bed. You could easily tell who the morning person was in that relationship. The other two couples in Olive's family trailed behind them.

"My friend Cooper will warm you guys up. I'm going to take Olive to gear up, and we will be right back." I took a leap of faith that she wouldn't smack me and grabbed her gloved hand with mine. Even with thick gloves between our skin, I could still feel sparks from her touch. Olive's mouth was slightly open, she looked down at our hands and back up to me.

"Okay." She said quietly.

With her hand still in mine, I walked us to the small building that served as a rest area for people to change clothes or use the bathroom. We had an extra locker room in the far back that was much nicer than the one at the original resort. I led her to the room and pulled out the clothes I brought for her.

"Hopefully they fit you. If not I have some zip ties, and I can probably make it work." Her mouth twitched in a small smile, but she quickly shut it down. Even if it was only a millisecond, I knew she had a gorgeous smile, and I would make it another goal of mine to see how I could get her to do it again.

"Okay." Olive grabbed the winter clothes from me then placed them on a bench. She reached down to unzip her windbreaker jacket and then looked up at me.

"Aren't you gonna turn around?"

"Do I have to?" I wouldn't mind seeing what's under all those layers, peeling her back like an onion. No, not like an onion—that's not sexy. Like a present. She was like a present with a bow on top. That was it.

Her eyes narrowed and she twirled her pointer finger in a circle, telling me to turn around. I rolled my eyes and reluctantly faced the other wall. I heard her zippers sliding down and buttons being undone. Even the sound of it was hot.

"You know, if we're gonna fake date, you might as well let me look. It'll help us bond so we'll seem more realistic."

A shirt was thrown at my back.

"We are *not* fake dating after today, and there is no way you will ever see me naked."

Well, I wouldn't say that just yet. I focused on the white brick wall in front of me as I listened to her slipping on the expensive new ski clothes.

"Why can't we keep going just for a while longer? They liked me, didn't they?"

Her groan filled the locker room. "Ugh. Yes, they did. They all kept going *on* and *on* about you." The amount of irritation behind her tone amused me, as if her family liking me was the worst part of her week.

"Ahh, I see. You're scared to catch a case of the Becketts."

She was quiet for a moment. "The *what*?"

It just hit me, she didn't know my last name. "Beckett. My last name is Beckett."

A zipper closing echoed through the room. "Huh," she said.

She was probably thinking the same thing I was: how odd it was that we didn't even know each other's last names.

"Okay, I'm ready."

Turning to face her was like a punch to the gut. This girl was always drop-dead gorgeous, but seeing her in white ski pants and an insulated pink Patagonia jacket with her braids slightly disheveled was like a dream come true. Her cheeks were slightly flushed from peeling off and putting on tight layers. I reminded myself to follow the moves Cooper told me about.

"I, um." *Jesus, what is wrong with me?* "GOGGLES."

She cocks her head to the side, confused. "Huh?"

I reached beside her to grab the beanie and reflective goggles from the bench. I shot back up so fast I nearly smacked her in the face. I held the beanie above her and hesitated, giving her a beat to deny me. Instead, she reluctantly tilted her head forward, and I placed the black beanie over her blonde braids. She adjusted it where she wanted it then looked at the goggles in my hand. I handed them to her and let her put them on herself.

Olive turned to a mirror so she could see better. "So, what's the plan?" She asked me in the reflection.

Welp. "I didn't really have a plan, I thought we could just wing it."

She swiftly turned from the mirror to look at me as though I had grown a second head. "We can't just *wing it*." I looked from her to the wall and then back to her in confusion. "What if they ask you my favorite color? Or what movies I like? Or what my go-to order at Chick-fil-A is?"

I smiled down at her. "Then I would say maybe you should've played twenty questions with me on the plane."

Olive smacked my arm but even that gesture made my stomach feel all messy.

"I'm serious! We need to set some ground rules." Her stern expression reminded me of a toddler getting mad because her mom told her no.

"Well, go on. What are the ground rules?" I crossed my arms and leaned against the wall of lockers.

She tapped her foot like she was making a mental list.

"Okay. If you don't know the answer to a question, let me answer. No embarrassing me." Well, that's out the window. "No flirting when we're alone. No physical touch unless it's necessary. No kissing. And don't find yourself alone with Sarah."

Man, I had some plans for some of those. But the last one puzzled me the most. "Why can't I be alone with—"

"Just promise me you won't." This time her sweet face turned more serious, and a gut feeling told me there was more to this story, but I nodded.

After a beat, I attempted to lighten the mood. "So that means you agree? I can woo you for the next two weeks?"

She rolled her eyes and cut me a look that said *don't even think about it*. "Sure. And it's only twelve days now. And I said no flirting when we're alone."

I stuck my hand out for her to shake. "I doubt that will last long, but I will do my best." She hesitated but eventually reached out to shake my hand. Her soft fingers lingered on my calloused ones and I studied her hands, with her rounded nails painted a soft pink. There is absolutely *no* reason for me to be turned on by her hands. Nope.

When her hand left mine, I checked the time. We had been in here for over ten minutes, and I'd hoped her family didn't think we were in here doing the hanky-panky.

"We should probably go." I nodded my head to the door on my right.

Olive nodded back and picked up her gloves. "You ready?" I asked her in hopes she'd say yes.

She nodded again. "I guess so."

I opened the door for her. "Well let's do this."

She gave me the tiniest little smile and although it wasn't much, I would take it. She walked past me, and I couldn't stop myself.

"Go team." I playfully smacked her butt like we were a couple of football players going to the playoffs. She turned to me and gave me another stern look.

"Too soon?"

"Way too soon."

TWELVE
OLIVE

You know how some people say skiing is like riding a bike? Okay maybe nobody said that. But in my mind, I could have sworn it would be the same thing.

I could not have been more wrong. I went skiing once when I was around seven years old. I remember I was not great at it, but after a couple of hours I got it down and thought today would be the same. Unfortunately, that was not the case.

When Finn and I came out of the facility and joined the rest of my family, his coworker—Cooper—was already warming everyone up. Cooper was the definition of a pretty boy. He had warm, golden hair and was nearly as tall as Finn. He had deep blue eyes and a smile that could make your knees go weak. But he wasn't Finn.

Cooper had the whole family doing some odd stretching that involved lifting their ski poles in the air rhythmically to cheesy '80s music. It was like we walked right into an SNL sketch.

Finn, being the flirt he was, graciously offered to put my skis on. He grabbed my glove-covered hand and led me to a bench, where he took the sleeve of his jacket and wiped all the snow off so I could sit. I couldn't hold back the tiny grin that spread my lips when he did, but I quickly tamped it down when I caught him looking up at me.

I sat and he grabbed one foot in his hand. "Are they looking?" He asked, his voice like rich honey. Due to my job, I listen to people talk all day long, and I could appreciate the fact that he had a great voice.

I forced myself to glance away from his deep gaze to see where my family's eyes were. Mom and Dad were in their own world, holding hands and looking at each other like they were on their first date. Sarah and Taylor were off in their own spot stretching. Matt was talking to Logan, but his eyes were on me and Finn. I cleared my throat uncomfortably.

"Um. Kind of."

Nerves climbed up my throat, my heart pounding like the drum at a Foo Fighters concert. My anxiety rose, climbing to a height I was scared to crash down from. *This was a mistake,* I thought. *I can't be here with them.*

"Hey. Look at me." Finn's soft voice drew my attention back to him, where he was kneeling in the snow with both of my feet in his hands. The tip of his nose was pink, and I knew he had to be freezing. "Just follow me, okay?" The smile he gave me wasn't his usual flirtatious one, but careful and calm. Finn was carefree and wild, no worries in sight. He was Pocahontas, painting with the colors of the wind, but in this moment, as if he could sense I was struggling, he was a rock I could lean on.

I nodded, and he took the approval to continue attaching my skis, his strong hands buckling pieces of metal and hard plastic together. When the skis were clipped on, he tested the security by lightly pulling on them. With his eyes glued to mine, he trailed his fingers from the skis up to my calf. His touch was delicate but firm enough that I could feel it through my layers. It wasn't much, only a small, light movement up my leg, but with his dark brown eyes gazing into mine, it was incredibly intimate. My cheeks and ears flamed despite the freezing cold weather.

"Are they tight enough?" He asked, his tone coarse and rigid.

I hummed softly, my eyelids half open. "Oh yes. I think they are." I looked down at the skis on my feet. Finn stood and wiped the snow off his knees, then grabbed both of my hands and helped me stand.

I wasn't expecting to agree with Finn on this whole charade, but after listening to Mom and Taylor talk about how great he is, there was no way I could dump him like a pile of trash. I wouldn't hear the end of it until I left home. At least this way, when I got back to Florida, I could call them in a few weeks and break the news over the phone.

When I stood up with Finn's help, my feet slid up and down the patch of ice I was on, and my arms instinctively shot out with my fingers spread wide for balance. My chest and shoulders adjusted, trying to find a comfortable posture to do more than stand, but I leaned too far forward and nearly smacked my nose on the ice.

"Woah. Hold on there, Grinchy." Finn's hand came up to my waist, and I found myself wanting equally to push it away and pull it close. It was like my ovaries were at war with my brain, and I was trying to stay neutral like Switzerland. The ovaries shouted, "Look how hot he is, take him home!" while my brain said, "Run! Now!"

Respectfully they were both annoying me.

When his hand left my side, I forced myself to straighten up and lifted my chin. I turned to where everyone else stood and saw all eyes were indeed on us now, including Cooper, whose grin was undoubtedly mischievous. I cleared my throat and grabbed the ski poles from Finn's hands.

"Wait. Let me fix this first." He grabbed the snow goggles and brought them down to my eyes. The new shades provided the comfort of being able to see more than blinding white everywhere. With ski poles in hand, I pushed myself forward, one tiny foot in front of the other. I clearly couldn't *glide* my way over there, so I had to awkwardly lift my skis each step to walk them over to my family.

Behind me I heard snickering and swiftly turned to see Finn, fist balled up and covering his mouth to hide his giggles.

My cheeks burned with embarrassment. "Shut up! It's been a while."

He looked past me to my family then effortlessly floated to me. He reached my side and playfully tapped my leg with his ski poles. "Wait right here." He made his way to Cooper and spoke quickly, pointing at random spots in the mountain.

I awkwardly made my way to my family, ignoring Finn's request for me to stay put. Matt laughed at my attempted skiing and Taylor elbowed him in the side.

Mom had her hand on Dad's arm while she talked with the other. "Cooper said that Finn is the best skier over here! Said he won a bunch of medals and even almost went pro. How amazing is that?"

I glanced back at Finn and Cooper, who were still talking. Almost went pro? That *was* impressive, and the fact that he was so good but chose instead to work with kids slightly warmed my frozen heart.

"Yeah, he is really good," I said as if I'd seen him do this a million times. *Yes, see, I'm a wonderful girlfriend! I have seen my boyfriend at his job multiple times! See how real we are?*

Cooper and Finn fist bumped and headed toward us. "We were just mapping out where we should go. We're going to take this ski lift up," he said, pointing to the lift closest to our right, "and then I'll guide us from there. So, pick a partner and stick to them." We paired off naturally into our couples, leaving Cooper as a ninth wheel.

Finn held both my hands and pulled me along like I was one of the kids he worked with. He dragged me to the ski lift entrance and bypassed the lines that were full of tourists. The guy operating the lift nodded his way and let us through.

As soon as I was settled into the lift seat, Finn took the poles from me and set them on his side, then lifted his strong arm and placed it over my shoulders. The sudden affection made me stiff. "Relax, Olive. It's going to be fine," he said as he toyed with the edge of my braid. "Your family is watching, so I'm just doing what I normally would with my girl."

Heat raced through me and my stomach turned. It had been so long since I was with a man. Not that I'm *with* Finn. But since I moved to Florida, I had been out of the dating game, and I refused to have casual sex, so celibacy it was. The sudden physical affection from Finn just had me reacting stronger than I normally would.

"Are you nervous? You look flushed." He brushed the backs of his fingers across the small sliver of my warm cheek below my goggles.

"I'm not a fan of heights. Or skiing. Or any of this." *Or that you're touching me, and my body is losing its mind.*

"Well, I can't help with the heights, but I can say you'll enjoy skiing by the end of the day, I promise." His grin was small and confident, and it eased my anxiety a little.

Speaking of skiing... "Mom said that Cooper was talking you up. He said you almost went pro or something?"

Finn's smile widened and he leaned his head back. "Sounds like Coop... I mean yeah, I was serious about it for a while. I ended up tearing my ACL and was out for two seasons. It freaked me out a little to go professional, so I switched to teaching beginners and kids." His nonchalance was admirable, as if it was only a small bump and not something so monumental it changed the entire course of his life and career.

"Wow, that's crazy. Do you ever miss how it was before the injury?" His hand was still playing with my braid, and he was staring at it like he was trying to reconstruct how it was made.

"Nah. Everything happens for a reason. I was definitely meant to be where I'm at." His arm left my shoulder and cold, snowy air replaced the warmth he brought me. He reached his hands up to my face and I flinched, unsure of his next move. I told him I wasn't going to kiss him, and I meant it.

He huffed out a small laugh. "I just wanted to lift these." His fingers rimmed the edges of my goggles. "If you were *actually* mine, I would want to be able to see your eyes when we're talking."

Something about the way he said *if you were* actually *mine* had my heart racing like I recently ran a marathon. My mouth gaped open slightly, and I mumbled something unintelligible in response.

He grinned as he loosened the strap of my goggles and pulled them away from my eyes. Surely I had a weird outline of them pressed into my skin, but he looked at me like nothing was there.

"There. Now I can see you." I glanced away awkwardly and saw Matt and Taylor in the seat behind us, Taylor waving excitedly while Matt gave me a head nod.

Our seat was significantly higher than the last time I looked around. The wires above us were dragging us higher, and my stomach twisted in discomfort. With Finn playing with my hair and lifting my goggles, I hadn't paid attention to the overwhelming height. My mind was too occupied by his sturdy posture and strong muscles that you would think would be hidden by his jacket. Unfortunately for me, even under all those layers, Finn Beckett was still able to show off his body.

But for now, my mind was only able to comprehend the fear that was lacing its way through me; it was weaving in my veins and taking over my every thought. *What if we fall? Or get stuck? Or if a cable snaps? How would they get to us? They don't make ladders this tall, right?*

"Olive." I turned my head to the owner of the deep and rich voice. "You're fine. I promise, it's all good. I ride this every single day." I nodded, unsure of how he managed to calm me with one sentence.

"Where's the Finn who was telling me about plane crashes during takeoff?" His chuckle rumbled through the metal seat.

"He's trying to give you a break. I didn't know you were that scared of heights back then or I would've shut up." I narrowed my eyes at him. "Okay, I probably wouldn't have shut up, but I would have at least toned it down…a little."

My mouth twitched in a tiny smile, and his eyes crinkled in reaction.

"Well, I guess I didn't think about getting *up* the mountain in order to go down." I let out an embarrassed laugh.

"By the time we're done you'll be begging to go up again." His head was tilted down to look at me and his goggles showed me my reflection. My braids were a little looser and my makeup was partially rubbed off. My cheeks were still flushed from his touch, and my lips were full and swollen from biting them anxiously.

We were at the max height up the mountain we had been so far, but with Finn telling me details of his job and the light touches he was giving me, I didn't even care.

"So, what's up with Sarah and Logan?"

I stilled, my eyes widening. "What do you mean?"

"You get weird every time they come up. And they stare at you all the time. It's...odd."

That was such a loaded question. I couldn't even have a two-minute conversation with them, much less talk to Finn about them.

"Oh. I haven't talked to Sarah since I left. We kind of got in a big fight so it's a little awkward." That was all true, with several missing details. And who needed details really?

His lips twisted, and he cut me a look that showed he didn't believe me.

When it came time to finally get off the lift, my heart raced with anxiety. I pictured my knees locking up, falling headfirst into the snow and creating a giant snowball as I rolled down the hill, taking every living thing with me.

"So just sit on the edge and point your skis up," Finn demonstrated, and I followed his movements. "When it's time for us to get off, lean forward a little and the lift will give you a teenie push."

"It *pushes* you?" I yelled loud enough for the couple in front of us to turn around and give me a dirty look.

"It's not what you're thinking. Just let it do the work for you."

I scoffed sarcastically. "Oh yeah, I'll be sure to let this raggedy metal bench *push* me down a snowy hill."

Finn's laughter wasn't enough to distract me this time. I was fully prepared to faceplant in front of God and everybody here. The couple in front of us jumped off, and Finn tapped me with his elbow as a signal for me to get ready too.

The chair reached the top of the snow-covered mountain, and the smooth hill was lined with curved tracks from previous skiers.

The lift slowed. "You ready?" Finn asked as he smiled and pulled my goggles down for me, tightening the strap. I didn't speak in fear that it would be obvious I was most certainly *not* ready. I simply nodded and pulled my lips into my mouth. Finn handed me the ski poles and nodded back. "Try to have fun, Grinchy." I couldn't see his eyes, but I was willing to bet there had been a wink under those reflective goggles.

When it came time for us to jump, Finn eased off and drifted down effortlessly. I hesitated but pushed myself off, or the chair pushed me. I don't know, it all happened so fast. I was stiff as a board sliding down the steep mountain; my knuckles were probably white underneath my gloves from gripping the poles so hard.

Finn looked back at me and surprised me by completely turning around. He was skiing *backward* down this terrifying hill like it was nothing. His grin was undeniable, and he looked like a fish in water, gliding down like this mountain was a mere hill.

"Let loose, Olive. Let the snow do the work for you."

He slowed himself so we were side by side. I could hear Matt and Taylor laughing behind me, so I assumed they got off fine. But right now, I didn't care about them or anyone else; I was in survival mode. If I ever made it off this forsaken mountain, I was going to kill Finn. We were going so fast there was no way this was a beginner slope.

"Finn! This is not the bunny slope!"

He smiled brighter at me. "Yes, it is, Grinchy. This is the first slope I take all my students down." *What?* Absolutely not.

Matt passed us and waved, then Taylor. Soon Mom and Dad went down and even Sarah and Logan flew by. How are they not sick? I'm hurtling down a mountain and they're *passing* me?

"Finn, I think I'm dying," I shouted over the wind blowing in my face. His answering cackle made me feel equal parts better and worse.

"We're barely even moving, Olive. I can do this hill with my eyes shut. Your family's already down at the bottom and everyone is passing us."

He lifted a hand and pointed it to a group of kids that blew past. One of the boys turned around and gave us a middle finger with his black glove-covered hand before taking off. I gasped loudly, and Finn laughed so hard I was sure people back at the resort heard him.

"Even the kids are telling us to go faster. Come on, let's pick it up."

"No! I refuse."

A couple of terrifying minutes later we approached the bottom of Mount Everest and Finn gave me instructions on how to slow down. I couldn't hear a word he said over the pulse pounding in my ears.

When we reached the bottom, Finn swooped in front of me and threw his poles. He confidently opened his arms to catch me, and I smacked into him. He must have thought I wasn't going all that fast, so he was taken aback when the impact landed us both in the snow. His back landed on the cold, hard ground with an *oof* slipping from his lips. We were chest to chest, and

I suddenly wished I had three more layers of clothing on. Anything to distance us further from each other, because now my ovaries were winning the battle with my brain. They officially had control, and I was a goner. I was nestled between his muscled thighs, and our skis were awkwardly tangled together. I could feel his muscles tense below me, he was stiff under my touch like he was afraid for me to move. When I lifted my head, his eyes were on me. His mouth gaped, matching mine, and we stared at each other for a minute. My head was pounding, and my fingertips were going numb. He was *right there.* His face inches from mine, his lips calling mine to them. He was a magnet with a pull strong enough that it could reach me back in West Palm. I licked my bottom lip, and his eyes darted down to the movement.

"Alright, lovebirds. Come on," Matt mumbled from a few feet beside us.

Mom hit his arm. "Hush! Look how sweet they are." She had her head tilted comically like we were a couple of puppies in a pet store.

I carefully sat up and scooched away from Finn. He effortlessly stood in his skis and grabbed my hands to pull me up.

"Thank you." My voice was quiet and sheepish. I looked down at the snow, unwilling to meet anyone's eyes.

Cooper, who I had forgotten was even here, spoke up. "You guys good? Do you want to go again?" Amusement lined his voice, courtesy of our little show.

I shook my head and quickly said, "No!" and gave Finn a look that said *do* not *make me go back up there.*

Finn looked between me and my family. "Uhh. Yeah, I think we will hang back here for a while. You guys can go with Coop, and he can take you to the next hill."

I nodded my head so fast my eyes shook, and he held in his laughter.

THIRTEEN
FINN

Olive skiing was the most awkward and adorable thing I had ever seen. It was like a baby giraffe trying to walk for the first time; I couldn't look away.

"Oh man...and when that kid shot you the bird." My laughter filtered between my words as I relived the memory.

Olive and I rode the bus back to the resort, she changed into her previous clothing, and we went to lunch at White Mountain Cafe. I came here often for breakfast or lunch after my shift was over.

"It's not funny, Finn. That was mortifying. Where were his parents anyway?" She played with the straw in her drink

"It was absolutely hilarious, and they were probably going down the yellow hills like every other adult."

A crumpled-up napkin was thrown at me in response.

After Olive's family went skiing with Cooper, I told her I would get her warm, dry, and fed so I could go back to the slopes to get my time in for today. Instead, I've spent two hours sitting in a tiny metal chair and learning more about her.

Everything passed so fast it was like I was in a time vortex of Olive. Not to sound self-absorbed, but I had dinner with women pretty often. I wasn't shy or quiet by any means when I found a girl attractive, so they usually loved my honesty and would jump at the opportunity to go out with me. It wasn't a luxury I had before tearing my ACL. I stayed in my own lane and never ventured out, but after that life-changing injury, I decided from then on I wouldn't take a single moment for granted. That being said, when I *did* take women out, I was never this enraptured. With Olive, I was glued to the table like I had nowhere else to be in the world.

And Olive seemed like she was enjoying herself too. It's hard to say with her, because she definitely keeps her feelings locked in tight. But every now and then she would give me one of those sweet smiles, and I felt like maybe I was doing something right.

What wasn't clicking for me was why she hadn't found her own date to visit her family. Or why she didn't already have a boyfriend. She was drop-dead gorgeous, and even though she wasn't quick to open up, she had a solid personality. Surely she would have no problems getting a guy from Florida to come up to stay with her and meet her family. Wait. Can you be jealous of an imaginary person? *Ugh, douchebag.*

"So, why aren't you dating someone?" I blurted.

"Um. Just don't have much time. I work as much as I can. I edit for ten different podcasts and each releases one episode a week. If the schedule falls behind on them, they'll blame me for it."

"Yeah, I get that. But still, nobody? No guy friends or one-night stands? A cool ex that liked your family?"

"Nope. Nope. None of that." Little liar. She answered *way* too fast.

"Oh, come on there's got to be somebody. What does it take to qualify as *the* Olive Moore's boyfriend?" I took on an accent to lighten the mood.

"I don't know," she said, trailing off. "I want someone who will look at me like I'm the only person in the room." There was sorrow in that answer. A past, a history I was completely unaware of and would likely never discover. All the same, I wedged her answer into my memories—just in case.

"So, what other plans do you have while you're in town?"

"I dunno." She shrugged. "Probably work mostly. I'm sure Mom will make plans for us all on Christmas Eve." She said it like that was the most torturous thing to ever happen.

"That's it? You're here for two weeks—"

"Twelve days."

"And that's your plan? Just work?"

I could think of a hundred amazing things she could do here in twelve days and only a couple of them involved us possibly getting naked. Which is when it hit me. The greatest idea I'd had in a long time.

"I'm gonna give you the twelve days of Christmas."

"What?" She looked up from her drink with her cute mouth in a frown.

"I'm. Going. To. Give. You. The. Twelve. Days. Of. Christmas." I repeated it word for word. What was so hard to get?

"I don't want a bunch of birds."

I scoffed. "Who said anything about birds? I'm talking about keeping your plans completely open, and I'll give you the best Christmas ever. It's the twelve days of Aspen! No. It'll be the twelve days of Finn. All inclusive." I winked at her.

It was her turn to scoff. "It sounds stupid."

"Well gee, thanks. You are really bad for my ego, you know?"

"I think you have enough ego to spare."

She was probably right but still, it was odd to have someone consistently say no to me. I had cute cheeks with a dimple as a plus. Combine that with sweet manners, and I could get just about anything I wanted. Which is why I got ice cream before dinner at least once a week growing up.

"Well, you may be right there. But, seriously, what do you have to do that's better than my wonderful idea of twelve days of me, or Christmas. Same thing."

Suddenly her drink must have become very interesting, because she played with her straw and stirred the ice around, ignoring me.

"It's not that I have anything better to do, and it's nothing against you. I just was planning on coming here and working from my laptop, seeing my family a few times, and dipping out. I didn't plan for any of this extra Christmas event stuff." She said it like I told her we were going to a cheese museum or something.

"Olive. You act like this is going to be torture. It's called fun! You don't have to *plan* fun; you just go have it."

She crossed her arms and leaned back in her chair. "Tell that to anyone who showed up to Disney World without reservations."

"Come on, Grinchy. Give Cindy-Lou a chance."

That made her give me the small, one-corner-lifted grin I had become so fond of the last couple of days. "I'm not saying yes...but I'm not saying no. We'll see."

I smiled brightly at her; she was *totally* saying yes. And thankfully, I could read between the lines to see that. I had a million ideas running through my mind of where I could take her.

"Do you want to— "

"Hey, love!" I couldn't finish my sentence before Olive's sister-in-law came running up to our table.

"Do you want to ride back with us?" Taylor ran a hand through Olive's crazy hair.

I was a little jealous of Olive in this regard. She had two siblings, who were both married to really cool people, and great parents. Growing up, I always wished I'd had a family like this, where everyone got together during the holidays and our kids would all be best friends. My parents tried to have another; they knew it would be great for our family. But God had other plans. They tried everything but nothing worked. By the time they gave up on having one I was graduating high school. At that point they figured they were too old to adopt, so they retired early to travel. Mom always said that I didn't have a sibling because it wasn't in their cards, but I always said it was because they made the perfect kid on the first try so there was no need for another. But looking at Olive's family brought all those feelings back.

"Oh, um." Olive looked down at the half-eaten sandwich in front of her and up to me. "Yeah, I can." She seemed almost disappointed to go and a part of me took a lot of pride in that.

"Sorry to interrupt! I just didn't want to leave you here without a ride." Taylor smiled down at Olive lovingly.

"No, no it's fine we were almost done anyway."

When Olive stood, I did as well, intent on saying goodbye. Which was awkward because what was I supposed to do? With a friend, I'd settle for a little side hug or a bro-handshake, but this was Olive. To Taylor, I was her boyfriend and if she *were* mine, you best believe I'd snatch her tiny waist up in my hands and kiss the daylights out of her. But, this wasn't real so what was I supposed to do?

I settle for a front hug, my hands affectionately tied around her hips right above her behind. She instinctively wrapped her own around my neck, and when I got a whiff of her perfume, it shot straight through me. She smelled of florals and spice, a combination that matched her perfectly. With her feisty attitude and sweet looks, it was one hundred percent Olive. Her chest pressed against mine, and I tried to ignore how perfect she fit in my arms.

"Text me, okay? I'll let you know when I'm done with my shift." She pulled her head from my shoulder, and I raised a hand to lightly brush my knuckles against her cheek. My favorite rosy blush tinted them, and I couldn't help but grin.

"Okay. I'll um…text you." I could tell she wasn't sure where to go here either. Taylor grabbed her hand and looked up at me. "Thanks again for the invite today! Everyone loved it. Well, except this little pansy."

Olive rolled her eyes and mumbled, "That was *not* a beginners hill." Taylor and I both laughed and said our goodbyes as they walked away.

Once Olive was gone, I was overwhelmed by a sense of *what now?*

FOURTEEN
OLIVE

When we got back to the house, everything was eerily quiet. Matt and Taylor left for their own home, Sarah and her husband knew better than to hang out here, and Mom and Dad were quietly hanging out in the living room.

I took advantage of the peace so I could get some work done. I had my laptop opened, my noise-cancelling headphones on, and my coffee next to me ready to go. But I couldn't concentrate. I figured maybe it was the podcast I was listening to, so I switched to my favorite one.

It was a true crime podcast hosted by two young women who dissected and theorized crime mysteries starting back in the thirties. I usually loved this one, not only for the suspense, but because both women had beautiful vocals. They were feminine enough but not high-pitched with a bit of a rasp to them that made me excited when they said words like "victim" or "hatchet." But for some reason, this afternoon I couldn't focus. Even with the comforting sound of women talking about dismembered bodies and bloody crime scenes, I couldn't get in the zone. *What is wrong with me today?*

It had to be because I was in Colorado. I've never worked on podcasts from anywhere other than my cute little apartment in West Palm. I'm outside my usual routine, so my mindset isn't right. It's too dang cold, and I don't have a margarita in my hand, that's all. Thankfully, I was ahead of schedule on all my editing, so this wouldn't affect anyone else that I work with. Editing podcasts wasn't my first career choice, but I left Colorado in a tizzy. I had no plans and no luggage, only my phone, laptop, and car. I saw an ad for this job and figured as much as I listened to podcasts and audiobooks, I would like it. Soon, I became talented enough that I had a handful of clients who used me for every show. After that, I was able to make a good enough living.

For now, I sat in my childhood room at my old desk wondering where to go from here. I forced myself through another hour of cutting *ums* and *ahhs* out of the conversations, or taking out any repeated phrases, but I left enough for it to sound natural. After I pushed through one podcast, I let myself check my phone.

Hottie in 15B: So should I start my twelve days of Christmas tonight?

I have *got* to change that contact name. I thought to tell him no, to say I had plans and ignore him. But clearly no good was going to come of me being here all afternoon.

Me: If you did, what would day one include?

Did I want to know? Probably not. Surely it involved helicopter rides or rock climbing.

Hottie in 15B: If I tell you, you won't go.

Me: That's true. Let me see what my parents have planned.

I padded through the living room where Mom had her feet in Dad's lap. Dad had one hand on her foot, the other holding his coffee. They were watching *Christmas Vacation,* and a wave of déjà vu came over me. They were always this way, so sweet and affectionate to each other. It could make you sick—in the best way possible. They set my expectations for romance too high when I was young, and I learned quickly the chances of finding a love like theirs was nearly impossible.

"Hey, my little Olive tree! Are you all done with work?"

I took a seat on the opposite side of the sectional and propped my feet up. "Yeah, I am for now. Do you guys have plans tonight?"

Mom looked at me in shock and paused like she wasn't sure how to respond.

"Well, we were hoping to go get a tree tonight, if you want...to go?"

"I'm surprised you don't already have one up, normally it's decorated by Thanksgiving Day."

Mom shrugged nonchalantly. "I was planning on waiting till you were here. I was thinking maybe we could all decorate it together again? But I wasn't sure you would want to go with us to pick it out."

I really didn't want to go pick one out. Walking down rows of identical trees in the freezing cold at the end of the day was not my definition of fun. But clearly being stuck at home was doing me no good. And if Finn was going to bother me with his crazy plans, then I might as well.

"Yeah, I think I'm going too. Is...everyone going?"

Mom looked at Dad then back to me. "I think so. But bring Finn! We would love to have him."

I wasn't sure I'd make it through without him anyway. After dinner and our ski trip, I learned pretty quickly that distractions were the way to go when I was near Sarah.

Me: We're going to a tree farm in a couple hours if you want to come. You can come pick me up at the house?

Hottie in 15B: See you soon, Grinchy.

I smiled down at my phone, and when I looked back up both my parents were staring at me with puppy dog eyes.

"What?"

Mom answered, "It's so refreshing seeing you like this. All happy and dating someone." Dad simply nodded alongside her with a small smile.

My cheeks flushed. "Oh, yep. Mhmm."

She continued. "I mean we thought for sure you would end up as a lonely cat mom with the road you were headed down—"

"Denise." Dad patted her knee.

"No, really. We figured you went into a deep depression and would start with one kitten and then lead to two and eventually an apartment full of hair balls and wet cat food. I mean we prayed and pray—"

"Honey. I think she gets it," Dad said a little louder.

"Oh right." She smiled sheepishly. "Well you know."

And for the first time, I found myself *extremely* thankful to have met Finn.

When we arrived at the tree farm, it was slim pickings. There was the classic Charlie Brown tree with about three branches and a dream. Or there were the twelve-foot trees that would take a whole village of elves to get in the house.

Finn went with Matt and Dad to get us hot chocolates before we all began walking down the aisles. He came back with two red cups and a bright smile on his face.

"What are you smiling so big for?" I asked.

He took a sip of his drink and licked his lips. "Your dad told me I was a 'stand-up guy.'" It took everything in me not to tell him my dad tells *everyone* they're a "stand-up guy."

I took a sip of my own scalding-hot drink, wishing I'd cooled it off first so I could've saved myself from burning the tip of my tongue.

"Well maybe he'll be your fake boyfriend next Christmas." I said, and Finn chuckled next to me loudly.

"What's so funny?" Logan asked as he walked up to us.

"Olive thinks she's a comedienne." Finn placed a hand on the small of my back and my stomach flipped with his touch.

"Oh yeah." Logan looked at me and I glanced away to avoid eye contact with my sister's husband. "She was always a funny one."

I choked on my drink and coughed loudly. I bent forward and leaned my hands on my knees, trying to catch my breath.

"You okay, babe?" Finn asked, his hand rubbing soothing circles on my back.

I let out a strangled, "Yep," and thanked God that Mom came by right after.

"Is everyone ready?"

"Yes!" I answered for everyone even though my voice was still strained. I laced my fingers through Finn's and pulled him with me to quickly escape any more talking with Logan. Like the good little fake boyfriend he was, Finn strolled alongside me with my hand in his. His tall frame gave him an advantage for seeing farther down the aisle, and my shorter stature could see the fullness of the tree.

"Olive, why don't you pick the tree out?" Dad suggested from behind us. "Since you're not in town often."

Finn leaned down and whispered in my ear, "Oh, see this is the part where the Whos invite the Grinch to dinner."

I let out a tiny snort but zipped my lips closed quickly.

"Yeah, I can," I told Dad and walked through the small selection of trees with Finn by my side. None of them called to me like they used to when I was a kid. I used to come here and be so excited for every tree we walked past. It was the highlight of my week, and since we usually went before Thanksgiving, it always put me in the Christmas mood.

I walked down the row and nothing stood out; it was one scrawny tree after another. I was about to pick a random one and call it a day when there it was. The most perfect tree ever. It was around the corner tucked away where no one could see it. I paused in my tracks and admired the beauty. For a split second, I felt like Clark Griswold, and this was the tree we would rip right out of the ground. It was probably ten feet tall, with a full round bottom that tapered up to a high point. A light came down from the heavens and I could practically hear angels singing. It was the Beyoncé of trees, and I had to have it. But I didn't want to seem too excited. I felt the need to keep my emotions at bay—stay neutral. I had a reputation to uphold here.

I was about to say something aloof and dispassionate like, "This one's fine, I guess." Or, "I don't know, I guess we can do this one."

But Finn spoke up and said exactly what I was thinking instead. "You love this one don't you, Grinchy?" He smiled down at me.

I shrugged. "I mean, it's nice enough." Did I answer too fast? Was it obvious that this tree and I had a special bond like I was a Navi member and this was the tree of souls? That might be an exaggeration, but it was a good time for an Avatar reference.

Finn turned to the bearded salesman who was patiently walking behind the rest of my family. "Is this one taken?"

"No, sir. This here is a Fraser fir. It will make your whole house smell good and the branches are really strong too." I held in my smile.

"Let's get this one then." Finn looked down at me and gave me that flirty, bright-toothed smile.

The tree was huge, and I wasn't sure how we would ever fit it on any of our cars, but I was looking forward to seeing it in the house. The last time I was this excited for anything revolving around Christmas, it ended miserably with a long road trip to West Palm and a passenger seat filled with empty tissue boxes.

I looked to see what the rest of my family's thoughts were. Mom and Dad were in their own world, not paying attention to anything other than each other. Matt was off to the side on his phone and Taylor was beside him smiling at me and nodding. I hesitated to look at Sarah and Logan. Logan was looking at Sarah with loving eyes as she stared at me. She seemed nervous and seeking approval. I knew she had a million things to say to me; she could probably talk to me for the next twelve days straight and still have more to explain. But I wasn't ready.

I swiftly turned back to the salesman, who had no idea the love I felt for this tree. "Yeah, this one will do."

He smiled and shouted at a coworker to help him get it ready for us. I looked up at Finn to find him already glancing down at me with that sweet grin on his face, and I couldn't help but smile back, my eyes softening and teeth flashing.

"You should do that more often," he said confidently.

"What?"

"Smile like that."

I didn't respond or move. I simply smiled wider but looked down to my feet, embarrassed that for the first time in years I had butterflies in my stomach. It felt like I was looking at the ocean: there were beautiful waves crashing against the shore and a sunset lighting the back like a perfect portrait, but there were sharks in those waters. Sharks with luscious brown hair and eyes that said, *take me, I'm yours.*

FIFTEEN
FINN

Remember when I said I was blessed with good luck? Still rings true.

I drove my loaded SUV, which held an unreasonably large tree on top of it, a beautiful blonde in the passenger seat, and a damn good hot chocolate in my cup holder, back to Olive's parents' house. See—good luck.

Olive wasn't a talkative girl; I learned that within five minutes of meeting her. But if you paid attention, her face broadcasted every thought running through her mind. The way her eyebrows raised and lowered, how her lip twitched, the small dimple that popped through when she got excited but didn't want to admit it. All you had to do was watch and her gorgeous, tan freckled face would tell you anything you needed to know.

Olive sat high and straight, feet crossed like she was the queen of England. When she saw that tree her entire face lit up; it was like watching a kid open a jar of cookies for the first time. And although it didn't last long, I could feel her excitement. I loved her small twitch of a smile and the way her pupils widened, like she found a tree that spoke magic words to her. She sealed the emotion away, but it was enough to show me she could still enjoy the holidays, or at least parts of them. Olive was warming up to me like a frozen lasagna in a 2001 microwave. Slow and steady was not the easiest route, but we'd get there.

"I can't believe you managed to get this tree on top of here," she said as she twiddled her thumbs beside me. The rest of her family drove separately so we could have some 'privacy', according to her mom—who seemed far too eager to have grandkids already.

"I lift heavy equipment all the time so it was nothing." I flexed my long arm a little underneath my dark jacket and saw her glance at it. *That's right, baby. You can look—but don't touch.*

She rolled her eyes at my flexible bicep. "You had three grown men helping you. It's not like you were the only one."

Womp womp.

"Yeah, but if I hadn't driven here we wouldn't have anywhere else to put it. That's your fault for picking the biggest tree, Grinchy."

She flushed. "Do you think I should've gotten a smaller one?"

I quickly backtracked because Olive letting her guard down was out of character, and I didn't want to reverse our progress. "I think you should always follow your instincts and trust them. You hesitate too much. Life isn't that serious, just let loose a little and have fun."

She scoffed beside me. "The second you don't take life seriously it will knock you on your ass."

Woah. I didn't ask for an elaboration; I assumed she wouldn't have provided one anyway. After my injury, I was devastated. The thought of not going pro or possibly not skiing again at all was a stab to the gut. It was my lifeline, my first thought in the morning and my last at night. But after a two-week pity party in bed with a torn ACL, I realized life is short. Injuries happen, people leave, life passes—and I'd be damned if I let an injury hold me back. I vowed that I would live each day gratefully, because there wasn't enough time to overthink or hold back.

Olive was a scared little kitten left out in a storm. Lucky for her, I was the good samaritan neighbor who found her in the street and took her in to give her warm blankets and Christmas cat toys.

To ease the conversation, I reached over to play some music. The first station had *All I Want for Christmas is You* by Mariah Carey. I looked over at Olive, and she gave me a death glare.

"Oh, come on, this is a classic." I turned the volume even higher and saw her throw her head back.

I belted out the lyrics and they bounced off my car walls. Olive groaned. "You know you're a much better skier than you are a singer," she said.

As I sang the lyrics of the song we played frequently at the resort, I couldn't tell if Olive was amused or annoyed. I was notoriously known for being the best at Christmas karaoke during our work holiday parties. Coop could testify.

I spent the entire ride to her house serenading Olive, and although she pretended to hate every second, I noticed her little foot tapping to the beat on the floorboard and a twitch of a smile on her face.

When we got to the house, she hesitated to get out of my car.

"You good, Olive?"

She nodded. "I just don't know how this is going to go. I can't be held responsible for whatever happens in there."

I chuckled. If she knew how Christmases on my dad's side of the family were, she would not be worried.

Being an only child was lonely until holidays with my dad's family came around. With so many cousins, aunts, and uncles—all rambunctious and wild—it was like a zoo there on Christmas Eve.

I got out of the car and ran around to open the door for Olive. "What are you doing?" She asked with a frown.

"Opening...the door for you?"

"Oh..." She hesitated but eventually hopped down to the snow-covered driveway, and I thought I saw the corner of her mouth move up.

Matt, Logan, and I managed to get the tree off the top of my SUV and carry it inside. It wasn't particularly heavy, mostly awkward to get through the narrow wooden door frame. Thirty minutes later we had the tree set up in water and needles covering the hardwood floors.

Olive brought me a water bottle and placed her tiny hand on my back. I whispered a quiet "thank you" in her ear.

It amazed me that Olive never expected help from anyone, that something as small as opening her door or brushing her back nearly had her malfunctioning. I could practically see her wires disconnecting one by one with every gesture, like she didn't understand what my goal was. It seemed that Olive's love language was acts of service, and I was here to deliver. When she blushed at my whispered gratitude in her ear, my lips brushing against the soft spot behind her lobe, I couldn't hold back my grin.

I couldn't help but notice Logan tracking every move we made, like he was sizing me up, or like he didn't actually believe we were a couple. So when Olive tried to walk away, I reached out, grabbed her hand, and pulled her toward me. Her eyes widened, but I kept grinning like we did this every day. Like her dainty fingers wrapped in mine didn't make me light a fire in my stomach. I was simply an actor, and a professional one at that. One that pretended like the soft brush of Olive's fingers against my calloused ones was an everyday experience.

"Come sit with me," I said, scooting over on the tiny loveseat to make more room. She nodded slowly and made her way over, sitting close enough for our legs and hips to brush. Her black leggings looked soft and warm compared to my basic denim jeans. I fought the urge to run my hands over those leggings, to see if she was dying for my touch the same way I was for hers. Between those and her cropped sweater, I knew I would be fighting with the zipper of my jeans all evening.

I looked up at Logan to see if he was still studying us, but Sarah was there now, her hands on his arms, looking like she was comforting him. No one in particular was looking our way, so it shouldn't matter if we acted like a couple or not. But I still felt the need to wrap my arms around Olive and pull her close.

Olive's dad was stringing lights on the tall tree in front of him. When any of us offered to help he told us to "hush and worry about ourselves." Which made Olive chuckle quietly next to me. It was a sweet sound I'd missed since we got off that plane.

Olive's mom excitedly pulled out different boxes labeled *Christmas ornaments* and told us to get busy. Olive and I grabbed one and sorted through it. The box we picked was filled with all homemade ornaments, done by Olive and her siblings when they were kids. With each ornament we withdrew, Denise explained the backstory as she placed it on Olive's tall tree.

I pulled out a tree made of colored popsicle sticks, then another of Olive's tiny handprint from second grade, and one from Matt the year he graduated high school. With each one, Denise looked as though she would tear up.

At the bottom of the box, I found one that was a homemade frame with glitter and macaroni pieces glued to it with a blurry, dated picture. I peered at it and saw a young girl standing in snow with her arms up and big red rain boots on her feet.

I looked to ask Olive who it was, but she was talking to Taylor by the tree. Turning the frame to Denise, I asked, "Who's this?"

She looked down at the frame and sighed, then glanced across the room at Olive before coming back to me. "That's Olive when she was probably in third grade."

I studied the picture closer, thinking there was no way that was Olive. Except, it was her. Only it looked nothing like her save those sweet doe eyes. Her hair was short and brown, her cheeks round and full, and she was more filled out than now. Her contagious smile was brighter than the lights downtown.

"Wait, which one is that?" Olive peeked over my shoulder and stopped speaking abruptly when she saw the tiny homemade frame in my hands. Her shoulders fell. "Oh yeah. I forgot about that one."

Olive reached to grab it from my hands, and I lifted it higher. "Oh no. I think I have to take this with me. Sorry, Mrs. Moore."

Olive jumped up to grab it but with my height advantage, she wasn't even close to reaching it. Denise laughed while Olive fumed. "You are welcome to it, honey," she said to me.

"Mom!" Olive shouted and the room filled with laughter. I looked back to the picture in my hands and smiled. "You look cute." It made me wonder if we would've been friends back then. Probably not. I would've pushed her down on the playground and tugged her ponytail as a way to flirt with her.

"I look like I ate the whole class," Olive said jokingly, but I knew there was a deeper meaning behind it. I glanced between her and the picture, realizing she still held that insecurity under her tight and toned body.

Quietly, I said, "Olive, you—"

"All done!" Taylor shouted from across the room, where the tree was now fully decorated and covered in sparkly ornaments and stringed lights. It wasn't the best-looking tree ever, but it was covered in their childhood mementos, and I could tell that alone made Denise excited.

"Alright, my little Olive. You know the rule," Denise said as she reached in a different box and pulled out a tree topper in the shape of a huge gold star. The tree was ten feet tall, and Olive couldn't be more than five-five. For several long moments, she stared at the tree, sizing it up, searching for a way to get the topper on. As fun as it would've been to watch Olive attempt to scale the tree, I put a stop to her planning with a hand on her shoulder.

She turned to me, brow furrowed. I knelt, patted my shoulders, and said, "Hop on, Grinchy."

Olive hesitated but slowly wrapped both of her toned legs around my shoulders, and I lifted her with ease.

It seemed like a good idea at the time; we would be all coupley in front of her family, she could reach the tree, and it was an excuse to have her near me. It seemed smart...until it wasn't. Shortly after I stood with her on my shoulders, my brain wrapped around the fact that her legs, her thighs, her perfect backside were sitting right on top of me. Suddenly, all the blood left my head to go...other places.

No, no, no, I thought, willing myself to calm down. *Not when her dad is six feet away from you.*

"Can you get a little closer?" She tapped my abs with her tiny heel, and I inwardly groaned. I took a step closer to the tree and she leaned forward, her soft sweater rubbing against the back of my neck and her sweet, floral scent encircling my nose. I felt like I was floating, and I desperately needed a distraction.

Snails. The voice of the coach on Water Boy. *Grandmas. Dead grandmas.*

By the time I got myself under control, Olive had already put the star on the tree. *Thank God,* I thought as I started to kneel so she could get her annoyingly perfect body off of me. Then I heard, "Wait! Let me get a picture."

I cussed under my breath and faked a smile as Olive's groan reverberated against my skull. Maybe she was as miserable as I was being this close. But for her, I'm sure it was disinterest; for me it was complete desire.

"Say cheese!"

Olive's mom held a phone up to take our picture, but paused, her brow creasing. "Oh, wait. How do I get it off me?" She pulled out her reading glasses and everyone in Colorado groaned. "Tom! Come fix this, honey!"

She pulled the phone away from her face to see it better and thankfully, Matt stepped in before she could take any longer.

"I'll get it, Mom," he said, grabbing the phone and snapping a few pictures.

I smiled like I didn't have an entire rave happening in my pants. It would be a miracle if I made it through this night. When Matt finished, Olive tapped my shoulder, signaling me to put her down. I crouched and grabbed her soft hands to steady her as she climbed off.

She whispered a shy "thank you" to me, a blush spreading across her cheeks and down her neck.

"You don't have to thank me, Grinchy. I'll gladly lift you up anytime." I winked, and the blush deepened, stroking my ego a bit.

I checked the time and realized how late it had gotten. I wanted to stay, but I had to be up early to get ready for another day of lessons.

The rest of Olive's family made their way to the kitchen where her mom was cutting and serving pie, but I grabbed Olive's hand, holding her back.

"I should probably go. I have to get up super early."

"Oh, right." She seemed disappointed, and that tiny "oh" had me wanting to call in sick the next day, but I knew in the long run it wasn't a good idea.

"I'll see you tomorrow, Grinchy. I have plans for day two." I smiled when her eyes widened.

"I'm afraid of what those plans are," she said.

I grinned wider and said, "I'm really good at surprises."

I popped my head in the kitchen to say bye to the rest of her family, all of whom had mouths stuffed full of pie and whipped cream. They tried to say goodbye, but it came out as, "BUUEE FENN!" But I'd take it.

I came back through the living room to say goodbye to Olive. She had the sleeves of her sweater pulled down past her hands, and she tugged on the hem anxiously. I felt a deep need to put her in my lap and wrap her in a warm blanket, but I shoved that urge down with all my other inappropriate thoughts.

"'Night, Little Grinch." I approached her slowly, hesitating briefly before kissing her forehead softly. She let out a tiny squeak, a clipped, "goodnight," and pushed me to the door. I laughed at her rush to get me out.

Maybe she wasn't as unaffected by me as I thought.

SIXTEEN
OLIVE

When I eased into the kitchen, every eye in the room turned my way. I walked past the table and barstools, ignoring the wall of eyes as I cut my own piece of pie, careful to take only a paper-thin slice. I placed the sliver on one of the plates Mom had left out and turned around, hoping they would no longer be looking my way. Unfortunately, I was not so lucky.

The creepy smiles on Mom and Taylor's faces told me they would be asking inappropriate questions later. Dad and Matt both leaned back in their chairs with their arms crossed, which was normal. Sarah and Logan looked at each other, then me, then back to each other as though speaking some language no one but them understood.

"What?" I asked no one in particular.

Taylor answered for the room. "It's just nice to see you happy with someone."

That was laughable for two reasons.

1. I was not *with* anybody.

2. I was the furthest thing from happy.

Tonight was a fluke. A slip-up. A random coincidence. Had I been happier tree shopping with Finn by my side than I would've been alone? Sure. That didn't mean anything though. I probably would've had as much fun with a beaver.

I filled my mouth with pie to avoid replying.

"And he's so sweet," Mom said.

"And handsome," Taylor added.

"And strong."

"I *know,* did you see how he lifted that tree up—"

Matt coughed and gave his wife a stern look. She leaned over and kissed him on the cheek.

I couldn't help but let out a tiny, appreciative grin. As much as I wanted to hate everything about Finn, he *was* sweet—and easy to look at.

"I'm happy for you, too," Sarah said quietly, and the room stilled. It had been more than she said to me all day.

Quietly, I thanked her, then self-consciously looked down to the piece of pie on my plate. Even though there were barely two bites left, I threw it away. The room suddenly felt smaller. Although the extra fat I used to carry was now trimmed down, I still had the urge to wrap up in a larger oversized sweater. It didn't matter how much weight I lost—I would always feel this way.

Matt broke the silence. "So...what are you and Finn going to do while you're in town?"

I fiddled with the edge of my short sweater and improvised a response. "He's got a bunch of Christmas stuff planned around his work schedule. He really loves the holidays, so he wants to take me to do a bunch of stuff in town." This much was true, and one of the few things I knew about Finn; the man did not hide his love for all things Christmas.

"Did he say where? Can we come?" Matt asked, and I couldn't decide if he was interested in our plans because he liked Finn or he wanted to protect me. Possibly both.

Taylor answered for him. "No, honey, they probably want to be alone. Why don't you and Finn go to a hockey game sometime or something?"

Matt grumbled an incoherent response and leaned back in his chair. Without meaning to, I met eyes with Sarah. Neither of us broke this time. We stared into each other's similar eyes—both with two completely different stories to tell.

I wiped my sweaty palms on my leggings. "Excuse me," I said and squeezed through the small entrance and crossed the house to the back porch. Even in the open space, with the view of the city lights and snowy mountains, I still felt constricted. I needed a warm beach. I needed an Adirondack chair and a cold drink in my hand. I needed palm trees, not pine trees.

When I was in Florida, I was the new Olive. I was the Olive who didn't care about anyone's opinion and focused on herself. I was the girl who walked in a room and pretended to ignore all the eyes on her. But in Colorado, I was thrown back by a wave of insecurity and dejection. Even when I was heavier, I was a confident girl. I knew I wasn't the prettiest sister, and that was okay. I didn't have the perfect figure or the nicest hair, but I *was* the most fun. I could make a room erupt in laughter or come up with the best ideas for groups of friends. But then the real world hit, and I realized that wasn't enough.

I used to sit out here often, imagining the future and how *perfect* my life would be. I would lie back and look at the stars, thinking that one day I'd do this with my own family. It was amazing how much could change in three years.

Tiny snowflakes kissed my nose as I looked up to the night sky.

"Are you okay?" I didn't have to turn around to know who was behind me. I heard Sarah's boots smacking against the wooden deck as she made her way to the chair next to me.

"Yeah." My tone was clipped and short, but what was I supposed to say? I needed more time. More ways to run through explaining why I left without even talking to her, or why coming back here was the last thing I ever wanted to do.

"Olive, please just give me five minutes. I can't deal with things like this between us for the next two weeks."

"I—" I couldn't finish. I didn't want to snap at her, not really. I wanted to cry to her, to tell her how painful it had been for me to lose her from my life. Or for her to know that when I left, I didn't think I'd go this long without seeing her again.

"We were so close...you were my *best* friend." Her voice was wavy, and I could tell she was holding back tears.

Without sympathy, or pain in my voice I gave a monotone reply. "You were mine too."

Sarah turned in her chair to look at me, but I couldn't face her. "Olive there's something I really have to tell you—"

The loud buzz of my phone ringing interrupted her. I pulled it out and saw Finn's contact name—Hottie from 15B, which I still had to change—on the screen.

I didn't look at Sarah as said, "It's Finn."

She nodded and I answered.

"Hey...babe..." I would never get used to that.

"Oh, we're doing that now. Hey, honey." I could hear the smirk in his voice.

"What's going on?" I tried my best to sound natural, but I was sure it came out robotic.

"Just got out of the shower." *I didn't need that image in my mind...* "I was going to ask you what time you're available tomorrow. Turns out I have to buy tickets for what I'm planning, and I figured I'd get them now."

If whatever he had planned involved tickets, chances were I would not enjoy it.

"Should I be scared?" I asked flirtily.

Sarah got up from her seat and whispered, "I'll talk to you later I guess," as she went to walk back inside.

The sliding glass door slowly shut, and Finn asked, "Was that Sarah?"

I leaned back further in my seat. "How did you know?"

"You're always a little different around her."

Finn was far too perceptive for his own good, so I ignored him. "I don't have any plans tomorrow to answer your question. Although if you're planning on taking me somewhere that involves heights again, I think I'd rather stay here."

Finn's responding chuckle was oddly comforting.

"No heights this time, Grinchy. I'll text you when I get off tomorrow, alright? Be ready around 4:00 and dress...comfortably."

I did not want to know what that meant.

SEVENTEEN
FINN

"Alright, today we're going to make our first jumps." I projected my voice over the group of young kids surrounding Coop and me. The morning class was always the busiest, so we had to share the students between the two of us.

Today, we had a select few who we had been working with for a couple of months. They all passed beginner levels and different slopes, and they were ready to move on to skills like jumps.

"Everyone watch Mr. Coop very carefully, alright?"

I moved out of the way and let the children all see him slide down, bend his knees, and do a small hop in the air. It was slow enough that they could all witness his actions but fast enough to make them collectively say, "Wow!"

When he rejoined our group, he asked, "Did you guys see my start up? We're going to build speed, crowd down, straighten when you're ready to jump, then land with your feet straight! I want you all to practice that." Coop demonstrated his actions as he spoke, and the kids mimicked him.

Alea, my recent favorite, pouted in the back row with her skis pointed "pizza style" and her arms crossed. I slid down the row of children until I reached her.

"Alea, what is it this time?" Alea was always a troublemaker; she was moody and had an attitude like you wouldn't believe. She was also the most skilled of this group and one of the smartest kids I'd ever taught.

"I don't feel like doing jumps today. I wanted to do spins or go down the yellow hill. You said we'd do something new this week." She stomped her right ski in the snow.

"Jumps *are* new." I nudged her with a gloved hand.

"No, they aren't. I've been doing those for weeks. I want to do something cool and fun like you and Coop. I want to do a one-hand jump or go backward."

I couldn't help but laugh, because of course she wanted to do something crazy. She'd been pushing my buttons like this since she started here.

"Well, the rest of the class hasn't learned jumps yet, so why don't you show them how it's done?"

Alea perked up a little at that, the corners of her mouth twitching slightly.

"I *guess* I could teach them." *Little show off.*

I smiled down at her and backed away to meet Coop up front.

When the kids had practiced the motions sufficiently, I clapped my hands. "Alright. Let's go try it for real this time."

***

Two hours, and many words of affirmation later, I slumped against the row of lockers back in the resort. I had one white towel wrapped around my waist and another smaller one rubbing my wet hair to dry. I stopped to check my phone, hoping Olive had replied to my previous text. I may have pushed her a little too far by flirting a tad more this morning, but you couldn't blame a guy for trying.

I stared at the unanswered message.

Me: Ready for these two turtle doves?

At the time, it seemed cute. Like a reminder of the twelve days of Christmas, but the Finn version. I may or may not have had to look up the lyrics to the original song to find it but oh well. That was over three hours ago, and I still had no response. Maybe if I sent one more...

Me: Not legit doves.

I hit send before I could think. Who says that? Obviously, I'm not bringing her doves. What is it about this girl that makes me lose all of my game?

Okay, let's try again—some casual damage control.

Me: Unless you want my doves.

Did that sound sexual? Oh no.

Me: By doves I do not mean my balls.

It was official. I was going to die. I would be laid to rest with a tombstone that said *cause of death: embarrassment*. I used to be so cool with girls. I don't think I've double-texted someone since high school. But here I was, *quadruple-texting* Olive.

Here was the problem: she was too hot for her own good—and mine. I started to send another to clear up the air when my phone buzzed, screen flashing her name. Frantically, I stabbed the green button to answer.

"Hey, Olive. Sorry about all of that."

Her voice seemed amused when she replied. "It's okay, I was just letting you know I didn't answer 'cause I was at the gym."

Oh. "You were at the gym for three hours?"

I heard a car door close and an engine starting. "Yeah, I had to work off some of the food I had last night. Plus, it's leg day."

Food from last night? She barely ate. Unless she had an entire pie, I didn't see what she was talking about. Olive's body was perfect—fit but feminine. She was toned without compromising her sweet curves. Honestly, she was every man's dream girl, so I wasn't sure why she felt the need to work out for three hours straight. Then again, I was blessed in that department. I had a metabolism that allowed me to eat whatever I wanted and not gain a point, plus, a job that involved regular physical activity.

"Damn, that's commitment. Do you go every day?"

I heard her swallowing a drink in the background, and she huffed out a breath. "Not every day. But I'm consistent enough where I won't ever slip back into my old body."

That comment intrigued me. Last night, I noticed several pictures of Olive when she was younger, and she looked completely different. There was a high school senior portrait in the hallway that caught my eye on the way to the restroom. Olive was wearing a flared red dress, and her short, dark hair was perfectly combed. She was more filled out back then. The combination of her curvy figure and bright smile was, to me, as attractive as her body now. Which proved to me that *she* was my type—whether curvy or toned, I wanted this girl through and through. I couldn't help but wonder what made her lose weight in the first place. If some frat boy douche bag fostered that insecurity, I would make it my mission to track him down and shove a stem of broccoli down his throat.

"I think you looked cute back then," I confess, I wanted her to know I think she's as attractive now as she was before.

She sucked in a breath, and I swore I heard her mumble, "You'd be the first," but I couldn't be sure.

Before I could interject, she continued. "Is tonight just me and you, or is my family supposed to come?"

Honestly, I was excited it was only me and her. Then again, she did say no flirting or touching when we're alone. But maybe it could be for practice's sake? In order to learn more about her so we look more comfortable in front of her family. That was the best excuse my brain could come up with. It was safer than the truth, which was that I wanted her around me all the time.

"Um, actually I could only get two tickets since it was sort of last minute." *Shit. I'm actually terrified of her saying no.* "Do you think they'll be upset about that?"

"They'll probably be jealous. Mom and Taylor won't shut up about you, and Matt and Dad have been talking about taking you to hockey games with them next season."

The thought made me smile. Tom and Matt seemed like cool guys to go to the games with. We could probably even get season tickets in a box if we split it three ways. Then maybe one of us could—

My thoughts come to a halt. *Next season?* Next season I probably wouldn't even have any contact with them. For some reason that thought alone killed my good mood.

"That would be cool," I said with a laugh to cover my disappointment that it would likely never happen.

"Well, I'll let you finish up at work and I'll go get ready for tonight."

Something about the thought of picking her up in front of her whole family felt odd yet strangely domestic. Like I was a teenager about to go on my first date. I wondered if I should pull out my cheap old cologne like back in the day. Olive was a high-maintenance girl and could probably tell the difference between American Eagle cologne and Paco Rabanne. I had always been easy going, simple. But picking her up for a date—even if it wasn't *really* a date—made me want to take that extra step. Like a schoolboy putting on his dad's aftershave so he could impress his crush at recess.

"Sounds good, Little Grinch."

I swore I could feel another one of her tiny grins through my speaker when she quietly said goodbye.

EIGHTTEEN
OLIVE

"Do you think my butt looks big in this?" I turned in the mirror to look at my behind in my thick black leggings. I lost a majority of my figure when I left Aspen, but my curves never quit, which was why pants usually fit too tight around my behind and too loose around my waist. It was a problem the old Olive would've loved to have.

"I think you look hot," Taylor said as she laid back on my bed, listening to the podcast I edited today. She was as addicted to them as I was and, although I wasn't one hundred percent sure it was legal, every now and then I'd let her listen. I considered it feedback.

In addition to the leggings, I had on thick socks under my boots and a Colorado Avalanche shirt I stole from Matt with a black jacket on top. It was possible I wore the shirt to impress Finn, though I would never admit that to him. In my head the outfit gave *girl next door meets hot chick you met on a plane* vibes. But now, standing in front of the mirror in the full outfit, I felt ridiculous.

"Alright. That's it." Taylor paused the podcast and got up from the bed.

"What are you doing?"

"Performing my duty as your sister-in-law."

She pushed me to the full-length mirror and turned me so I was facing my reflection.

"Repeat after me," she said. "My name is Olive."

I looked at her tall figure in the reflection. "This is stupid."

Louder, she repeated, "My. Name. Is. Olive!"

I rolled my eyes but played along. "My name is Olive." My voice was monotone and dry.

"And I am sexy." I glared at her in the mirror, but she tapped my shoulder telling me to continue.

"And I am sexy."

"I am fun."

"I am fun."

"And my boyfriend is going to think I look amazing."

I struggled with that one the most. "And my…boyfriend is going to think I look amazing."

Taylor smiled sweetly at me. "There. Now, don't you feel better?"

I turned away from my reflection and faced her. "I feel like I just attended an insecurity intervention."

She frowned at my joking because she knew my issues rooted far beneath a simple confidence exercise.

"Don't let her do this to you."

I started to ask who she meant, but I knew better. Taylor straightened my jacket. "Maybe you should give her a chance."

I flinched away from her touch, and she held her hands up in surrender. "I'm just saying, it may be time to hear her out."

I didn't respond. I simply nodded along, because I knew I wasn't ready for that conversation. Taylor leaned over my bed and pressed play on the podcast again. I finished my hair and makeup as the mystery retelling filled the silence.

I pulled out my phone to text Finn that I was ready. My nerves were strung high. I hadn't been on a date since I'd moved to Florida. Not that this was a *date*. It was an experiment, a practice, a three-hour trial to the subscription of Finn. A way for us to get to know each other better and to keep my nosy family at bay. Despite knowing that, I still experienced all of those first date emotions: butterflies in my stomach, a constant urge to pee. It was like my body realized something new was happening and was rebelling.

"Why do you seem so nervous? You've been seeing each other for a while, right?" Taylor asked, picking up on my anxious habits of staring off into space and twiddling my fingers.

"Oh, you know...We're still in that honeymoon phase, so I get a little nervous about our dates." I prayed that sounded believable.

Taylor's smile told me everything I needed to know. "Young love is so sweet. I remember those days with Matt, when everything was so fresh, and you'd stay up late talking and just holding each other. And other stuff too, you know." She winked, and I cringed.

"Okay, one—" I said and held up my pointer finger, "—you are only three years older than me, so don't act like a grandma. Two, ew. I didn't need that mental image of you and my *brother* together."

She shrugged. "I'm just saying. If you need any tips for the bedroom, I could hook you up. I have read so many articles that I'm pretty much the master. These hands have some magic in them."

She gave me a jazz hands pose, and I shut her down quickly. "Okay, perv. I'm good, no thank you. I do just fine in that department."

My cheeks burned as I pictured doing any of that with Finn. A man hadn't touched me in so long that when I hopped on Finn's shoulders yesterday, arousal stirred deep in my stomach. My palms sweat and the hair on my arm raised. I figured that kind of intimacy was common for him, judging by his charming and flirty attitude. But for me, when I had my thighs around his neck and my hands in his hair, it was like having a big red button that said *don't push me*. But oh, did I want to push that button. Me and that button could have a good old time together.

"Hey, Olive, Finn is here!" I shook myself to the present at the sound of Mom's voice.

Taylor looked at me. "Just remember, whenever you guys get to the bedroom—"

I pointed my finger at her. "Don't even think about finishing that sentence. I mean it."

She giggled and hopped off the bed to follow me in the living room. Finn was there, dressed in a black jacket over his grey shirt. He had on dark denim jeans that hugged him in all the right places, and his hair was perfectly styled as opposed to the mess it usually was. He leaned against one of the wooden supporting columns at the entrance to the living room, talking to my mom. Although I couldn't hear exactly what they were saying, judging by her shy smile, I assumed he was charming her with that sweet accent and perfect smile. It almost irritated me how good he looked, whether dressed up for a date or casual on a red-eye flight, Finn Beckett caught the attention of every female in the room.

My footfalls on the floor had Finn turning his head to me. For only a second, he was speechless. The same Finn who talked my ear off on a plane and randomly spouted facts about the *Titanic* on our ten-minute drive was in front of me, staring like I was clad in only my underwear, his jaw dropped and eyebrows raised. It wasn't long, but under his lust-filled stare, I felt all of the things that I told myself in the mirror five minutes previously. *I am sexy. I am fun. And my boyfriend thinks I look amazing.* He quickly turned his open mouth into a twisted smile.

"Hey, Grinchy. Love the shirt. You ready to go?" He winked at me, and I felt blood pooling in my cheeks. I looked down at his favorite team's shirt and felt like I was in high school going on my first date.

"Yeah, I am." I tilted my head when, from behind Finn, Mom gave me two thumbs up, looking up and down Finn's posterior. I widened my eyes and gave a look telling her to stop checking him out. She only grinned back.

Taylor spoke up. "Did you call her Grinchy? Olive, I thought you loved Christmas?" My body stiffened and my face turned red.

"This girl?" Finn laughed. "Absolutely not. She wouldn't watch any holiday movies with me on the plane."

The way he spoke made it sound like we planned to fly here together, and I was grateful.

"Okay, let's go. Don't want to be late!" I interrupted their conversation before anything else could be leaked.

"Have fun! Be safe kiddos." Taylor's wink made me roll my eyes as I grabbed Finn's wrist to pull him out of the house.

NINETEEN
FINN

This seemed like a good idea in hindsight.

I stayed up late the night I told Olive I would give her Twelve Days of Christmas, writing down every romantic thought that came to mind. When this one popped up, I thought it would be sweet. I was wrong.

I bought us tickets to the movies in one of the main theaters downtown. They had huge seats that reclined back, and they served dinner. It was a nice way to spend an average Friday night, but during the holidays, it was incredible. They would have Christmas movie marathons and give out popcorn tossed with M&Ms. They strung lights in the lobbies and had theme nights. I usually attended the animated Christmas ones, where they featured *Rudolph the Red-Nosed Reindeer*, *Charlie Brown*, and of course my new favorite, *How the Grinch Stole Christmas*. But I knew my own Little Grinchy—not that she was *mine*—would have hated that. Thankfully, when I checked the online schedule and saw this showing, I knew she would love it. I was flexing my romance muscles, if you will.

Tonight's feature was Christmas movies that weren't exactly Christmas-themed. Therefore, we were going to see *Die Hard*.

Again, it seemed like a great idea at the time I booked tickets. It was meant to be innocent fun—me and Olive dressed all cozy watching a good action movie. Maybe I'd get a little action myself by casually letting our elbows touch and eventually wrapping my arm around her, just to have her close to me. Afterward, we could go to dinner. I'd drop her off at home at the end of the night. Move on to the next day, no sweat.

That all sounded great, until she walked into the living room at her parents house.

Olive looked like a living, breathing teenage-Finn's dream.

She was wearing those leggings I couldn't stop thinking about topped with a Colorado Avalanche shirt and jacket. Her cheeks flushed when our eyes met, like she was nervous to see me. Which was ridiculous because one glance of her in that shirt and those leggings, and I was ready to throw all caution to the wind and take her right there. Her blonde hair was effortlessly curled and framed her tan face. Though she was wearing more makeup than usual, her gorgeous freckles still dusted her cheeks. She looked almost shy—her cheeks were a perfect shade of pink, and I loved that she looked so innocent. My mouth was caught open. I had told her to dress comfortably. I did *not* tell her to wear a shirt with my favorite hockey team on it and leggings that made her look perfect enough for me to grab.

Which is what had me sweating in the twenty degree weather. My crotch was in a constant fight with my zipper, and my mental strength would be tested all night. Olive was perched in my passenger seat, seeming as nervous as I was. She tapped her feet together, and we were both quiet most of the drive, the only sounds that of the Christmas music from the stereo and the vents blasting warm air. I usually filled the silence, as I always had something to say, but I was scared whatever came out of my mouth would end in me telling her how hot she looked.

"Can I—"

"Are you—"

We both let out a small laugh, and I tipped my head to her. "You go first."

"I was going to ask if you were going to give me any hints about where we're going."

I smiled. "Not a chance, *babe*. But we'll be there soon."

She looked out the window, and her curly blonde hair swished my way, filling my nose with her sweet scent. I inhaled sharply.

"I was thinking..." Olive turned to me and although she wasn't smiling, she wasn't exactly scowling at me either. "Taylor said you loved all things Christmas earlier." Now may have not been the best time to bring up the topic, but I only have so much time with this girl.

She let out a sarcastic chuckle. "I guess I used to, yeah."

I took a quick glance at her. "And now you don't?"

Without meeting my eyes, she glanced in my general direction. "I got in a fight with my sister a few years ago on Christmas Eve, and now it's just like every year it brings it all back."

Ahh. Another piece to the gorgeous puzzle sitting a foot away from me. After she let it slip, Olive began nervously talking about random things like, "Oh, have you eaten there yet?" or "I think it's supposed to snow a lot tomorrow." I understood her attempt to change the subject and decided to leave her alone, but I knew in the back of my mind I had found a sore spot in Olive.

We both went back to our quiet state when she finished babbling. Every now and then I would glance in her direction to find her already looking at me, then we quickly turned away from each other.

It was comical really—how we both were so anxious. It was such a contrast to our first meeting on the plane. She was all independence and strong-willed attitude; I was all charming and flirty, trying to break through those walls. Somewhere along the way, we faded from those original characteristics into balls of hormones and anxiety. I felt like I was sixteen taking my crush on our first date. My heart pounded, and my palms were sweaty. The whole way to the theater, I tried to distract myself from glancing over at her. She was too sexy for her own good, especially in that Avalanche shirt, and it was going to take everything in me not to make any moves.

When I pulled into the theater parking lot, Olive laughed when she laid eyes on the marquee, which read, in bold letters: ***Tonight's Showing: Die Hard.***

"I figured we would come see this, in honor of watching not-so-Christmasy movies." I grinned at her, and the corners of her lips pulled up.

When we stepped inside, I noted the oversized Christmas wreaths that adorned the tall glass windows and trees that filled the lobby, exactly like I remembered. Olive spun in a slow circle, taking in the cathedral-like ceilings and all the Christmas spirit present in the lobby. She had a tiny smile on her face, and I felt like maybe I was doing something right tonight.

I liked good action movies, and I'd always heard *Die Hard* was great. Unfortunately, I couldn't focus a single bit on what was playing in front of me. About halfway through the movie, Olive's shoulder rested against mine. That slight contact had heat spreading through me. The movie was two hours and twelve minutes of pure torture, as Olive's hand brushed mine when we both reached for popcorn, or my knees accidentally bumped hers. The audience audibly gasped at certain scenes, so I knew when something important was happening, but I couldn't tell you anything specific. I glanced at Olive to find her already looking at me, but when our eyes met, she quickly looked back to the screen. Her hand rested palm up on the armrest, *so* close to mine, and I'd wondered if it was an invitation. I wanted to find out, but I remember her earlier comment: *no touching or flirting when no one else was around.*

But maybe we needed a little bit of practice. I took the leap and grabbed her hand. Her tiny fingers wove through mine, and I let my thumb lightly brush against hers. She tensed slightly but then eased into my affection.

When the movie ended, I reluctantly let go of her hand, and we made our way back out to the parking lot.

"Good movie?" I asked, instantly wishing I hadn't because I wouldn't remember any of it.

She looked up at me. "Huh? Oh. Yeah, yeah. Really...good."

She walked toward my car, but I stopped her by grabbing her upper arm. "We're not done yet, Grinchy."

I cocked my head toward our next destination, and she looked surprised. The truth was I didn't have many other plans tonight, but I didn't take into account that sitting in a movie theater for two hours meant it was two hours of not talking to Olive, and talking to her was one of the reasons I was here. So impromptu hot chocolate and people-watching it was.

A few stores down from the theater was a coffee shop with outdoor seating warmed by electric heaters. It had a view of the ice-skating rink and was lit with strings of twinkle lights. We took a seat in the corner near a heater. I pulled out her seat, and she slipped in her chair. We both glanced at the swarm of people attempting to skate on the ice across from us. The sounds of conversations around us mixed with holiday music and the laughter from the rink.

I pointed to a group of teenagers trying to skate but hugging the outer rim of the rink and said, "That's how you know it's their first time."

She looked at the group I was talking about. "That would be me. I've never been coordinated enough for that stuff."

Judging by her skiing skills, I knew that to be true. Watching her scream while going down a slope I took six-year-olds down daily was the cutest thing I had ever seen.

"Well, objectively speaking, your skiing talents didn't exactly tell me you were very coordinated."

Her tiny nose scrunched up, and she opened her mouth in a chuckle-gasp. "I can't believe you didn't give me more of a heads up on that mountain."

I laughed, warmth spreading across my broad chest. "You act like I took you down the black diamond! It was a children's hill."

She rolled her eyes but smiled, and I felt like a lovesick puppy at the sight of her pretty mouth curling up and flashing me those beautiful teeth.

We sat like that for a bit, pointing out different people and watching them skate around in circles. The tip of Olive's nose was tinged pink from the cold, so on a whim, I took off my jacket and wrapped it around her shoulders.

My knees bounced against the table when a waitress came up to us. She was wearing a tight pink top that showed off her chest and black pants that accented her waist. She had short black hair and gave me a devilish smile. I knew that look. It was a look that I had seen before, eyes trailing up and down me and lashes blinking innocently. I used to not mind it. I liked the idea of attracting women my way and feeling like I could have them without any complaints. But now that I had met Olive, I was at the mercy of a woman who acted a little disgusted by my presence. Apparently, my taste buds were maturing.

"Good evening! What can I get you?" She smiled at me, not acknowledging Olive. I frowned, putting my hand on the back of her chair and scooting it closer to me. The metal scraping against the floor captured the attention of other diners, but I didn't care. Olive deserved to be more than a second thought or complete ignorance. Affectionately, I placed a hand on her legging-covered thigh. The tiny waitress looked between Olive and me, down to my hand and back to my face.

"We would both like a hot chocolate for now. Thanks." I said in a clipped tone. I had no interest in anyone other than the Grinch sitting on my right. The waitress hesitated a beat before leaving to get our drinks. Olive stared at the rink, ignoring my hand on her leg. The mood had shifted since the waitress took our drink order. I tapped my finger on her leg to get her attention.

"You all good?" I tilted my head and looked into her pretty green eyes.

She hesitated but said, "Yup, I'm fine."

Oh gosh. That was not what I needed to hear. If I learned anything from my mother, it was that when anyone said they are *fine,* it usually meant they weren't.

"Did I do something?" I leaned closer to her, hoping she would meet my eyes.

"No, no. It's just...does every girl flirt with you the second they see you?"

Ahh, so that's what it was about. I grinned mischievously at her. "You jealous, Little Grinch?"

Olive opened her mouth like she was offended, and I grinned harder. "Absolutely not. I just think it was rude of her, if we were together, I mean."

Her arms crossed, and I tried to avoid looking at how her chest moved when she did so. I gave her a look that said *suuuuure,* and she continued. "I'm serious, Finn. I don't care because we're not actually together. I just think it was rude."

I looked her up and down and couldn't help but laugh. Olive was one of the most, if not *the* most, beautiful women I had ever seen before. The thought of Olive being insecure about or jealous of any woman was ridiculous. Sure, Olive had perfect blonde hair and a body that most women could only dream of. But more than that, her personality was incredible; she was smart, witty, funny and damn if she didn't make me smile every time she looked at me.

Her eyes met mine, and I felt compelled to make a confession.

"Olive," I breathed out her name. "If you were mine, you would never wonder how perfect you are."

Woah. Even though I meant every word, I hadn't planned to let something like that casually slip. I wanted to backtrack but honestly, who was I kidding? I was completely caught up in this girl.

"Finn, I—"

"Two hot chocolates!" Our obnoxious waitress came back and cut off Olive's reply. This damn waitress was close to making me write a bad review on Yelp or some shit. Well, probably not. Only assholes wrote public one-star reviews. But I certainly wouldn't give her the time of day. I said a quiet thanks and turned my body fully to Olive, giving her my undivided attention. Giving her what she deserves.

"What were you saying?"

I took a sip of my hot chocolate and regretted it as the tip of my tongue burned. I pretended like it didn't affect me on account of trying to look normal in front of her.

"I was just going to say thank you for tonight. It was...fun." She blew on her own drink and took a slow sip.

"So do you admit Christmas isn't overrated?" My grin was wide and confident.

She puffed out a laugh and although it may have been sarcastic, it was music to my ears. "Absolutely not, Finland. I'm telling you, you don't know what you're up against."

Her nickname for me made the pain in my tongue slip away. "Don't worry, Grinchy, we've still got ten days." I winked, and she lifted her cup up to her full lips.

"I'm not sure I'm ready for the next ten days," she said, but the accompanying grin told me she *was* ready. She was excited.

"Oh, honey. We're just getting started."

TWENTY
OLIVE

I tossed and turned for hours. I couldn't be sure why. Maybe it was the amount of caffeine I'd consumed that day, or too much screen time. Possibly the fact that I had an amazing date with my hot fake boyfriend who I was slowly developing feelings for.

Nope. Not that.

I reached for my phone in hopes of a distraction. I mindlessly read my ebook, escaping into a wild fantasy. I slipped in between the rich words and fell into murder mysteries, romance, dragons, and faeries. It was far better than anywhere on Earth.

As I was reading, a notification popped up on my phone that I didn't expect.

Hottie from 15B: You still up?

I still have to change that contact name...

I checked the time, noting it was one in the morning, and wondered why Finn was up so late.

Me: Sure am.

A moment later my phone rang, and I didn't hesitate to pick up.

"Hello," I said, my voice hushed like a teenager who was scared of their mom catching them on the phone late at night.

"Hey, honey." *Oh no.* Finn's voice was even sexier late at night. It was rich and creamy and reminded me of caramel. It clung to my brain and weaved its way through me. Between the deep and thick tone and his use of the word *honey*, I was a puddle.

"What are you doing up?" In comparison to his sexy tone, my voice was small and squeaky.

"Couldn't sleep." *Me either.* "I thought I'd see if you were up too, and I lucked out."

I reached over and turned on my Bluetooth headphones so I could hear his voice better. "Well, you did, I'm up and can't sleep for anything."

"Have you tried counting Maxes?" I could hear his grin through the phone.

"Huh?"

"You know...like counting sheep. Counting Max... since you're my Grinch?" I liked the way he said *my Grinch* as if I really was his, as if we had known each other as long as we claimed. As if the time we'd spent together had been real and not him doing me a favor.

When I didn't answer right away, he continued. "Crap, it sounded funnier in my head."

It made me giggle, thinking of Finn lying in the dark, making his little jokes. I wondered where he was, and figured he was probably in bed like me. But what was he wearing? Did he sleep naked? Oh no, no. No. Between his deep voice and *that* mental image, my brain was shot.

"You there, Olive?" His use of my name brought me back to reality.

"Oh yeah, sorry. I was just thinking."

I heard a shuffle of what sounded like pillows being adjusted. "What are you thinking about tonight?"

You.

"Not much really. Politics, religion, taxes…"

Finn's laugh as it filtered through my headphones was oddly comforting. "Sounds like a fun time in that big brain of yours, but I don't believe you. Tell what you're *really* thinking." His voice dropped an octave, suggesting I had inappropriate thoughts, which was true, but I'd never admit it to him.

He continued when I didn't respond. "Do you want to know what I'm thinking about tonight?" His voice was husky and somewhat hoarse, and it resonated deep in my chest. It was like I was lying next to him in that bed, and I could feel the rumble of his words from here.

"What's that?" I whispered, scared to even ask. What *did* Finn Beckett lie awake thinking of?

He whispered back to me, so quiet I barely heard. "I'm thinking about how good those peanuts were on the plane. Or was it peanus? I can't remember."

I laughed loud enough to wake the house, and probably harder than I had in a long time. I wiped a tear from my cheek and said, "I have to say that was *not* what I expected." I sucked in a breath to calm my racing heart.

"Olive Moore..." He dragged out my name, those three syllables mellifluous in my head. "Are you thinking about having phone sex with me right now?"

I gasped audibly and my heart raced faster. "No!" I shouted louder than necessary. "I just thought you were going to say something different."

His deep chuckle was warm. "I mean if that's what you're trying to do I can help. I'm pretty good at it. You wanna know what I would do if I were there, I wou—"

"*Finn*!" I yelled, embarrassed. I longed to hear what he would do to me with those big hands of his, but if he did, I would never be able to look him in the eye again.

"I'm just messing with you, Grinchy. Unless you wanted me to?"

His voice was playful and flirty, making me blush all over. A shuffle came through the phone, and I imagined him shifting in bed. Part of me wished we were together right now, which was ridiculous because I *just* saw him. I looked at the time again, feeling a little guilty for keeping him up.

"Don't you have to work early tomorrow?" I briefly remembered him mentioning his early schedule at the resort.

"A little, but I can run on a few hours of sleep." For some reason, that didn't surprise me. A picture of Finn up bright and early running around like a golden retriever crossed my mind, and I grinned to myself.

"Are you sur—"

"Just keep talking to me." His breath hitched. "Tell me something no one else knows."

There was so much I could tell him, the ghosts of my past that haunted me at night. But I settled for something easier. "I broke my arm when I was little. A boy on the playground said he could go across the monkey bars faster than me, and I told him he couldn't. Turns out I was right, I just found out the wrong way. I got there way before him and slipped at the last second. My cast got signed by the whole class, and my mom bought me a new Gameboy."

Finn chuckled. "What color Gameboy did you have?"

"Pink. It matched my cast."

He laughed again, and I closed my eyes, picturing that sweet smile and bright teeth lighting up a room.

I wasn't sure how long we stayed on the phone like that, but I enjoyed every second of it. It was like talking to a long-time friend but also something a little more than that.

"I did not!"

"You totally did. You looked like you had steam coming out of your ears."

I *hmphed* out a breath. "You made fun of my favorite movie!" I tried my best to sound angry even though I couldn't stop smiling. "I can't let you do that and not be upset."

He laughed back. "It was cute, watching you defend why *Prisoner of Azkaban* was the best one in the series."

I blushed, and my cheeks ached from grinning so hard. "Man, I can't remember the last time I smiled this hard." The sentence slipped out before I could truly filter it.

"I think you have the most beautiful smile I've ever seen," Finn said casually, as if it wasn't the sweetest admission I'd heard in a long time. I smiled and played with my hair like a schoolgirl.

Finn yawned, and I reactively checked the time. It was half-past four. We had stayed up all night talking, and I didn't even think twice about it. For once I didn't second guess myself or overthink everything I was saying. I spoke with Finn like I had known him for years. For some reason, it was easier than being with anyone else I knew. Maybe it was because it had been so long since I had a friend, or maybe it was because he was so understanding. Either way, it was a lot like unbuttoning a pair of too-tight pants. Finn was loosening me slowly but surely, and my walls were slowly falling.

"I didn't realize how late it was. Do you need to go to sleep?"

He groaned. "Ugh. I guess I should. I've got to be up in two hours."

Guilt trickled over me. "I'm sorry, I guess I shouldn't have kept you up all night."

Finn quickly backtracked. "No, Olive. Don't apologize, I would lose all my sleep just to hear your voice." Gah, he was too sweet.

"I liked talking with you tonight," I said. "You make me feel...normal." It was a small opening, a crack into my feelings for him.

"You are far from normal, Grinchy. But I adore it."

A sleepy smile spread across my cheeks, and I shoved my face in my pillow to keep from audibly squealing. I was sixteen all over again with Finn.

"Well thanks, I guess."

"You are terrible at taking compliments. You need to be more confident. You've got a lot to offer. Flaunt it, Olive."

I muttered, "You can thank my ex for that," and cursed my broken filter, wishing I could retract what spilled out. But I didn't have the energy to watch what I said.

"Is he the reason you won't touch anyone with a thirty-nine-and-a-half-foot pole?" I picked up on the Grinch reference but didn't acknowledge it.

"We should probably go to sleep," I said, ignoring his question.

"I know what you're doing, and you're lucky I'm too tired to keep asking. But don't think this conversation is over." Finn yawned again, and I pictured his tired puppy-dog eyes.

"I'll let you go, goodni—"

"Stay on here. We can both go to sleep but just...stay here. It's comforting."

I tried to not overthink everything he was asking, but my heart kicked my ribs with his words. What was happening here?

"Oh. Okay." I didn't argue or protest, only sleepily laid my head on my pillow and drifted to sleep with my phone cradled in my hand like I was holding Finn.

When I woke a few hours later, I immediately checked to see if I was still on the phone with Finn. But our call had ended, and I had a text from him at six thirty.

Hottie from 15B: I had to hang up when I started getting ready, didn't want to wake you. Happy day three, Grinchy. I'll see you tonight.

TWENTY-ONE
FINN

I stretched my arms up and rubbed the sore spot in the back of my neck. I let out a loud noise that was a mix between a groan and a yawn.

"Did you not sleep?" Cooper asked, handing me my fourth cup of coffee.

"Nope. Too busy with Olive." My tone wasn't suggestive, but it could be misconstrued that way. And judging by Coop's sly grin, he took it as such.

"So, my moves worked then, huh?" He sipped his coffee and raised his brows.

I rolled my eyes and regretted it thanks to the headache I had from lack of sleep. "Not like that. We just stayed on the phone all night."

Coop looked at me confused. "So y'all didn't..."

"Nope."

"Huh. So, you *really* like this girl then."

"I mean, yeah. She's just different. This whole time I feel like she's been so closed off and last night it was like she was finally starting to open up, and maybe like me back. I'm kind of scared to see her tonight. She's been skittish, and I don't want her to backtrack."

We both got up from our spot in the cafe and walked to the locker room to change out for the day. We passed by a group of women who openly stared at the two of us, and Cooper tipped his head to them and smiled. They giggled and when he stopped to talk to them, I kept walking. It used to be a fun game for us, to see how many numbers we could get and brag about it the next morning. But now I couldn't even pretend to care if I tried. I wasn't interested in a single number any girl had to offer. All I could think of was a certain lithe blonde that captivated every fiber of my being.

I didn't stop when Coop called out my name, only kept walking to my locker.

"Finn. Wait up." He caught up to me. "Come on, you could've just said hi."

I shrugged. "I'm good."

He looked slightly taken aback but kept walking with me. When we got to the lockers, I rushed to my black The North Face backpack and pulled my phone out hoping to see anything back from her after sending the last text this morning. I was blessed with one small message.

Li'l Grinch: My family is going out to the Wild Fig tonight. Can you go?

I smiled to myself and felt the need to raise my fist in the air like the guy from *The Breakfast Club*. Maybe when I was alone.

Me: Give me a time and I'll be there.

I adjusted the collar of my button-up in the visor mirror and ran a hand through my dark hair. My scruffy beard was neatly trimmed, and I wore the most expensive cologne I owned. I felt like James Bond about to go do some spy shit. I resisted the urge to raise my eyebrows and do a fake gun motion with my hand like a true 007.

I stepped out of my *mom car*, as Olive liked to call it, and walked to her parents' large wooden front door. I hadn't even raised my hand to knock before the door swung wide, revealing Denise.

"Hi, Finn! You look so handsome!" Olive's mom excitedly waved a hand for me to come in. I sent her a bright, charming smile

"Thank you, Mrs. Moore. You look wonder—" I couldn't finish my sentence before she wrapped around my midsection and squeezed the life out of me.

"We are so excited to have you here. Olive has been needing you."

I tapped the top of her head and said in a strained voice, "Thank you." I wanted to show more gratitude but she was currently depriving my lungs of necessary oxygen.

"Mom!" Matt's deep voice rumbled along the walls of their entryway as he came up behind her. "Give him some room."

He lightly touched her shoulder, and she released her death grip. I took a step toward Matt and shook his hand.

Matt was as tall as me, which said a lot considering I usually towered over everyone. If I were anyone else, he would have terrified me. His dark eyes scanned me head to toe, sizing me up—trying to intimidate me. Lucky for me, I knew better than to fall in that trap. James Bond didn't get nervous around his crush's older brother. We shook hands and his glare lessened slightly. I scanned the large living room for Olive, but she was nowhere to be found. Before I could ask, Matt answered my question.

"She's with Taylor in her room." He jerked his head in the direction of the long hallway covered in family photos. I nodded and made my way past him and Denise.

I glanced at the framed pictures and smiled to myself. There were some of each kid at different events. Graduations, football games, academic awards. It gave me a small pang of jealousy. I had always wished for a single sibling, but having two would've been incredible to me. I stopped at a picture of Olive and her sister, Sarah. Posed in front of the same house I stood in, they had their arms wrapped around each other in a tight embrace. Big smiles spread across their cheeks, and Olive appeared to be mid-laugh. She had the prettiest smile I'd ever seen, and the picture made me wish I saw it more.

Laughter filtered into the hall from behind a closed door at the end of the hall. I assumed it was Olive's, so I leaned closer to the light filtering through the crack to listen.

"You totally should!" Her sister-in-law said, laughing through her words.

Olive's stern voice followed. "Um. Absolutely not. Please just stop talking."

I'd heard that same tone before on the plane, when I initially suggested helping her with her family. Out of curiosity, I stepped closer.

"Why not? He would love it. You could go over there and get some *privacy*." Taylor's tone was suggestive, and I grinned.

"Because it's rude! And I can't do that, we just—" Olive cut whatever she was about to say short, and I wondered if she was going to spill the beans that we'd only met recently. Before she could go further, I opened the already cracked door and leaned against the frame. Olive was on her small bed, and Taylor sat on a white desk chair. Her room looked youthful. It was covered in rose gold and sparkles, which was a surprise compared to the Olive I knew. She was laid out on her stomach on the bed with her arms propping her up. Her black dress was tight on her upper thighs, and I fought to keep my eyes from trailing across her body. Her blonde hair was in a braided updo, and I could admire her like this all night.

"Just man up and do it!" Taylor raised her voice a little.

They had clearly not seen me.

"Taylor! I am not staying with him when I have a perfectly good place to sleep here," Olive said.

Taylor leaned her head back and groaned. "Live a little! Just go stay at his house. It's your chance to put all my tips to good use."

What tips? I assumed they were talking about me since Taylor thought we were together.

I cleared my throat, alerting them to my presence before they could say anything else. Both women turned their heads to me faster than I could blink. Olive struggled to sit up, and Taylor looked between the two of us.

"I'm just gonna…" Taylor jumped off the fancy desk chair and ran past me in a hurry, avoiding my gaze.

I looked back to Olive, where she sat properly on her bed with legs crossed and hands in her lap. Her round cheeks were a shade of deep pink that faded over her freckles, and I couldn't hold my grin back.

"We were just talking about a podcast I'm working on." If if I hadn't heard her and Taylor talking about me, the pitch to her tone would've told me she was lying.

"Sounded like a good *podcast*."

"No, no. It was just—" she said, jumping to defend herself, and my grin widened.

As she stuttered excuses, I studied her room. It was feminine and sparkly and so unlike Olive.

She was still going on when I said, "I'm surprised. This doesn't seem like you." Not that I knew her that well, but from what I did know of her, I didn't see her as the type to be so girly. It was cute.

"It's not. Mom never changed it when I left for college." She scanned the room like she was placing memories through it.

"So, what's your room like back in Florida?" I settled into the chair Taylor had vacated when she fled the room. Olive shifted to be more comfortable on her bed and in doing so forced me to confront the fact that I was in her *room*. It was where she grew up, where she laid her pretty blonde head down to sleep, where she talked to me on the phone for hours, where she got ready this afternoon in that killer dress. It was overwhelming, her classic scent everywhere. And everything was so *soft*. The rug under her bed, the blankets lying at its foot, the tiny pillows that served no purpose, the candles with black wicks on the desk—it was all so comforting, like a warm hug.

"A lot more neutral," she said with a small laugh.

"I can picture that."

And I could, but I hoped she still had pieces of this Olive in her current bedroom in Florida. Would I ever see that bedroom? I had a feeling I wouldn't, and that thought was a cloud of dread hanging over us. She twiddled her fingers like she was thinking the same thing, and I felt the need to put my own hands over them.

"Are you ready to go?" I looked down at her form-fitting black dress and heels. She certainly looked ready—ready to drive me crazy all night.

She nodded her head slowly, careful not to muss up her hair. Even in heels, she was incredibly short when she stood, and it made me smile. She was like a doll I wanted to scoop up and carry with me everywhere. I stood too and closed the distance between us. The top of her head came up to my chest, and I struggled not to pull her closer. *Was that Lionel Richie playing in my head?* I didn't even care because I *was* stuck on her. After talking so much last night, things felt *different*. I had always been attracted to Olive. Hell, the second I saw her on the plane—eye mask and all—and realized she was my seat mate, I nearly dropped my luggage on my feet. Now it was like everything was multiplied. Something told me she felt the pull between us too because she wouldn't even look me in the eye.

"Olive," I said, her name like a prayer. I didn't have anything else to say; I only wanted her to see me.

Her bright green eyes lifted to mine, and I melted. My hand reached under her chin and rubbed my thumb across it. *So beautiful.* She took a step closer, her chest brushing my midsection, and I nearly groaned from the simple contact. She leaned into me like she was on autopilot, and I was her only destination. I cautiously slid my hand from her chin to the back of her neck. She swallowed, and the movement of her throat pulled me in like runway lights calling me home. I moved closer, hesitantly, our faces only inches away. She would have stopped me, right? She would have given me that sassy attitude and pushed me away if she didn't want this. The Olive I knew wouldn't let me get this far. I paused, unsure.

"Tell me to stop."

I needed to hear it. To hear her yell at me. To have her say, "I told you no kissing," and give me a shove. If she didn't, I would take her on this bed right now, without a care of who else was in the house.

She grabbed my white button-down and pulled me impossibly closer. "No."

It was quiet, barely a whisper. I tightened my grip on her neck and leaned forward.

This was it. Everything you have thought of nonstop since that flight. I was going to kiss the hell out of her. I was going to leave her lips swollen and numb until she was dizzy and floating.

I tilted her head up with my spare hand and inched my lips toward hers slowly, ready to throw all caution to the wind.

"Finn." She moaned my name before my lips were even on her, and I forced my heart not to explode. We were a dyad, two halves of the same whole. She was the best I ever had, and I hadn't even *had* her yet. My lips were a centimeter from hers. Finally. *Finally.*

"Let's go!" A loud voice boomed from down the hall. I didn't know who it was, but they clearly had a death wish to interrupt what was supposed to be our first kiss.

Olive retreated, and I nearly whined like a toddler when her warmth left. My body still *burned* for her. I craved her, any way I could have her.

"We should go," she whispered like it hurt to come out of her mouth. It sure hurt to hear. I nodded my head though all I wanted to do was pull her back to me. She'd effortlessly wrapped me around her tiny finger, and I never wanted to let go.

TWENTY-TWO
OLIVE

My body was on fire. The restaurant was on fire. The whole world—on fire.

I couldn't stop shifting in my seat at the long table. The white tablecloth softly brushed my thighs, and I was thankful for the coverage so no one could see my restless legs. Finn was sitting so close I could smell his cologne. His shirt was partially wrinkled where I'd fisted my hands in it earlier, and I blushed looking at the lines, remembering.

Our almost kiss earlier replayed in my mind ever since we left my room. I couldn't erase it from my memory; it *owned* me. Our lips hadn't even touched, and my knees nearly buckled. Finn's strong hands were on my neck and my chin; he was pulling me into him, and even if I should have told him to stop, there was no way I would. I couldn't. He was *right* there, and I *wanted* him to press his perfectly full lips on mine. But then, in a flash, we pulled away. The denied contact made my skin tight, and I was equally aroused and annoyed.

Finn sat close to me, a long menu in his big hands and his knee bouncing against the tablecloth. I looked up into his face at the same moment he turned to me. Our eyes met, and my mouth went dry. I quickly turned away, back to the conversation across the table. Dad was telling us all about the trip he and Mom went on a couple of weeks ago, but I couldn't retain a word he said. I was focused solely on Finn's body being *right there.*

"And for you, sweetie?" An elbow to my left poked me, and I looked up to see our waitress was staring at me with a notepad in her hand.

"Oh, sorry. I'll just get whatever he got." I cocked my head toward Finn, too wrapped up in thinking about him to count calories. The waitress took the rest of our orders and soon brought a bottle of wine to our table.

"Are you okay?" Finn leaned into me, his mouth brushing my ear.

I looked up at him and smiled. For the first time in years, I wasn't anxious about anything. I wasn't wondering what could go wrong or who was around me. I didn't care about my makeup being perfect or if my hair was placed just right. For the first time since I got here, I didn't care what Sarah was doing or if anyone in my family was watching me. I was focused solely on Finn. And judging by his soft eyes and wide smile, he felt the same. He made me feel like I was something real to him, and I soaked it up.

"Finn, tell us about some of the kids you work with," Mom said from across the table.

"I've got a couple of groups that come regularly and some that are just here on vacation. My regulars are my favorite, of course. I've got a couple that are hard to control, but they're usually the most talented." Finn continued on for who knew how long while I stared at him. His eyes sparkled with passion, and you could tell with every word he spoke, he loved his job.

I was proud to have him here, to bring him around my family. It was such a contrast to our last dinner together when he popped in uninvited. I was a ball of anxiety and anger last time, but now I was basking in a wave of reassurance. It took me until that moment, watching him laugh and talk to my family as if they'd known each other for years, to truly realize how much I needed him on this trip. I would've probably already fled by now and been back in Florida, drinking margaritas on my living room floor and watching nineties sitcoms. Instead, I sat next to one of the nicest guys I've ever met, with his hand on my leg as he and my family joked about sports and their jobs. Finn fit at the table like a missing puzzle piece, and I was thrilled...and terrified. Because the past lingered over me, following me wherever I went.

Finn trailed his thumb across the skin just above my knee, and I leaned closer. I felt Finn looking at me as I watched Matt talk about stories from when we were younger, and I couldn't help the corners of my mouth lifting ever so slightly.

After our wine was poured, we each grabbed a glass. Dad said to the table, "Would anyone like to toast?"

To no surprise, Finn raised his glass, looked me dead in the eyes, and without wavering said, "To the red-eye."

I swore my Grinch heart grew three sizes.

TWENTY-THREE
FINN

Dinner with Olive's family was like seeing friends you hadn't seen in forever, like we had known each other for years and were catching up. I noticed how Olive loosened up over the night too, and as much as she wanted to blame it on the wine, I knew it was because of the company around her.

"That is not what happened!" Olive smiled next to me.

"Oh yes, it is! You were all 'Guys watch this!' Like you were about to do the coolest trick then you jumped and busted your chin." Matt explained the story of Olive's tiny scar under her chin and how she thought she could fly off their balcony at a young age.

Olive's mom wiped tears of laughter from her face. "Oh, she was a mess to deal with, but that's just our fearless little Olive. Always the craziest one in the room."

I looked down to the five-foot-four blonde beside me and raised a brow. This girl? Fearless? The one who nearly cried going down a hill made for children? Or the one who nearly had a panic attack when I said we had to get off the ski lift?

"Olive Moore? Fearless?" I elbowed her side, and she stiffened. "I have a hard time picturing that."

Olive shoveled her pasta in her mouth, not looking up when her mom continued. "Oh, yeah. Our Olive was always the most fun one in the family. She was known as the town troublemaker for her age, always getting into something. She would have her entire grade over for parties when she was younger."

I couldn't hold in my laughter. "Are we talking about the same Olive?"

The rest of the table was clearly uncomfortable, and Olive gave a strained response. "A lot of things have changed since I've been back here."

Thankfully, the waitress came back to check on us before I could make the conversation even more uncomfortable. Topics were suddenly switched, but I couldn't help but notice Sarah looking at Olive with sympathetic eyes.

Dinner ended, and we made our way back to the car. I offered to drop Olive off at her house to give her alone time with her family. However, when I mentioned it, she whispered a comment along the lines of, "That's the last thing I need." And I figured since it was day three of my twelve days of Christmas, I still needed to deliver today's gift to her.

An idea came to mind, and I made a quick U-turn to head straight to the resort. It was late, but I had an all-access key, and I could come and go as I pleased.

Olive shivered beside me, and I reached over to turn her seat warmers on. She looked up and smiled, and it was like my own seat warmers turned on as a result.

"Where are we going now?" She nuzzled into the warming passenger seat.

I grinned back at her. "I've got an idea for my third day of Christmas for you."

She turned her head to the side, lips twisted and eyes squinted like she was thinking. "Three French hens?"

Whoever made that song had a bird problem.

"Nope. No hens tonight, Grinchy."

When we got to the resort, I pulled out my access key card and walked her down the marble-floored lobby to the employee locker room. I grabbed two navy towels with one hand then took Olive's in my other. I dragged her to the back door.

"Why would we possibly need towels?"

I smiled and put an index finger over my mouth, the universal gesture for *be quiet*. I opened the door to a gated area that had one of the largest hot tubs on the resort. I usually came here after my shift if I needed to relax, or on the off chance they had any parties or events back here that Coop and I were invited to. Since it closed two hours ago, according to the sign on the gate, I was left with no choice.

I threw the towels over the tall white gate and backed up.

"Finn. What are you doing?" Olive asked like she didn't already know the answer. I took a running jump and climbed the fence, dropping down silently on the other side. I opened the gate wide and waved my hand for her to come inside.

She had her arms crossed and legs tucked together, clearly freezing. "Are we going to get in trouble for this?" She asked, her teeth chattering.

"Nah. It's fine." *I hope.*

My hand intertwined with hers, and I pulled her along. There was a small walkway that led to a big hot tub, the snowy mountains serving as a gorgeous backdrop. Olive looked between the tub and me and raised her eyebrow in confusion.

"I don't have a swimsuit."

I grinned, thinking maybe it would be better if she didn't have a swimsuit. I lifted my eyebrows twice and winked.

"I am *not* skinny dipping with you in twenty-degree weather," she said, crossing her arms as if to seal her point.

Can't blame a guy for trying.

I shrugged. "You can just wear my shirt."

I had an undershirt beneath my button-down, and seeing her in my clothes didn't sound like a bad idea.

Olive watched me closely as I unbuttoned my shirt. I slowly peeled it off me then tugged off my white undershirt. I reached an arm out to her, my undershirt dangling off my fingers. Olive's eyes trailed across my abs and up my chest, her mouth frozen, and her cheeks that pretty shade of pink I loved so much. She opened her mouth and shut it, like she couldn't get out whatever was crossing her mind. Judging by the color spreading across her face and her nervous fidgeting, I could guess what was going on in that pretty little head of hers.

"Enjoying the view?"

She tore her eyes from me and turned to the real view of icy mountains and shining lights around us.

"Mhm," she mumbled in agreement, and my cheeks hurt from grinning.

She grabbed the shirt forcefully from me, and when I didn't make an attempt to move or look away, she spun her finger, gesturing for me to turn around.

"Ugh, fine." I reluctantly looked away, and after a brief moment, I heard her clothes shifting. She made a *brr* noise like she was shivering, and a small amount of guilt filtered through me.

I turned to hand her a towel, but before I could even say anything she shouted, "Turn around!"

I closed my eyes and held out the towel, which she ripped out of my hands, and I swore I heard her whisper, "Pervert."

I let out a belly laugh and said, "That's the last time I try to help you."

She groaned in pain and I asked, "What's wrong?"

My eyes were shut, but my arms jutted out in her direction, ready to blindly help.

She slapped away one of my hands and said, "Nothing. These stupid heels are killing my feet."

Once she was dressed in my T-shirt with the towel wrapped around her shoulders, I looked around the corner to make sure no one was around and unbuttoned my pants.

"What are you doing?" Olive whispered sharply through her chattering teeth.

I glanced around. "Um. Getting in. What does it look like I'm doing?"

She squinted her eyes. What did she expect? I wasn't getting in there with pants on. Realistically, I could have grabbed a pair of Coop's swim trunks from the locker room, but where was the fun in that?

I stripped down to my black boxer briefs and pretended to not notice Olive blushing in the corner. I dipped a hand in the hot tub and winced at the heat.

We both eased our way into the hot water and relaxed against opposite sides. I reached out and pulled her tiny sore foot into my lap, rubbing my thumbs deep into her soles.

Olive moaned the same way she said my name earlier in the night, and I fought to not pull her all the way to me.

"Why are you so good at this?" She asked in a frustrated tone. As if she was saying, "Why didn't you pay your taxes on time?" and not complimenting me on my massage skills. I huffed out a small laugh.

"I used to have to work out knots in my legs after skiing. I got pretty good at it over the years." I *may* have dug into the same spot where she let out that previous sweet moan, wanting to hear it again.

"Yeah, you did," she said in a strained voice that made my shoulders bounce with a chuckle.

Olive tipped her head back against the headrest behind her. The tips of her long blonde hair dipped into the hot water and darkened. I had a clear view of my wet T-shirt glued to her chest, and her exposed neck was laid out perfectly across from me. It was foolish for me to think the greatest views in Colorado were the snowy mountains. No, it was the rise and fall of Olive's soft curves that needed to be on a postcard.

I thanked the good Lord that she was wearing a bra under my shirt because the last thing I needed right now was my own Olive

Moore-sponsored wet T-shirt contest. My heart raced faster when she let out small whimpers as my thumbs pressed on the inner soles of her delicate foot.

My stomach seized and body temp rose—and not due to the water. I needed any kind of distraction.

"So...fearless Olive, huh?" I did my best to keep my voice calm so she wouldn't know how incredibly turned on I was.

She leaned her head into her shoulder. "Ugh. I know. I was hoping that wouldn't come up again."

"So, what's changed? Since back then, I mean." I took advantage of her relaxed state, sliding my hand from her foot up to her ankle and shin. Her skin was smooth but tight, and it was almost worse. I was incredibly grateful for the bubbles moving around my boxers, or this would be a lot more uncomfortable for her.

"Everything." She sighed when I dug my fingers into her calf.

Everything? I hummed. "It hasn't been that long since you've been here, right?"

Her head tipped back, and she hummed a moan. I knew she was over our conversation, but I clearly wasn't going to let up.

"Is it because of that ex you mentioned?"

Her arms, which had been swishing back and forth along the surface of the water, stilled. "Yes." She gave no elaboration.

I trailed my thumbs across her shin and tugged her closer to me, forcing her to lift her head from the rest behind her.

"Do you want to tell me what happened?" I placed her pink-painted toes against my abs under the water, loving how her skin felt against mine.

"Not really, no," she said, but didn't pull away.

From that response alone, I could have an idea of what happened. Olive's walls were high and strong, but I would chip them down piece by piece to get to her.

"Can I ask you something?"

"Just one thing?"

I actually had a million questions, and I smiled that she knew me that well. *Do you like cereal better in the morning or at night? How do you feel about sharks? Do you think aliens are real?* But those were far down the long list.

"For now...yes."

She shrugged as an answer and took a deep breath as I pressed into the ball of her foot.

"Have you ever been in love?"

"Once."

"And?" I prompted, but had a feeling I knew the answer.

"And it's overrated."

Whoever broke her heart was depriving not only himself, but the whole world.

Sighing, I continued sweeping my thumbs over her feet. What would it take for me to know Olive? *Truly* know her. Not the image, not the outer shell, but the real Olive. The one who sometimes snorted when something was too funny, or the one who secretly loved her mom's pie but hid it. That was the Olive I needed. The *real* one. Not whoever this woman in front of me was. Maybe if I gave her a piece of my own past, I would get some of hers in return.

"You know, I was cheated on once in high school."

Olive's eyes widened. "Really? *You?*" I liked how she said that, as if she couldn't believe anyone ever cheated on me. It puffed up my ego.

"Yup. I wasn't always this good looking, babe. I dated this girl for a few months and caught her with a guy from another school at a party. It broke my heart, but I was quick to realize if she didn't want me, I wouldn't sit around and mope about it. I was a scrawny little thing, but I was smart and funny. If she couldn't see that, it was her fault. Not mine."

Olive relaxed under my touch, and I inched a little closer.

Give me something, Grinchy, I silently pleaded.

Finally, she whispered, "I was too, you know."

I dipped my head and raised my brows, telling her to continue.

"A long time ago, when I still lived here, I was cheated on. Walked right in on him with another girl after we graduated college. That was one of the reasons I was scared to come home."

I couldn't picture someone cheating on this girl in front of me. She was *everything*. It was comical, how I didn't care about my past girlfriend cheating on me with some basketball player at a stupid party, but I was ready to break a man's fingers for ever hurting Olive.

"Does he still live here?" My deep voice was rasped.

"Oh, no. He moved away almost right after. I'm not sure where he is, but that's probably a good thing."

It *was* a good thing. If I had any clue this guy was in town, well…I would hate to end up in jail before I could finish my twelve days of Christmas with Olive.

"Well, it sucks to hear, but it was for the best. If there's something you can't control, it's because you weren't meant to control it. All we can do is manage how we react to what inevitable pain life brings us."

Olive lifted her chin to meet my eye and squinted, like she was trying to figure something out about my philosophy.

"Think about it, if you were still with that douchebag, you wouldn't be here in this hot tub getting the world's best massage." I grinned at her in an attempt to lighten the mood and hoped the rage in my chest would burn out.

She smiled ever so slightly. "I guess you're right. You *are* pretty good at this."

The admiration in her voice only bolstered me more. "Wow, is that what it's like to hear Olive Moore compliment me?"

She poked a finger into my bare chest. "Don't get used to it." Her words said one thing, but her threatening smile said another.

I grinned harder and made my move. I grabbed the back of her exposed thighs under water and pulled her onto me, her legs straddling mine. Her wet t-shirt clung to her smooth curves, and I fought to keep my hand from running over them.

Her cheeks flushed, mouth slightly agape. I raised a hand to her chin, the same chin I touched earlier tonight, when I'd been about to kiss her, before we were interrupted.

This time, there were no interruptions around us. I traced my thumb down her throat as she swallowed. I made small circles on her sensitive pulse point. With my spare hand, I trailed from her knee to her upper thigh. I appreciated every soft, feminine curve she had.

Olive breathed in a puff of air when my hand slipped to her backside as my other thumb pressed slightly on her throat.

"Finn." She spoke my name like it was something she had longed for, like at this moment it was all she could think to say. I soaked in the syllable as though it was the first time I'd ever hear it.

"Tell me, Olive." I pulled her closer to me, only a wet t-shirt separating us.

"Please," she whispered, almost like she was embarrassed, but it was enough for me. My hand at her throat moved under her hair at the back of her neck, and I pulled her mouth to meet mine.

Finally. I pressed my lips against hers and slid into home. She tilted her head slightly and our lips meshed together, a perfect fit. I was gentle despite everything in my body begging me not to be. I kissed her soft and slow, my hands gripping her. I craved more, but Olive was like a scared kitten that you had to let come to you. So, I fought every instinct I had.

When she made the sweetest whimper against my lips, all control abandoned me. I gripped her harder, pulled her closer, kissed her deeper. I wanted her to forget any memory of some idiot cheating on her. I wanted her to be here with me with no regrets.

I pulled away enough to whisper against her lips, "If I could, I would never let anyone else hurt you." *If only you were* really *mine.*

I knew I would be a mere two-week hook up for her, and she would gain her confidence back and go back to Florida, to all the tan surfer boys. But if I could give her enough to remember me.

Enough to make me not some guy she met on a plane. I wanted her to still think of me long after she was married and with kids. Was that terrible? Probably.

I needed to be etched into her mind, the way she was in mine.

I shifted Olive closer to me, and her hands traced my chest up to my hair. She ran her wet fingers through the strands, dampening them. She pulled away, and I fought to bring her lips back to me.

"Finn, we can't do this here." I was grateful that she ended that sentence with *here* and not *ever*. I press one more kiss to her lips. "Come home with me." I prayed my luck was still gracious enough to allow her into my bed.

She kissed me back and pushed her thighs against mine. A deep groan filled the air around us, and I realized it was coming from me. I was having an entire out-of-body experience by having her in my lap.

Olive slowly pulled away again. "I...can't."

I draped both my long arms around her small waist. "Why not?"

She looked down to my lips and back to my eyes, like she was considering changing her mind. "I have to go back home soon."

I shrugged. "I'm sure your parents don't mind. You're what, twenty-five? I doubt they think we are just innocently driving around."

She bit her swollen bottom lip. "No, I mean I have to go back to Florida soon and I—" She paused to take a deep breath. "I don't want to be just a two-week fling."

Something about that gave me comfort. She *was* thinking of me as more than a fling and although she was denying me a night in bed together—I agreed with her. She was far deserving of more than a two-week fling and a quick goodbye. At the same time, I knew if I had the knowledge of what Olive tasted like on my lips while she was here, I don't think I would survive when she left.

"Do you just not want a long-distance thing or..." I dragged my sentence out in hopes she'd finish it for me.

"No, it's not even that long distance is the problem. I just can't be in a relationship right now, and I don't do casual hook-ups." I hoped that hook-up rule applied when she went back to Florida too and didn't apply only to me.

"So, when you leave, that's it?" It made sense, but my heart was heavy.

"I don't like to come here often, and I'm just not in a place where..." She didn't finish her sentence, but I picked up on the cues that this was not going anywhere. My shoulders sank a little, but I grinned down at her.

"You're right." I sighed and tapped her thigh twice. "Come on, Grinchy. I'll take you home."

She smiled at my nickname for her and reluctantly got off my lap. The freezing cold air had both of us shivering, and we each turned around as we got dressed. I cringed, taking off my wet boxers and putting my clothes back on. I heard her whine then a loud wet smack on the ground, which I assumed was my t-shirt. I gave her a minute to get dressed, and when she tapped my shoulders, I turned back around. She had on her tiny black dress again and the soft towel wrapped around her shoulders. Her blonde hair dipped under the towel, and the wet ends clinging together. Her tiny nose matched her red cheeks, and I wanted to wrap her up in a blanket and bring her close to me. Instead, I gave her my thick coat and held her hand as we exited the restricted area.

When I dropped Olive off, all the lights were off except the front porch. I walked her to the door, my hands in my pockets—unsure what to do from here. She reached around her shoulders to take off my jacket and I stopped her. "Keep it. It looks better on you." I was rewarded with her dazzling smile, and I drank it in.

"Thank you," she said quietly and looked down from my gaze.

"I'll see you tomorrow, Grinchy."

She cocked her head to the side like she didn't know what tomorrow was.

"For day four. If our time together has an expiration date, I'm really going to get you in the Christmas spirit." I winked at her and took my hands out of my pockets. Instinctively, I reached for her but stopped myself. She studied my frozen gesture and could see I wasn't sure what to do. Do you kiss the girl you are pretending to see, but are kind of—not really—seeing goodnight?

She gave me a soft, sympathetic smile and stretched onto her tiptoes to give me a kiss on the cheek. "Goodnight, Finn." She patted my arm and turned to go inside.

Biting my lip, I walked back to my car feeling the need to run around like Rudolph after Clarise kissed him. *She thinks I'm cute! She thinks I'm cuuute!*

That night I went home and settled into bed with a smile plastered on my face—all due to my Little Grinch.

TWENTY-FOUR
OLIVE

I hadn't stopped smiling since last night. I woke up early, went for a run, edited a few podcast sections, and caught up on my reading before anyone else was up. I was showered, dressed, and ready before nine, feeling proud of my accomplishments so early. This morning made me feel like one of those productivity influencers who cleaned their whole house in thirty minutes. Watch out, Aspen—I was getting. shit. done.

When I left my room, Mom was perched on a barstool at the kitchen island. I walked around her to the coffee maker and poured myself a cup.

"You're in a good mood today," she observed. I hadn't realized I was sporting a small smile the whole time. I took a sip of my hot coffee and leaned against the counter.

"I had a good morning."

Mom had a big grin on her face. "A good night too, I'm assuming?"

"Mom!" It was great having a mother you could always reach out to about anything, but in moments like this I wished she was a little more uncomfortable about the subject.

"I'm just saying you got home late. And with wet hair."

I squinted at her. "Were you watching us?"

Her bedroom was adjacent to the front porch, and I should've assumed her nosy eyes were on us. A mental image of my mom splitting the blinds open and squinting to watch Finn and me while Dad told her to back away came over me.

"I just happened to check if the driveway had snow while you guys were out there." *Sure.*

"Well, *eavesdropper*. If you must know, it was a fun night." I left it at that, no need to describe any hot tub action I got.

Mom wrapped her hands around her own mug and leaned into it for warmth. "It is so refreshing seeing you like this. I can't tell you how many times I prayed you would find someone like Finn."

Of course she did; she was always thinking of her children. Even when I was a kid, Mom prayed nightly over the three of us and our futures.

"Well, he's a great guy." And it terrified me, because it would break their hearts when we eventually had to *break up*. Unfortunately, it wasn't going to only be me that would take the inevitable downfall with Finn harshly; the whole family would.

"Even Sarah last night was going on about how nice he seemed. Speaking of Sarah..."

I took a larger sip of my coffee. "I see what you're doing, Mom."

She shrugged her tiny shoulders. "I'm just curious if she has talked to you at all."

"We talked briefly yesterday. I just am not sure what she could say that would make us go back to normal."

Mom nodded. She knew every part of my old self was ripped out the last time I spoke to Sarah, and one conversation wouldn't bring that back.

"Maybe you should go shopping or something with her. Clear the air a little?"

I had no interest in clearing any air with my sister, but I knew Mom would keep pushing if I didn't say yes.

"I'll consider it." She saw through every bit of me, as always.

"I'm not taking her side. I am merely a neutral party who wants to see her children getting along."

I nodded my head. "I know, Mom."

I sat with her for almost an hour, laughing and catching up over the missed time. When I was in Florida, we spoke every couple of days, but there were so many things I didn't realize I needed to say until I saw her in person. And being the precious mother she was, she sat and listened with no judgment or unsolicited advice.

My phone buzzed and saw a missed text from Finn.

Hottie from 15B: Is it possible to die of a caffeine deficiency?

I chuckled to myself.

Me: Maybe. What are your symptoms?

Hottie from 15B: Exhaustion. Fatigue. Crankiness with a group of children.

Me: Sounds fatal. What is the treatment?

Hottie from 15B: A coffee date with a certain green-eyed blonde that hates Christmas.

My heart skipped a beat, and I felt my smile creeping back up.

Me: You're in luck, I happen to know one of those.

An idea crossed my mind, and I hugged mom briefly and asked to borrow her car before slipping out the door.

TWENTY-FIVE
FINN

"Okay, everyone! Up and down and up and down!" I shouted across the group of kids as they copied my movements.

Some stumbled as they practiced raising and lowering their legs with their skis attached. Several of them had helmets and goggles on that were too big so they looked like tiny aliens—it was adorable.

We had already run our practices for the day and were wrapping up what they had learned in the last week. When we finished our final exercises, the kids were dismissed, and I was wrapping up by picking up the orange flags we had placed down earlier in the morning. But I'd be lying if half my mind wasn't thinking of what Olive was doing.

I pictured her lying down on that tiny bed under a pile of covers that were pulled up to her chin. Or maybe she was sitting on her back deck looking at their perfect Colorado view. I could even see her at her desk, back hunched over her laptop, editing her podcasts. Her long blonde hair dripping into her face and sticking to her ChapStick-covered lips, and she would get irritated and huff as she kept pulling the strands away. I could picture her every movement.

What I didn't picture was her in an adorable layered ski outfit heading my way with two coffee cups in her hand.

Which was exactly what she was doing.

I rubbed my eyes with a gloved hand and refocused my gaze. But it didn't change. The mirage of a beautiful, shapely blonde with both of her hands full was moving toward me. It was like seeing a giant pond in the middle of the desert. Her small smile lit up the view, cheeks rosy and hair twisted into two long braids that I wanted to wrap my hands around. She was a dream. *My* dream.

I put down the flags I was holding and met her halfway. She paused in front of me, with a big grin on her face, and I was giddy like a child on Christmas morning.

I took a cup from her to free her hands. "What are you doing here?"

Olive nodded to the coffee in my hands. "I figured I couldn't let you die from lack of caffeine. And since you've been treating me all week, it was my turn."

I happily put my arms around her and pulled her into a hug. "Thanks, Olive. That's very un-Grinchy of you."

She laughed and hugged me back. "I was trying to make up for you doing so much for me since we got here."

The Olive in front of me was entirely different from the one I met on the plane. She was light and airy, like warm sunshine after all the clouds had gone away.

"Well, I'm very grateful. Come on, let's go inside. I have thirty minutes before my next group gets here." I nodded my head to the resort behind her.

"I didn't mean to take you away from work," she said, pointing at the flags I had dropped like they were on fire when I saw her. "I just wanted to stop and say hi while I was out."

"Come on, I've always got time for you." I grabbed her free hand in mine and walked us into the resort lounge area.

I sat us on an uncomfortably modern leather couch.

She breathed in loudly through her nose and leaned back into the cushions. "It's so relaxing here."

Relaxing? Maybe it was because I worked here, or because I had gotten used to it over the years. The lobby was filled with the chatter of people checking in and out, and the scent of coffee and orders being called out drifted from the cafe behind us. I looked around and breathed deeply as she had. Clean leather and vanilla clung to my nose, something I'd long since grown accustomed to. The fifteen-foot Christmas trees were lit up, and there were wreaths and stringed lights everywhere.

"I guess it is kind of relaxing. I'm just used to it now." I shrugged and sipped my coffee. She scooted a little closer, and I couldn't help but smile down at her.

We caught up over our coffee, even though it hadn't been twelve hours since we saw each other last. She told me of her morning with her mom, and I talked about the group I had right before she got there.

I relaxed back into the couch with her, and it was like we were the only two in the whole resort. When she spoke, nothing else around me mattered. I hadn't realized how gone for this girl I was. Since the moment I first saw her, I found her attractive, but watching her talk and smile was fascinating, and I would gladly sit on this uncomfortable couch all day.

"Excuse me," a sassy voice interrupted Olive, and without turning my head, I knew immediately who it was.

There stood tiny and feisty Alea with her arms crossed and her eyebrows furrowed. She looked like a teacher that caught Olive and me kissing under the bleachers.

"Oh, hey, Alea." She was staring Olive down with a fury only a fifty-five-pound, nine-year-old girl could manage.

Olive's eyes shifted from me to Alea uncomfortably.

Alea turned back to me. "You're late. Class was supposed to start five minutes ago." I checked the giant clock on the wall and noted she was right.

"Shoot. Sorry, kid, I'll be right there." I didn't attempt to get up since I wanted to say goodbye to Olive in private. Alea didn't move either. She stared Olive down like a mafia boss about to ice someone.

"So, what are you, his *girlfriend*?" She looked Olive up and down and curled a lip in disgust. Alea spit out the word *girlfriend* like it was poison.

"Well..." I began.

"Yup," Olive answered for me and crossed her arms, staring Alea down. Neither girl budged. It was a staring contest of epic proportions, the battle of the century, Scar versus Mufasa. And I was an innocent bystander who was about to witness the fight that should be televised by all boxing stations. It was violently uncomfortable watching it go down, but I couldn't look away. My twenty-five-year-old *girlfriend* and my nine-year-old student, both with attitudes that could drive you up the wall—having a stare down. I could've sworn a tumbleweed rolled in the background of their duel. This resort was clearly not big enough for the both of them.

"Well, Finn, *my teacher*, needs to come to class now," Alea sassed Olive.

"Well, my *boyfriend* will be there shortly." Olive stared her down.

What is happening right now?

"Um, guys," I muttered but neither of them acknowledged me.

Olive stood, towering over Alea, but what she didn't know was that Alea's attitude was taller than this entire building.

Their staring contest continued until I touched Olive on the shoulder. "I probably should go, Olive. I'll see you tonight though, right? Day four?"

Olive didn't look away from Alea, who smiled at me and said, "Yeah. He should probably go."

Olive finally tore her gaze away from the little girl. "I'll see you tonight." She planted a big kiss on my cheek, her lipstick undoubtedly leaving a mark, and I made no endeavor to remove it.

"Bye, babe." Olive turned to leave but not before giving Alea a cold stare.

These two girls would be the death of me.

TWENTY-SIX
OLIVE

The last three days had been some of the best I could remember. Finn made Christmas plans for us each day, and his excitement was adorable. It was like a child dragging you to go meet Santa; it was cold and you didn't want to stand in the lines, but seeing how excited they got when they finally met him made it worth it.

Day Four

After I stopped by the lodge to surprise him, he took me to a bonfire that Cooper had at his house, where he excitedly introduced me to all of their friends and their girlfriends. One of the girlfriends brought her dog, and I stuck by his side all night; dogs that were fluffy and begging to be squished were my kryptonite. Finn eventually pulled me away and brought me near the fire. I sat in his lap—due to limited seating of course—close to the warm glow, and every time the smoke came my way, he would pick me up and move me. His friends ribbed him about being whipped, and he never once denied it. It was a tiny view into his personal life, and I smiled the whole way home.

Day Five

He took me to see *The Nutcracker* ballet in theaters. He made comments every time the male dancer would do a high jump or an impressive spin with the ballerina in his arms.

"I could do that."

"Pshh, that's easy."

"Why is everyone freaking out over this guy jumping?"

Afterward he proceeded to take me into the parking lot and do high jumps under the street light lamps. He would kick his leg out in poor form and tell me to rate it on a scale of one to five. By the end of the night, he had convinced me to get a running start and leap into his strong arms while he lifted me in the air. We looked like a couple of drunk idiots, but neither of us had a care in the world.

Day Six

Finn invited me back to the resort when his shift was over, and we went to an open area away from all the tourists. He took his backpack off his shoulders and unzipped it to pull out two carrots, a few black rocks he stole from the lodge landscaping, and a tiny red bow tie. I squinted my eyes at him, and he said we were going to be making a snowman. I hadn't made a snowman since I was a kid, and I would be lying if it didn't spark happiness in my chest. We rolled up each section of the body and stacked them on top of each other. He handed me the rocks for buttons and eyes. I reached a hand down to grab a carrot, and when he held two out, I questioned him. His mischievous grin was shining bright at me, and he explained. "One for the nose, and one so he can be a man and come to life." I laughed loudly and told him I would take the nose, and he could take the phallic-shaped carrot since he was so adamant. He shamelessly placed it below our snowman's buttons, and we both took a step back to take in our creation. He was tall and lumpy with crooked buttons and a very pointed reproductive organ, but he was ours. We smiled and decided to leave him to scare people away from what we now called our spot.

Day Seven

Day seven was probably my favorite. After Finn saw how much I loved *The Nutcracker*, and how I reacted to the dog we saw at the bonfire with his friends, he did some research and brought me to the most spectacular event I had ever seen. With no hints as to where we were going, I sat on pins and needles in Finn's car as he drove us thirty minutes outside of Aspen. He told me to dress nice but comfortable, so I was completely unsure what to expect...until we pulled up and walked inside an arena full of every dog you could imagine. I looked around and soon saw the large sign hanging up above the arena entrance: **The Muttcracker**.

My knees buckled at the sight, and when I saw one tiny puppy in a gingerbread costume, my eyes watered.

"Are you really going to cry?" Finn snickered next to me.

"Shut up." I sniffled, and I hurried to our seats to watch the show.

There were ramps, hoops, rings, and slides for the dogs to perform tricks on. We watched each dog with amusement, and

I couldn't remember the last time I'd smiled this much. Finn bought me a souvenir t-shirt featuring a puppy dressed as a ballerina. I even got a picture with a group of five French bulldogs. Finn said he was going to make the lockscreen on his phone.

Day Eight

He made plans today for the whole family to go ice skating. Of course, when I told them all, Mom and Taylor lost their minds, Dad, Matt, and Logan looked slightly miserable, and Sarah stayed quiet as always. After the last seven days with Finn, I couldn't help but look forward to our eighth night. He always had something extra up his sleeve, and somehow over the course of the last week he had completely flipped my mood around.

Don't get me wrong, I still hated Christmas, but I didn't dread it nearly as much when Finn was around. Every time he texted me to say he was on the way to pick me up, my heart raced and my cheeks flushed. I was utterly spoiled by him, and I knew going back to Florida wouldn't be as easy as I'd once assumed.

When Finn came to pick us up, Mom shouted, "Okay! Matt and Taylor in our car, Sarah and Logan in Finn's. Bye!" She grabbed Taylor and Matt and shoved them through the door in a hurry. *Very smooth.*

I sat up front with Finn, and Sarah and Logan sat in the backseat. An awkward silence filled the air until Finn flipped on a Christmas playlist. *Feliz Navidad* drowned out the silence, which was almost worse. I couldn't wait to get out of this car.

"So... Finn." Logan's deep voice traveled from the backseat. "Have you been keeping up with the NHL this season?"

If I learned one thing about Finn since I met him, it was that he adored hockey.

Finn perked up. "Oh, definitely. MacKinnon's been killing it all season."

Logan and Finn rattled off stats on the drive while Sarah and I sat in silence. Finn must have sensed my discomfort because he reached a hand over to my lap. Gratefully, I threaded my fingers through his.

Sarah cleared her throat behind us. "Hey, Olive, do you still watch those reality shows you used to obsess over?" Her voice was soft and shy. "I saw a new one coming out this week where Instagram models are stuck in the woods for ten days with no phones or internet. It sounded like something you used to watch back in the day."

I picked at my long, painted nails. "Nope. I stopped watching that stuff a while ago," I snapped, harsher than I intended. But her attempts at bonding with me were useless, and I hated wasting my time.

"Oh, okay." I could hear her sulk in the back while Finn and Logan continued their own conversation.

When we pulled up to the same ice-skating rink that Finn and I people-watched at, I almost smiled at the memory. And if it hadn't been for the most awkward ride here, I'd probably be excited to get on that ice with Finn.

He came around my side and opened up the door for me. When I stepped out, he placed an affectionate touch on my hip, sending tingles all over my body. Instantly, he made me forget about Sarah and her husband, refocusing all of my attention on him.

We made our way to the booth where my parents, Matt, and Taylor already were standing. We each got our ticket and went to pick out our skates. Finn took me to a bench, sat me down, and knelt at my feet, replacing my boots with my ice skates. I smiled down at him, and he looked up into my eyes with a big grin that made my heart beat faster.

He pulled my laces tight and meticulously looped them so they fit just right.

"You're good at this," I said, giving him a rare compliment that only made smile bigger.

"Well professional skate lacer was always a backup plan for me," he said with a shrug. I let out a small laugh, and he smiled down at my feet, continuing to tie my laces. I felt the strong urge to run a hand over his head. He knelt down at my feet like the kind, caring man he was, and I felt unworthy of it. Instinctively, I reached out and brushed my fingers through his short, dark hair, and he looked up at me with that big smile. He leaned into my touch like a puppy wanting to be pet, and I bit my bottom lip as I smiled.

My nails scratched through his hair, making it a little messy, and he stood up when he was done. "I'd let you keep going but you are a little too good at that. And I'm not trying to embarrass myself in front of your whole family."

My family. In that brief moment the two of us shared, I had forgotten that my parents, siblings, and in-laws sat a few benches away. I blushed a little when I looked down and saw Sarah and Logan both staring at us. I tensed up, Finn oblivious as he laced on his own skates.

He tapped my leg with two fingers and held his hands out for me to grab for balance. We stepped onto the ice, and I held onto him tightly. I tensed and spread my arms and legs for balance, similar to when we went skiing.

Finn effortlessly glided beside me with a hand on my waist. "Just loosen up a little. I won't let you fall."

I clung to his words the same way I clung to his side. "That's easier said than done."

His warm laughter traced my ears as he pulled me closer. I turned around to see Matt and Taylor skating like they did this all the time. He gave her a small push on the back, and she turned around to smack him, both laughing at each other. Mom and Dad were sitting by themselves on a bench where they could watch us. And I didn't look long enough to see what Sarah and Logan were doing. Because when I turned around to Finn, he was there, looking at me with those beautiful dark eyes underneath his long lashes that I was only a *little* jealous of. When his eyes connected with mine, it felt like the most erotic thing that I had ever experienced. It was hotter than when we were in my room and in the hot tub combined. With his gaze on mine, the rest of the skating rink disappeared. There was no past with Sarah, no distance from my old self; I was simply me. And I was the best version of me when I was with Finn.

He leaned closer, still smiling at me, and I knew he was about to kiss me in front of this entire rink, but I had no cares.

"Olive," he whispered, "I think—"

Finn was cut off when he was shoved by a young boy in all red. The boy pulled down his mask and said, "Don't hold up the ice."

Finn raised his hands like he was the guilty one. "Sorry, kid."

When the boy skated away from us, I couldn't hold in my laughter. "Why is this town like *Children of The Corn*?" I wiped a tear streaming from my cheek as I laughed harder.

Finn joined me in our chuckling. "I am genuinely scared of them."

We skated for the hour we were allowed, and when we were done, my leg muscles were exhausted and tight. I took off my skates and pulled on my boots before joining my parents where they were seated.

"Looked like you guys had fun," Dad said as he looked back toward Finn, who was handing our skates back to the lady behind the desk.

"Oh, yeah. It was nice."

My siblings and their spouses joined us, and Dad clasped his hands together. "Alright. Let's all go eat. You guys hungry?"

One thing was certain: you would never starve in the Moore house. Food was Dad's love language. Some had words of affirmation or gift giving, but Dad had shoving well-seasoned steaks and an absurd amount of potato sides down your throat.

When we all made it to the restaurant, Finn dropped Sarah and me off at the entrance while he and Logan circled around to find parking. I pulled my jacket tighter around me so I had something to fidget with.

Sarah and I were apparently the first ones there, so we got a table for eight and sat at opposite ends. I could feel her eyes on me as I stared down at the drink menu. A Bloody Mary sounded incredible.

"Are you going to get the Bloody Mary?" She asked softly.

I shrugged. "I don't know."

"You used to love those."

Well now I'm definitely not getting one.

"Yeah. I did." I stared a hole through the menu.

"You've changed so much since you left. I'd really like it if we could talk. Even just for five minutes?"

How long does it take to park a car?

I nodded as an answer. It wasn't permission to talk, but I wasn't exactly in the mood to make a scene either. If I talked, I would undoubtedly be kicked out of the restaurant.

Sarah tapped her left hand on the table and my eyes fell to her oversized wedding ring. I had missed the wedding entirely. It was a year after she and I...argued, and I wasn't prepared to face her or her stupid good-looking fiancé.

"So, you and Finn must be pretty serious, you know, since you're bringing him to all this family stuff."

I sniffed and looked to the door, hoping for an interruption of the dark-haired ski instructor. "Yeah, it's really serious." *Seriously fake.* Except for the hot make-out sessions. *Those* were very real.

I lifted my eyes to her at the worst time because she was already looking at me, and we made eye contact for a brief moment. At that moment, I didn't see the sister I was ignoring, or the one who betrayed me, or the one who made my skin boil every time I heard her name in Florida. I saw my old best friend. The one I used to play fairies with in the backyard or who curled my hair for prom. She once was the person I looked up to for everything. And the thought that our relationship would never go back to normal broke me.

"You deserve that. A good guy that pushes you to have fun."

I gritted my teeth. "Yep."

"*Olive.*" Sarah said my name like I was a snake, and she was a charmer, ready to calmly put me in a box. "Please. I *know* what I did was terrible. Not a day goes by where I don't think of what I did to you. But was it worth losing everything we had?"

I nodded my head vehemently. "Yeah, Sarah, it was."

TWENTY-SEVEN
FINN

When I parked the car, I reached my hands up to the keys to turn it off, and his voice stopped me. "Hey, can I ask you something?"

Assuming it was hockey- or skiing-related, I shrugged. "Yeah, man."

Logan cleared his throat. "Did Olive tell you what happened last time she was here?"

My interest piqued, I turned to him, his eyes searching mine as I answered. "Just that she and Sarah got into a fight. She really didn't want to talk about it."

But *I* did. Sarah seemed sweet, though shy and quiet, but she was always checking to make sure Olive was okay. Between her protective nature and the pictures of her and Olive as kids, I was confused as to what could have possibly happened that Christmas years ago. And how it could have turned Olive into who she was now. I never knew the old Olive of course, only glimpsed bits and pieces here and there, but what I had gathered didn't add up.

"Do you know what happened?" I asked. I mean, he *was* married to Sarah, so I was sure he did.

But Logan shrugged. "Not my story to tell."

He was right; I needed to hear whatever happened that night from Olive. Instead of answering, I nodded and turned off the car. We both stepped out, our boots imprinting the snow as we walked to the restaurant entrance.

Logan cleared his throat as we approached the door. "I'm glad you're with Olive. She is a really nice girl."

She was more than nice. She was everything. But I wasn't going to tell him that. I nodded and smiled. "She's the best."

I wasn't sure what happened between dropping Olive and her sister off to park the car and coming inside the restaurant, but whatever it was clearly shook her. When I found our table, Olive was standing, and she turned to walk to the exit. To me.

I rushed over to her, ready to pick up whatever pieces had been dropped in those few minutes. Olive wasn't paying attention and ran smack into me. I placed both hands on her shoulders. "Woah, woah Grinchy." I stopped her quick exit. and she looked up at me. She was clearly enraged, her eyes red and cheeks flushed. "Are you okay?" I asked, although the answer was obvious.

Without responding, Olive shook her head, and I let out a deep breath. "Come on." I grabbed her hand and without acknowledging the rest of her family, we left through the restaurant front doors.

Olive was breathing heavily and walking even faster than I was. She kept muttering to herself phrases like, "Never should've come here," "I can't do this," and "This was a mistake." They came out one after another, and she didn't care at all of what everyone around us thought. She walked fast to the parking lot, searching for my car.

"Olive, let's just calm down for a second. What happened?"

She looked up at me, and I thought she was going to break. Her hands clenched around her phone and keys. She looked tired and stressed, and I wanted nothing more than to provide any comfort that she would allow me to give her.

"I can't go back in there, Finn."

I nodded my head. I didn't understand why, but I hoped she would eventually tell me, so I didn't ask questions. I simply nodded. "That's fine. Let's just go."

She looked like she was going to fall apart at any moment, and I had no words left. So I simply stepped forward, wrapped a long arm around her shoulders, and pulled her into my chest.

She settled into me with no hesitation, her face planted onto my chest and her hands laid flat on either side of her face. Her shoulders shook, and I heard a tiny sniffle. That small sniffle, tiny but so mighty, broke a piece of my heart.

She shook against me as she let out her tears onto my T-shirt. She painted me with mascara and lipstick, and I couldn't care less; I would gladly be a canvas for her.

I could only imagine what must have happened between Sarah and Olive for her to react this way. My strong, confident, take-no-shit Olive was standing in a parking lot with her head on my chest crying so hard she was practically hyperventilating.

And I was…useless. I was no help at all. What could I possibly say or do?

I opened my mouth to speak. "Olive," I croaked. That was it. That's all I could think of? How about, "It'll all be alright," or "I'm here for you"? No. Instead I stuttered her name like an emotionally constipated teenager

But instead of looking up at me or commenting back, she simply burrowed into me further. She dug her fingers into my shirt and pulled me impossibly closer. I cupped her head with one hand and wrapped the other arm around her shoulders. Maybe words weren't what she needed. And in that case, I would be here. I'd be her fake boyfriend and shoulder to cry on as long as she needed me. When it came to her, I would be or do anything she asked. And in that moment, the only thing I could think of was how much I was falling for this girl—and how much I didn't even care.

Olive eventually lifted her head from my chest, her big eyes ringed with mascara and cheeks wet from her tears. I lifted a hand and wiped it all away. She gave one last sniffle and said, "Can we just go somewhere? I don't care where."

With no delay, I said, "Yes."

I opened the passenger door, helped her in, and strode to my side of the SUV. By the time I got on the highway in the direction of our destination, Olive leaned against the seat with her eyes closed and mouth partially open. Déjà vu hit, reminding me of when she fell asleep on the plane, and I smiled to myself. The most beautiful girl I knew was broken inside, and I would do anything I could to fix it.

TWENTY-EIGHT
OLIVE

In my dreams, Finn carried me up a path to a beautiful cabin. It was tiny, shaped like a triangle, surrounded by snowy woods, and had a large deck that overlooked the city. He shifted me in his arms and carried me to the front door, opening it with a key and gracefully taking me from the cold into the warm cabin that smelled of him. Like fresh-cut wood and cologne; I wanted to wrap that scent around me and never leave.

"Olive, baby," his warm, comforting voice said, and I opened my eyes. Everything was, in fact, not a dream. I was actually in Finn's strong arms in a beautiful, dimly lit log cabin.

I rubbed my tired eyes, not realizing how exhausting emotional breakdowns could be.

"Where are we?"

He chuckled and set me on my feet. "My house. I figured you'd want to go somewhere we wouldn't run into anyone you know."

I couldn't handle how thoughtful this guy was. I don't think I had anyone, even Mom or Taylor, in my life that did as much for me as Finn had done in the last week.

I stepped into the open living room, where a wall of tall windows faced the city and a simple gray sectional with a plaid blanket thrown across it looked like heaven. It was a little messy: a couple mugs were out on coasters, and I pretended to not notice the boxers sitting over by the recliner. I chuckled. "This is really..." I drug my words out as I walked to the large windows.

"Dirty."

"I was going to say nice." I smiled and took in the view of the city lights. It was gorgeous from all the way up here, even more so with it being Christmas. The flashes of white, gold, red, and green lit up the streets, setting them sparkling.

"I never get tired of the view. That's why I bought this." I heard a thud and turned to see Finn was holding a telescope that pointed down at the streets.

I chuckled. "So you could people-watch?"

He smiled. "No, little perv, so I could see the lights better and the mountains behind it." He pointed to the snowy peaks beyond the town. I sighed and leaned in. I had loathed this town for so long, but looking at it from here made all the bad memories go away.

When I pulled away from the telescope, my back bumped into Finn's chest, and we both sucked in a breath. The last several days of hardly any touching had us both charged up and ready to go, and the simple act of my back touching him made me electric. His right hand lifted to my hip and gently caressed it. Goosebumps rose on my arms, the room suddenly suffocatingly warm. I turned my head, and he was looking down at me. His deep eyes bored into mine, and I forced myself to break the contact.

"Soo…" I turned from him to walk to his fireplace. Along the mantle were pictures of Finn skiing, some of him and Cooper out on the snow, an older couple that I assumed were his parents, and one of him kneeling down with a group of kids surrounding him, smiling. I couldn't help but pick it up and brush my finger over the glass.

I walked around the house in small circles, looking at the nice light fixtures and the updated kitchen features. "Dang. Do they really pay you this much over at the resort?"

I wanted to laugh at his Keurig sitting on the counter. I could see him getting up each morning, groggily making his coffee and sitting on the sectional to watch the sunrise.

Finn laughed behind me. "Absolutely not. I received a pretty big settlement after the injury, and I used a portion to buy this."

I turned back to him and found him leaning against the counter casually in those perfect jeans and a black Henley. I bit my lip to avoid jumping on him.

"That's really impressive, Finn. I'm glad you made such a good choice and didn't spend it all on strippers and booze."

He gave me a crossed arm shrug. "Nah. Only like thirty percent of it went to that." I smacked his shoulder, and he grinned.

"Come on." He brought me to the living room, and we sat on the sectional. I curled up in the corner of it and pulled my knees to my chest. Finn reached for a remote and pulled up what used to be my favorite movie of all time: *It's A Wonderful Life*.

I didn't groan or moan as I wanted to. As his guest, and considering how sweet he was, I let it slide. He eyed me when he clicked play, but I didn't even flinch.

The familiar black and white picture filled the screen. "What are you doing all the way over there?" Finn questioned, opening his arms, and I tilted my head. "Come on, Grinchy. We all know we're both going to cry by the end of this. I need my emotional support Olive."

I laughed and scooted closer. He pulled my legs into his lap. Finn Beckett was a smooth criminal.

He traced circles on my shin, and I tried to focus on the movie. A few minutes in, he paused it. "Wait just a second. We're missing something."

Finn hopped up from his seat, and my legs chilled from his missing touch. A moment later, he returned with two mugs in his hands and a bag of popcorn dangling from his perfect teeth. I smiled and grabbed a mug from him.

The scent of apple cinnamon wafted up from the mug, and I realized it was cider. We settled back into our previous position, but he wrapped a blanket around us. I took a sip of the drink, surprised by the burn.

"It's spicy." I noticed the liquid had a light red tint.

He smiled. "Oh yeah, I put Red Hots in there."

I paused and gave a sad smile. "My ex used to put Red Hots in his coffee."

Finn chuckled next to me. "Seriously? In coffee?"

I nodded and laughed. "He said it added a *kick*."

Finn took a sip of his own mug and pointed at me. "That should've been a red flag."

We both laughed and shifted our focus back to the movie. He put both of our mugs down and snaked his hands under the blanket, one on my legs, the other tracing circles on my hip.

Two hours, and too much popcorn later, and I was snuggled into Finn's lap, both of us silent as we focused on the movie. Rewatching a classic, which used to be a favorite of mine, brought back unexpected memories.

"*To my brother, George Bailey, the richest man in town.*" The TV played my favorite quote, and I couldn't hold in my tiny sniffle as my eyes watered.

Finn lifted a hand to my face. "Ahh come on, Grinch. It'll be alright." He wiped my tears. "It's got a good ending."

I nodded and sniffed again. "I know."

He pulled my head into the crevice between his neck and his shoulder. "Who knew my Grinch had such a soft side for George Bailey?"

I let out a sad chuckle and pushed his chest.

With the movie over, he wrapped both arms around me. I turned my head to check the time and noticed how late it had gotten.

"Do you mind if I stay the night?" I asked sheepishly. I don't think I'd ever asked a guy if I could stay the night, and it felt weird doing so. Like inviting yourself to the third-grade sleepover that you overheard about during recess.

"I was planning on it. When else would you have shown me all the tips Taylor gave you?" He winked, and my cheeks flushed. I made a note to kill Taylor the next time I saw her.

Finn tapped my leg, and I moved it off his lap. "Go ahead and pick whatever you want to watch next. I'll get you some clothes." He handed me the remote and stood.

I set the remote down when he walked away, instead standing and making my way over to the large windows that overlooked the city. I felt like we were in a museum, looking out into the display of art that was Aspen. Finn shuffled back in the room with dark sweatpants and white t-shirt for me to sleep in. I swept down the hall to the bathroom to change and when I came back, he was moving two chairs in front of his big windows.

"What are you doing?"

Finn turned around at the sound of my voice and looked my ridiculous outfit up and down. I was at least a foot shorter than Finn with a lot less muscle so I practically drowned in his clothes, and I couldn't help but laugh, my cheeks burning with embarrassment. But seeing him now, the way his eyes twinkled and lips twisted into a smile, I no longer cared what I wore as long as he always looked at me like that.

"You look like you're being swallowed. It's cute." He jerked his head to the seats he'd moved, and I hopped in the one on his right.

And so we sat, watching the cars and lights pass by as we talked over our hopes, dreams, aspirations, regrets for who knows how long. Finn told me of his days skiing, how he loved the crisp snow beneath him and the wind whipping him as he flew down mountains. He told me stories of his tricks and motioned with his hands every bit of how he moved. I went on to tell him about my college days, how I used to have a great group of friends, and how talkative I always was. I told him about how close I used to be with Sarah and how after our last fight—what a terribly underrated word for what actually happened—we had a huge falling out.

Finn continually checked his watch, and I questioned him. "Are you worried about staying up too late?"

He hummed back to me. "No, nope." He tapped my leg with his long fingers. "So, are you anxious about going back to your family tomorrow?"

I sighed. "Yeah, not so much for my sake but for them. I'm sure it's hard to deal with Sarah's and my past."

"It must've been pretty bad for you to run off when you're alone with her."

I shrugged and picked at my chair arms. "It was rough. I left and deleted her number, and we didn't speak again until this trip. I don't know, it's just uncomfortable being in the same room as her."

Finn listened to me rant about Sarah and never pushed or asked why. He checked his watch again, and I finally asked. "What are you waiting for?"

Without looking up, he said, "You'll see in about... seven minutes."

Finn reached out and pulled my chair closer to him, like he had in front of that waitress. It made my heart pound in my eardrums. Finn took what he wanted when he wanted it, and I had no complaints. He was a no-hesitations kind of guy, and I couldn't help but adore it.

When our chairs faced each other, he reached a hand up to my chin. I nuzzled into his warm touch and hummed. Finn smiled down at me, and my heart raced.

"What do you want, Olive? You want the moon? Just say the word and I'll throw a lasso around it and pull it down." He quoted George Bailey with a cheesy accent, and I threw my head back to laugh.

When was the last time I felt this bliss? When did my cheeks last hurt from smiling so much? Or when pure euphoria enveloped me? When I was with Finn, the hours lasted minutes, ticking by like time was nothing. I was conflicted, because I loved my moments with Finn so much that I dreaded when they were over. As much as I wanted to say on cloud nine, *tomorrow* hung over my head like a guillotine. Despite that, I wanted to enjoy *tonight*, to stay here in this moment with Finn.

With my gaze, I traced a path from his eyes to his lips and back. "You might just be my favorite person in the world."

It was an almost embarrassing confession, the fact that my truest friend was a man I had met only a week ago. But it was honest, and judging by the huge grin that broke out on his face afterward, he appreciated it.

"You've been mine since I found out how terrible you are at skiing." He smirked, and before I had time to take offense to his joking insult, he yanked me from my chair and settled me on his lap. I giggled and leaned into him. He tucked a lock of hair behind my ear, and heat and warm fuzzies settled in my stomach—and on my lady parts, too.

"This is crazy, right?" I asked with an incredulous laugh. I didn't know my heart could feel like this, that it could palpitate at the mere sight of Finn's smile. It was ridiculous, the idea of me falling for a guy I hardly knew. I knew my parents fell in love fast, so I couldn't say it was inconceivable, but it seemed impossible. This was never supposed to be in my cards. After my ex, I planned to avoid love at all costs. But sitting on Finn's lap, his lips so close to mine, I knew we had to be at least a little crazy for this.

Finn's eyes never left mine as he said, "No. I think this is the most sane I've ever felt."

And with that, his lips were on mine in a slow slide. He kissed me like we had all the time in the world, like we didn't have an expiration date. He gripped my body in his large hands and held me close. I brought a hand up to the short hairs at the base of his skull and scratched my fingers over his scalp. He groaned into my mouth and shifted his hips below me. With a hand on my behind and another on my upper back, he pulled away from my lips, and I almost whined at the missing contact.

"Olive. You have no idea how bad I want to—"

BANG.

I jumped like a skittish cat and looked out the window to see bright greens, reds, and sparkles covering the sky. It took my brain several moments to catch up to my eyes, but when it did, I repositioned my body on his lap facing the window as fireworks lit up our view.

"Oh my gosh." I held a hand over my chest. "I think I just had a heart attack."

Finn chuckled behind me. "I guess I didn't plan that out so well."

We watched in silence, me curled into a ball in his lap, him with both arms wrapped around me. As if this was something we did regularly.

"I forgot they even did this," I said quietly. Every year the city would have fireworks each night starting on the twentieth until the start of the new year. It was supposed to be like a grand finale.

"We used to all go up on the gondola and watch it from the mountain. We would wrap up in blankets and Mom would take a million pictures. I remember being so excited when I was little. It was my favorite week of the year."

From behind me, Finn said softly, "I've always just watched them from here. They were always nice, but I never really took time to watch them *with* someone."

I turned to him in surprise. "And now?" I questioned.

He gave me that charming smile I loved. "And now it's like I'm seeing them for the first time."

TWENTY-NINE
FINN

"I insist."

"No. I insist."

"Olive. Take the stupid bed."

She huffed and crossed her arms, turning her head away from me and going to the couch. After the fireworks show, Olive and I argued for ten minutes over who would take the bed. My tiny cabin only had one bedroom, an office, and one bathroom. I rarely had guests, and the times I did have people over...let's just say there was no need for another bed. The thought of Olive sleeping somewhere other women had once laid made me sick. I needed to take the mattress out to the road...or burn it. But I'd be damned if I let Olive sleep on the couch tonight.

Olive wasn't a sleep-on-the-couch kind of girl. Or a sleep with her at the first opportunity, one-night-stand kind of girl. She was the girl you woke up at four in the morning to make breakfast for, or the one you quoted George Bailey to. She was the girl you took home to Mom.

"Finn, I can't! You are like nine feet—"

"I'm six-two."

"—tall and I know this couch will not fit you."

It wouldn't, but I'd gladly sleep in a crumpled ball for her.

"Sorry, honey. This is nonnegotiable, now go on to bed. You've had a long day, and I can tell you're exhausted."

Plus, the longer I was around her the more I wanted her. But she'd been rubbing her eyes nonstop since the fireworks finished, like an overtired toddler fighting sleep. Eventually, Olive gave in, and her tiny feet padded down the hall to my room.

My mind raced thinking of her lying in my bed, wrapping my sheets in her warm sweet scent. I bet she'd lift the sheets to her bunny nose and scrunch up in exhaustion. Mental images of a tired Olive lying in my clothes, in my bed, in my room wer pure torture. I leaned my head against the arm of my couch and sighed. I wouldn't get any sleep tonight knowing she was *right there*.

A shiver raced down my spine, and I rose to turn up the heat, in case Olive was cold, too. I went to the thermostat in the hall and saw my bedroom door was wide open. I not-so-accidentally peeked in and found her sitting on the edge of my bed. My knees almost buckled. My beautiful Olive. She'd ditched the baggy sweatpants and was now wearing only my large shirt, those shapely, tanned legs extending from the hem. Her hair was tousled like she had laid down and tossed and turned for a while. Her fingers twiddled as though she was contemplating something, and I stepped closer. The hardwood floors creaked beneath my foot, and her head shot up, mouth gaping open and eyes bugged.

"What are you doing?" She asked quietly.

My response was just as soft. "I can't sleep." *I'm too busy thinking about you being in here, alone,* I wanted to add, but didn't. I didn't want to scare her, or make her uncomfortable.

"You could stay in here...with me," she said, tone sultry. I wondered if she did that on purpose, or if it was simply how she was. "I mean if you wanted."

And oh, I wanted.

"Umm..." My tongue felt swollen and fat. "I mean I could if you needed me—"

"Finn." *Man, I loved the way she said my name.* "Stay here. With me." She crooked her finger, and I practically floated across the floor to her, pulled into her orbit. I don't think my feet even moved.

Suddenly I felt like a teenager all over again. My heart pounded against my ribs, and my neck and face grew warm. The sight of her in only a t-shirt, *my* t-shirt, had me sweating bullets. It was comical, really. *I* was supposed to be the charmer. *I* was the one that made people weak in the knees. *I* was supposed to make *her* beg for *me*.

And yet there I was, speechless and perspiring, stuttering over my words, acting the opposite of *smooth*. But Olive didn't seem to care. She'd manage to look past all that to the *real* me. She didn't see a shameless flirt or a random guy to have fun with—she saw so much more than that, and I wanted to worship her for it.

I breathed deeply and lifted a hand to her neck. "You look so beautiful, my Olive."

She smiled and glanced at my mouth. "I love when you say that."

I placed my other hand on her waist. "That you're beautiful? Come on, darling, you hear that all the ti—"

"No. I love when you call me *my Olive*," she corrected me with a grin, and I thought my knees would give out. I was so gone for this woman. She had no idea what she was about to get.

"I'd gladly call you mine any time you want, honey." I pulled her to me and kissed her like I never had before. I slanted my head to meet her hungry mouth and settled my hands on her hips, gripping her tightly, as though she could slip away at any moment. I firmly locked our lips together, and she let out a small moan.

Okay so maybe I hadn't lost *all* my charm and swagger.

She smiled against my mouth and kissed me harder, wrapping her arms around my neck, and I fell further into her hold.

That night we'd laughed and danced. We'd watched movies and fireworks. We'd eaten too much popcorn and drank too much cider. And when my head settled down to rest next to hers on my pillow, watching her chest rise and fall as she slept, my memory flashed all of our moments together so far. How much fun we'd had together, how much I liked her family, and how much I enjoyed chipping away at her Grinchy exterior to the soft, sweet, *real* Olive underneath.

I knew then—I was utterly in love with Olive Moore, and nothing was going to change that.

THIRTY
OLIVE

I was on cloud nine.

Exhausted from spending the night with Finn, yes, and dizzy, my head spinning with those memories, but...happy.

I remembered Finn holding me after my fight with Sarah. Finn watching movies and fireworks with me.

Finn blowing my mind in bed.

I rolled over and found his side empty. Bleary-eyed, I sat up and rubbed my eyes before noticing a note on the bedside table.

Had to go to work early today. Last night was incredible. You better call me, or my ego is really going to take a hit. Feel free to hang around and wait for me to get off later, or I can have someone come pick you up.

-Your George Bailey

I smiled at the handwritten note and got up to stretch. Afterward, I reached for my phone and found multiple missed texts.

Matt: Do you need me to come get you? Finn texted me.
Taylor: Is everything okay? I miss you. Let's get coffee.
Unknown: Can I talk to you?

The unknown number grabbed my attention the most, so I replied to it first. Assuming it was my sister, I typed, **Sarah?** and waited for a reply.

In the meantime, I made Finn's bed and studied his room. The space was mature and masculine, with dark green walls and wooden furniture, but some of his boyish items were still scattered around. Like the giant jug of coins in the corner and a picture of him hugging a woman I assumed was his mom, Finn with a graduation cap on his head. He had several plane tickets on display in front of his mirror and an absurd amount of spearmint gum stacked beside it. I smiled at the sight, which was so very Finn.

Last night was one of the first times since my ex that I found myself picturing a future with a man. I envisioned us recreating these two weeks every Christmas, and walking around this cabin barefoot and giggling at his terrible jokes. I was equal parts terrified and excited by the prospect. I had been so numb for so long, purposefully building steel-reinforced walls and keeping everyone out. Now that I had been so spoiled by Finn, and now that he'd managed to tear down some of those walls, I wasn't sure how to go back to normal.

Normal.

I was leaving in five days. Reality was sinking in, and my stomach churned. How was I supposed to leave him? Leave everything we'd shared and built behind?

I shoved down the anxious thoughts and told myself it would all work out, because it always did.

I texted Matt back and shared my location, asking him to pick me up. I walked back into the living room and saw the title screen for *It's a Wonderful Life* still on the TV. I smiled to myself and bit my lip.

To the empty room, I whispered, "Maybe I don't hate all things Christmas."

I freshened up as much as I could without having any of my products and pulled on the clothes Finn gave me last night. I pulled the drawstring on my borrowed sweatpants as tight as possible and waddled my way through his house. Matt said he was thirty minutes away, so I decided to clean up while I waited. I wiped down his counters and coffee table, threw dirty laundry in the hamper in his bedroom, and generally straightened up. It felt oddly domestic, and I'd be lying if I said I didn't love it.

When Matt pulled up, he honked the horn, and I walked out of the house and hopped into his truck, smiling.

He scowled at me. "What are you wearing?"

I looked down at the men's long-sleeve shirt and sweats. "Oh, ya know. Just some casual workout clothes."

He eyed me as he backed down the long driveway. "He's got a nice place. That view is sick."

I excitedly nodded my head. "He bought it after his injury in cash so he wouldn't have a mortgage. And he has a back porch that is really nice when it's not super cold. Did I tell you that he—"

Matt scoffed, cutting me off. "I don't think I've heard you talk this much in years." He kept his eyes forward but shook his head. "I don't know what he's done to change things, but you are obsessed."

I laughed. "I am not obsessed, I just like him a lot. Besides it's not like it's serio—" I cut my sentence short.

"It's not serious?" He questioned. "It's the first time you've brought a guy home since that last dickhead, and you think it's not serious?" He was beginning to sound like his wife, meddling in my affairs.

"I just mean I like him a lot, but it's not like I'm rushing to walk down the aisle or anything." I shrugged in hopes that sounded believable enough.

"Whatever you say, kid."

I turned my gaze to the snowy road and wondered to myself, was I obsessed with Finn?

I mean I liked him…a lot. From the moment I first laid eyes on him, I thought he was attractive. But by getting to know him, I realized he's more than a pretty face. I really like how much he loves his job, and how kind he treats me. I like how he whispers sweet things in my ear when I'm anxious. I like the way his shirt smells on me, and how he carefully traces my legs with his long fingers. I especially like when he runs a hand through his hair so it fell perfectly—.

Oh no.

I *was* obsessed with him. Ever since I agreed to our crazy arrangement Finn was all I could think about. I widened my eyes as another thought occurred to me. Was I *in love* with Finn?

No way. You couldn't love someone after not even two weeks. It was insane, absolutely ridiculous. I'd been in love before, and it hadn't been anything like this. With Finn, the feelings burning up my chest gave me cardiology concerns, and my stomach felt like I was dropping down a steep roller coaster. I never experienced this with my ex. I never felt on fire for him, except when I walked in on him balls-deep into another girl. Back then I definitely wanted to *set something* on fire.

A buzz from my phone interrupted my thoughts.

Unknown: It's Logan. Can I see you?

THIRTY-ONE
FINN

I've had a smile permanently glued to my face since this morning.

Pulling myself out of bed with Olive's blonde hair splayed across my pillows was the hardest thing I've had to do in a while. She was beautiful as always, with her makeup rubbed off and my blanket pulled up to her chin.

I considered it for a moment—quitting my job to stay there with her.

But then I figured it probably wouldn't do me any good when she left.

So instead of quitting, I ended up at my usual nine o'clock class full of seven-to-nine-year-olds with so many personalities in the room it was like a circus.

Mr. Finn, can we take a break?

Mr. Finn, how can I do a backflip off the snow?

Mr. Finn, when do we get a snack?

You would think I was a walking Google search bar by the number of questions I was asked daily.

We finished our inside stretches, and I lifted my hand for them to stop talking.

"Alright, guys. Let's go out. Single-file line, and keep your hands to yourself. Tyler, I'm talking to you." The boy in question groaned in response and tilted his head back.

I opened the door for the kids and saw them walk in their line out into the snowy ground. They already knew to walk where I had everything roped off. Most parents stood on the sideline and watched as I taught their kids different moves before we went up the hill. I counted their heads as they passed to make sure everyone was accounted for. When they all filled out except one little straggler, I turned around to find Alea standing with her arms crossed and her eyebrows drawn in.

"Alea." She humped her foot at the sound of her name. "What is it today?"

Our last session she complained that I was five minutes late because I had been with Olive. Before then, it was her skis that didn't fit right. And before that it was because I hadn't paid close enough attention to her tricks.

"You didn't mention the MVP this week."

Gah, she could be a brat.

"Are you assuming it's you?"

Sometimes I'd pick the other kids when I knew good and well Alea knocked them all out of the water. She was always the best one, and this week's MVP *was* her, but sometimes I didn't appreciate her attitude.

"I deserve it the most. Maybe you wouldn't forget if you weren't around that *girl* all the time."

Her bright pink shoes made it hard for me to take her seriously, and I somehow managed to not laugh when I knelt down to her eye level. "Come on, squirt. You know it's you. Just 'cause I've got a girlfriend now doesn't mean I'm too busy for you guys. You know that, right?"

Saying I had a girlfriend felt odd, but comfortable. It may have started fake, but it certainly didn't feel that way anymore.

Alea nodded her head, but there was still fire in her eyes.

So, I nodded back, stood up, and ruffled her hair with my hand. "Now, let's go before those hooligans start an avalanche."

***

I was putting the spare children's ski equipment up in their room when Cooper walked in with a bag in his hands.

"Hey, man." I nodded to him, and he returned it.

I went back to hanging up skis and putting away the support bars, all with a small grin on my face.

"I'm assuming your girl is the reason you're smiling like that."

I laughed. "What makes you say that?" I questioned him.

"Mike from security called me yesterday and brought me these." He removed some wrinkled clothes from the bag. "He thought they were mine since I am usually the one bringing girls here." Coop held up my boxer briefs along with Olive's white thong and said, "But I know good and well these aren't mine."

I couldn't hold back my grin. I didn't want to brag to Coop about Olive, especially after last night, but I certainly didn't mind showing off that I got down in a hot tub with the most beautiful woman to ever walk through here.

"It was a good night." I smirked and snatched the underwear from him.

"I bet," he said, mirroring my grin. "I'm surprised to see you like this."

"Like what?"

He shrugged. "I don't know. All relationshippy. Like you can't wait to see her again. I don't think you've been like this as long as I've known you."

Receiving confirmation that my feelings for Olive had manifested physically in a way that even Coop noticed didn't bring me the relief I'd hoped. Instead, it brought dread. Because I *knew* I was in love with Olive. And unfortunately, I knew her flight back to Florida hung over us like a storm cloud. But what was I supposed to do—ask her to stay? To move back to the town she hated coming to in the first place?

I wasn't worth that. I was the one-night-stand guy. The guy you used to get over the ex. The guy who you could brag about to your friends the next morning then forget about.

I wasn't the guy you moved across the country for. And Olive needed that kind of guy in her life.

"She's pretty great. But she's leaving soon, and I doubt we'll keep in touch." The words were acid in my mouth.

"Whatever you say, Finny," Coop said.

"I mean. I can't convince her to stay. What would she get out of that?"

He laughed. "*You*, you idiot. She would get *you*."

I laughed derisively and said, "Yeah 'cause that is worth moving for."

I couldn't hold back my sarcasm. The idea of Olive sticking around was unfathomable, and I couldn't make her any promises about long distance. I had to face reality: whatever was happening between us would end, and soon. Most likely I would possibly be broken-hearted, but she would be fine.

Coop stared me down. "Whatever you say, man."

My phone buzzed in my pocket, and I withdrew it.

Lil Grinch: My parents are inviting everyone over tonight to watch *Christmas Vacation* if you want to come?

Me: Wherever you are, I'm there, honey.

THIRTY-TWO
OLIVE

I never answered Logan's text. I hadn't heard from Sarah either. It seemed like the whole house was walking on eggshells around me since I ditched dinner last night. Only Finn, Sarah, and Logan saw me rush out of the restaurant, so the rest of my family made their own conclusions about what happened. I eventually moved my work laptop from my room into the living room to try and make a point that I was fine. But this led to Mom bringing me hot tea and telling me everything would be okay, or Taylor sitting next to me and brushing my hair in silence while I worked. At one point, Mom even brought me a tray with the Pillsbury Christmas cookies: snowmen, reindeer, and trees. We used to ask her to make all three because we *swore* they each tasted different. I think the only reason she went along with it was to get us to hush.

"You guys know I'm fine, right?" Both of my favorite girls nodded but exchanged looks.

"Olive, honey. It's okay to not be okay," Mom said sympathetically.

I shrugged. "I know that. But I really am fine. I've got Finn." *For the next few days...* "And work is good. I promise I'm okay. I just had a momentary relapse last night."

The looks I received said they didn't believe me, but the truth was, as long as Finn was there, I was good. I forgot about Sarah or anything else surrounding me. It was all him. Which was why, when I heard his voice echo from the front door, I shot up from the couch and ran to him. Finn opened his arms for me, and I jumped into his embrace, not caring what we looked like to my family. He wrapped his arms tightly around me, squeezing.

"Hey, Grinchy," he said once he set me on my feet, and I smiled at him.

I pulled him to the couch where Mom and Taylor were, and soon they were swooning over Finn as he spoke. We all sat there, slack-jawed at his deep voice filling the room, telling us stories from his job and how his day was. I could listen to him all day.

My job was to listen to people talk and edit out every "um" or "ah" from a two-hour-long podcast, so by the end of the day, I was sick of hearing anyone speak. I looked forward to the silence, but with Finn, I wanted to listen to his warm, honey-rich voice until I fell asleep.

The front door opened, and I didn't have to look to know Sarah and Logan had joined us. Everyone stiffened and Finn's voice slowly died down. I turned around, and they were both staring at me. I shifted uncomfortably in my seat, thankful when Mom spoke up.

"Matt, Finn, Logan. You boys go help Tom flip the mattress in my room please."

Matt scrunched up his face. "Flip your mattress?"

"Just go." She spoke firmly and waved her hand in that direction. The boys shrugged and did as she asked. When they were gone Mom tapped Taylor on the shoulder. "I need your help fixing up snacks for the movie." Taylor didn't hesitate, hopping up to follow her in the kitchen.

I couldn't help but roll my eyes. Sarah quietly said, "She was always good at clearing the room."

I gave her a tight-lipped smile but didn't respond.

Then, guilt over running away from her last night settled over me.

"Look, Sarah," I said. "I didn't mean to make things all weird last night, but you have to know how hard this is for me to be here."

She nodded down at her shoes. "I know," she said. "I don't know how to fix this, Liv." Her old nickname made my skin crawl. "Tell me how to make it right between us, and I will."

I shook my head. "You can't just fix it overnight, Sarah. You broke my heart. I'm just not sure I can forgive you right now."

She leaned closer to me. "But could you one day?"

I let out a breath, unsure how to answer. "No. Yes. Maybe, I don't know. Look, let's just talk tonight after everyone is gone. I might want to yell at you before I let you speak."

She laughed and nodded. "I would *love* for you to yell at me. Anything is better than silence."

I smiled, a small tilt of my lips, stood, and headed for my parents' bedroom to get the boys. When I opened the door, I was shocked to find the four of them sitting in a circle on the floor with a deck of cards passed between them. They didn't even look up when I busted through.

"All in." Finn pushed three quarters into the pot, which consisted of random loose change.

"Ahh, come on, man," Matt complained.

Dad folded and Logan said, "I got nothing," then threw his stack down.

I cleared my throat, and the boys looked up. "What's going on?" I crossed my arms and eyed the circle.

"Poor man's poker?" Finn said, inflection rising at the end to make it sound like a question as he pointed at the circle of money that probably added up to seven dollars.

"Alright." I shrugged and plopped in a seat between Dad and Finn, ready to play.

THIRTY-THREE
FINN

Olive was snuggled into my side on our end of the couch as we watched Chevy Chase put up Christmas lights. The movie played brightly on the large TV in front of us, illuminating Olive's face. Several times throughout the movie I caught her smiling or quietly laughing and I knew, this girl may claim to hate all things Christmas, but there was a Holiday Cheermeister somewhere in my Little Grinch.

Matt and Taylor sat on the large lounge chair, her propped in his lap.

Denise and Tom had both fallen asleep on the opposite end of the couch.

Sarah sat at the foot of the chaise, and Logan was in between her legs as she pet his hair.

But Olive and I were in the corner of the sectional, my arm around her shoulders, her head on my shoulder with a hand in my lap.

It was blissful, being surrounded by a large family and having this kind and beautiful woman next to me. It felt like I was glimpsing into the future, with my wife curled into me with our family spread out around us.

The problem was that Olive wouldn't end up being that girl at my side. And the thought of that made me sick.

The movie faded to credits, and Denise stood and headed into the kitchen. She yawned. "Does anyone want coffee?" We all sleepily agreed and followed her.

Logan and I leaned against the kitchen counter with our mugs, while Olive and Taylor spoke to each other in the dining room. Olive laughed and reached a hand out to Taylor. She had her head thrown back and tears sprang from her eyes. She lit up the entire house, and I was caught in her trance.

Logan shifted next to me, pulled out a small red box, and dumped the contents into his coffee, and it caught my attention.

I nodded to his mug. "What was that?"

He looked down at his mug and chuckled. "Oh, I usually put Red Hots in my coffee. I always said it gave it a kick, you know?"

He stirred the contents in his mug, but my mind snagged on something Olive had told me before.

My ex used to put Red Hots in his coffee.

My ears heated. No. No way. It *couldn't* be him.

I looked up to Olive, and when I took in her bright red face and wide eyes—I had my answer. A fury like I had never known burned through my chest.

I turned to Logan. "It was you?"

THIRTY-FOUR
OLIVE

*C**hristmas Eve, three years ago***

"Please, stop. You're killing me."

Logan laughed in the driver's seat as I belted out the lyrics to Santa Baby *as it blared through the speakers in my car.*

"Come on, you love it!" I bumped his arm, and he shrugged.

"I love you, yes," he said. "But your singing..." I laughed but didn't stop. Judging by his smile, I knew he secretly enjoyed it.

Logan and I had been together for almost nine months now, and we figured it was time for him to finally meet my family. We started out as classmates in a study group in college, but soon enough, he became my best friend. We did everything together. One thing led to another, and soon we began dating. My closest friend and boyfriend were wrapped in one perfect package.

Excitement raced through me when we pulled up to my parents' log cabin, and I excitedly hopped out and ran to Logan's door. He flung it open, and I grabbed his hand. "Come on! I can't wait!"

I'd prepared him over the last nine months about how much I loved my family, and how I couldn't wait for him to meet them. I talked about Mom and Dad, Matt and Taylor, but I spoke of Sarah the most. She was my best everything. *The girl I could call with awkward sex questions or the one who would mail me a handwritten letter just because. She was the best sister I could ask for, so after going on and on about her, and the rest of my family, I knew Logan couldn't wait to meet them too.*

He laughed and held my hand to the front door. Without knocking, I flung it wide open and shouted, "Honey, I'm home!" in my loudest housewife voice.

Taylor rushed across the room to wrap me in a bear hug, squishing me as tight as she could.

"Oh, my little Olive!" Mom excitedly exclaimed from down the hall. Matt came up behind Taylor and gave me a quick side hug too.

I turned to Logan, who was standing shyly by the door. "This is Logan! The guy I've been talking about for months." I pulled him to me, and he smiled briefly before greeting my brother and sister-in-law.

I pulled him to the kitchen to meet my parents. Mom wrapped him in a hug, and Dad gave him a firm handshake. Logan was always the shy one out of our friend group, so I wasn't surprised when he cowered.

"Where's Sarah?" I smiled brightly and bounced on my tippy toes.

Mom laughed. "She's in your room. She stayed up all night because she was so excited to see you."

I shouted, "Sarrahhhh!" down the hall and laughed as a door flew open and feet shuffled in our direction.

Sarah came into the room, looking like an angel. She wore a flowy white dress that was about the size of my pinky, and her long brown hair was curled perfectly. Her makeup was flawless, and her long legs gobbled up the distance to reach me. Her brown eyes stayed on me with my arms open wide, ready for her. But she stopped when she saw Logan standing next to me.

"Logan, this is Sarah! Sarah, Logan." Logan's hand went limp in mine, his mouth opening wide.

Yes, my sister was gorgeous. She was the pretty one; always dressed impeccably and went to the gym every day. She used a shampoo that cost more than all my groceries and was known for her makeup skills. Instead of making me feel less than, or trying to dress me up, she always accepted me for who I was. I was the fun, curvy sister, and I would gladly take that role. My hips were far wider than hers, and my boobs stretched out my sweater, but if you wanted a good time, I was your girl.

I hadn't shown Logan a picture of Sarah previously because I was a little anxious. Guys in high school befriended me simply so they could get closer to her, and I guess in the back of my mind I was fearful that Logan would do the same. So of course, he was shocked to see we had a Victoria's Secret model look-alike in the family.

"Hi," Logan said quietly, his voice strained.

"Hi," Sarah whispered back, not acknowledging me.

"Um, hello?" I stepped between their staring contest and Sarah backed away.

"Hey, my sweet Olive!" She wrapped me in that familiar hug of hers. I caught a whiff of her signature apple scent and breathed in.

"I missed you so much." I lifted my head from her shoulder.

She looked between Logan and me. "I missed you too," she said wearily. Something was wrong, but I figured I'd ask her later.

Mom piped up from behind us. "Who's ready to eat?"

Dinner was perfect, Logan fit in with my family like a missing puzzle piece, and it was everything I could imagine. Sarah asked him questions about his work and how he ended up at the same college as me. He seemed flustered at times, but I think he got the hang of it. Matt and Taylor exchanged looks throughout the dinner, and I wondered if they had some secret they were all hiding.

I definitely *needed to ask Taylor about it later.*

But I enjoyed dinner and dessert with all the ones I loved. When Logan and I first started dating I wasn't sure we would be the best fit as my boyfriend. After all, we were friends first. But seeing him in my childhood home and getting along so well with my favorite people made my heart warm. I knew I made the right choice. He and Sarah laughed together, and I couldn't help but smile. My two favorite people were at this table, getting along, and I felt like everything was right at that moment.

***

The entire day was amazing. We ate till our stomachs pushed against the buttons of our pants, and I laughed, telling Logan different family stories throughout dinner. We watched Christmas movies and drank hot chocolate. It was the kind of day I'd always hoped for as a little girl, having a hot boyfriend at Christmas with my family and everyone talking and laughing. I couldn't stop thinking of how perfect it all was. Even though Logan was shy the whole time, he never left my side.

That night, I was shaken from my dreams by the sound of a loud bang from down the hall. I looked beside me and saw Logan was gone. I checked the time, noting it was one thirty, and figured he probably tried to go get his usual midnight glass of water and bumped into something.

I got up from my blankets and sheets to help him, but when I tip-toed down the hallway, I heard grunting. I walked farther and leaned against the wall.

"Logan," a woman moaned, the voice one I knew very well.

No. I let out a silent laugh. They would never—

"Yes, Sarah. Just like that."

My worst nightmare was confirmed with Logan's words. I turned the corner and saw my own sister perched on the island countertop, her legs wrapped around the waist of the man I loved. Sarah's nightgown was bunched around her stomach, and I didn't have to look close to see Logan's pants were pulled down just enough. In the dark room, the twinkling Christmas lights lit enough for me to make out the movements of his hips thrusting.

Acid filled my throat.

I paused in shock.

My boyfriend and my sister.

The two people I cared for most.

"What?" I said the question out loud. I barely whispered it, but it was enough for them to look at me. Sarah gasped, her eyes filling

with shock and sorrow, surely matching the expression on my own face. Logan adjusted himself back into place and pulled up his pants.

"Olive, I am so sor—" I didn't look at them anymore. I couldn't. I couldn't breathe. My whole world crumpled in the matter of a minute. Every insecurity I had ran through my head.

"Sarah was always the pretty sister."

"Olive was always best at...other things."

"Maybe your sister shouldn't come, Sarah."

Every backhanded compliment rushed to me, and I fought to keep my dinner in my stomach. Without thinking or hearing any more of the useless words that left either of their mouths, I grabbed my keys and sprinted to the front door.

I didn't care that I was in pajama shorts and a sweatshirt. I was getting out of here. Both shouted my name at my back, but I had nothing left for them. I ran out to my freezing cold car, already too numb to be cold. Adrenaline and rage would keep me warm.

I shifted into reverse, barely able to see due to the stacked up ice and snow. I pulled out of the driveway faster than I could think, clipping something and realizing I knocked down the mailbox in the process. I was too shocked to care. As I left, I saw them both come out onto the front porch in my rearview.

And I drove, leaving my heart right where it belonged—in Aspen.

And I vowed I would never allow myself to be hurt like that again.

THIRTY-FIVE
FINN

An anger burned through my veins like I had never known.

All those moments where Olive was insecure, or when she was anxious to see Sarah. Why she was so upset on the plane. Why she left dinner in a hurry after being alone with Sarah.

I was still in shock, and it took every bit of my control not to haul Logan out of here and slam his face into the snow.

Everything finally clicked, every piece of Olive that made no sense. The pictures of her when she was younger, why she felt the need to drop so much weight, why she constantly felt less-than, why she always checked to make sure her makeup was just right.

It was all because this douchebag in front of me, who I'd considered a friend, broke her heart.

When no one answered me, I repeated myself. "It. Was. You."

"W-What?" Logan stuttered. "What was me?"

I scoffed at his feigned ignorance and turned to Olive. Tears threatened to spill down her cheeks, and I knew from her face that this bastard was the one guilty of breaking her heart.

I reached over and grabbed a handful of Logan's t-shirt.

"What are you talking about?" He asked, as if he had no clue what he'd done to the woman I loved most.

"You were the one that cheated on Olive."

His eyes widened, and Olive said, "Finn, don't—"

Logan looked from me to her, his eyes asking for help. When she didn't push further, he looked at the other members of her family around me, clearly wanting someone to pull him out of my grip. None of them moved.

"Don't look at them. Don't look at her. Look at me." I raised a tightly closed fist. "If you so much as breathe in Olive's direction, it will be your last."

Logan flinched, and his eyes widened further, looking like a deer in headlights.

"Finn. Please, can we go?" Olive asked, voice unsteady as she stepped up next to me. Her tiny, shaking hand reached up to my shoulder.

I didn't respond. Truthfully, I didn't know how to speak to her when I was so filled with anger.

Without tearing my gaze from Logan's I said, "This isn't over. And you'll regret the day you ever come near her again."

I dropped both my hands, and he opened his mouth to reply, but nothing came out. I turned to walk to the front door, and the rest of her family stared at me.

An hour ago I considered each of them to be good friends, to be people that loved my Olive. But now it felt like a room full of liars.

Without speaking to any of them in particular, I said to the room, "How any of you can stand to be in the room with those two together is beyond me. She deserves more than you all." I got to the front door and put my boots on without tying the laces as I headed into the snowy driveway.

I could hear Olive's small steps behind me. "Finn. Please, can we talk for just a second?"

I shook my head. I was so exasperated, and this knot-like ball of rage inside of me would make me say things to her that I may not mean.

"I'm so sorry, Finn. I just couldn't—"

"Couldn't what?" I snapped. "Couldn't find the time in the last twelve days to say, *oh hey, by the way my ex cheated on me with my sister and now they're married?* Everyone knew but me, Olive. I thought we were closer than that. You *lied* to me, you said he had moved." Hurt ran through me, mixing with my anger. After every intimate moment we'd shared, I was gutted that she hadn't told me. Was I not worth that conversation?

"I know I lied, and I'm so sorry. I just...I didn't want you to think less of me." Her voice cracked, the combination of it and her sniffles hitting me in the chest. "I was scared to tell you. We were having such a nice time, and I thought if I didn't tell you, it would be easier when I had to leave." Each word she spoke was woven with regret and sorrow.

I was upset with her for lying, but at the same time, my heart broke for her. I was always the rational one, but after putting the pieces together, I lost all control. It was all too much. The lack of communication had me confused and hurt, and if I talked to her now, I'd say things I would surely regret tomorrow.

I sighed and unclenched my fist. It was freezing out, and she didn't have enough clothes on. One glance at her bare feet on the snowy driveway, and the red in her eyes tore me up.

"Look. I don't want to make any mistakes while I'm upset like this, alright? I'm frustrated and confused." I puffed out a breath and ran my hands through my hair. "But you need to know that you didn't deserve what they did to you. I'm just gonna go, and we'll talk tomorrow, okay? I'm not mad at *you,* I'm just mad in general." My voice rasped with rage, and it probably would until I beat something to a pulp. Olive opened her mouth then shut it. Tears stained her cheeks, and instinctively, I lifted my hand to wipe them away, but paused midair. "I just need to process this, alright?" She nodded and took a few steps back.

So, I got in my car and pulled out of the driveway that belonged to a family I didn't know anymore.

THIRTY-SIX
OLIVE

My chest felt tight, and my throat ached from holding back sobs. Guilt ran in my veins, and when I turned back in the house, I forced myself to hold it together. I bypassed the kitchen, where I knew my family had gathered, and went straight to my room.

I slammed the door shut and fell face first onto the bed. I quieted my sobs by hugging a pillow to my face, my tears soaking the fabric.

It was all too much. Everything happened before I was ready. I *knew* coming here was a bad idea.

Flying here. Meeting Finn. Seeing Sarah and Logan together with rings on their fingers.

I wasn't strong enough to handle it.

The hardest part was I wasn't necessarily upset by the fact that they were together. What upset me was that neither of them tried to talk to me about it. Okay, and I was upset about walking in on them while he was still mine for sure. But the thing was, Logan and I were friends first, and if he or Sarah had spoken up about it, I would have gladly stepped aside. Because I had loved them both dearly.

Someone knocked lightly on the door, and I mumbled an incoherent, "Go away."

Whoever was there ignored me and opened it anyway. The bed dipped by my feet, and I didn't bother looking up.

"Olive," a deep voice said, one I instantly recognized as Logan's.

"Can we talk for just a minute?" When I didn't respond, he continued. "I really am sorry. You never even let us explain. I tried calling you so many times after..."

I knew he tried to call. They all did. Instead of ever facing them and what happened, I got a new number and never gave it to them. After I discovered them, I kept driving until I ran out of gas, finally pulling into a small coffee shop in the middle-of-nowhere Oklahoma. The only thing I had on me was my laptop. I withdrew it and searched for a job that would get me as far as possible from Colorado. Eventually, I found an ad for a podcast editor, and although it didn't pay much, it seemed like a good option. It was remote, so I could work from anywhere, and I wanted to choose someplace where I was my happiest. I remembered when I was nine and we went to West Palm Beach. I figured until I got my crap together, that's where I would go. And I stayed there as long as I could without Mom making me feel terrible for not visiting. This year was the last straw. All bad blood with Sarah and Logan aside, I missed my family.

"I know neither of us deserve your forgiveness, but I do miss you being my friend. I did love you, Olive. I know it seemed like I didn't after that. But I can't explain it, I just fell in love with her the moment I met her. I didn't want to, but it was inevitable. I wish I could say I was drunk or that I had a momentary lapse in judgement. But I didn't. Don't get me wrong, I regret it. Every day I regret how we went about it. It was wrong, and Olive I am *so* sorry. Nothing was going to stop us from being together, but I never planned to hurt you."

I knew neither of them wanted to hurt me, and that neither of them made a plan to rip my heart out that day. But they did, and one day I could possibly forgive them, I couldn't erase the memory that replayed in my head all the time. I sat up, wiping my tears and forcing myself to meet his eyes. I'd missed my best friends. Both of them. I missed the people that I loved so dearly, and I wanted that relationship back with both of them. But it felt too late.

"I know you didn't mean to break my heart. But you did. You both did. And maybe one day I can look back on all of this and forgive you, but that day is not today." I kept my voice strong even though my throat was tight and scratchy.

Logan nodded. "I am so sorry, Olive. I'll see you later. " I didn't respond, and he left.

That night I felt incredibly empty. I felt the strong urge to text Finn, but I was unsure what to say. If anything, this mess showed me I should've stayed in Florida. When I was there, I could numbly focus on work, reading, the gym, eating healthy, and working on myself. But the moment I arrived in Colorado, I was bogged down by agony and eventually, something that felt a whole lot like love. But Finn ran for the hills when he saw my dirty laundry, and I doubted anything was going to change that.

I checked my phone every few minutes, hoping each email notification buzz was a text from him. I typed out a message multiple times.

I am so sorry... *delete*.

I didn't want you to know because... *delete*.

Can I talk to you for just a... *delete*.

Nothing felt satisfying enough to send, and my mattress felt stiff and cold. The time on my phone said it was eleven, and I knew I wouldn't sleep until I expended this pent up energy. So, I suited up with thick leggings and a sweatshirt, laced on my favorite tennis shoes, and went out the front door.

I ran down the well-lit street, alone with my thoughts. I pictured the days with Finn that felt too good to be true. I imagined we were still at his cabin, bundled under blankets and watching Christmas movies. Every once in a while he would whisper a dirty joke in my ear and make me laugh as his hands trailed to my waist. It had been so blissful at the time, so domestic and sweet.

When I was tired and out of breath, I walked back to the house. The front door opened with a creak, and I quietly took off my shoes. I turned to head down the hall but paused when someone cleared their throat. I turned on my heel and found my mom in her pajamas on the sectional, a mug in one hand, the other on the table in front of her.

"Let's talk." She gestured to the couch, and I knew better than to argue. My shoulders sunk, and I plopped into the cushion next to her. She handed me the spare mug that I knew had her English breakfast tea in it.

"Thanks," I mumbled and took the mug.

"So, Finn didn't take the news well." She took a sip.

I let out a sarcastic laugh and shook my head. "No, he didn't. To be fair I didn't take it so well when I found out either."

She sighed and placed a hand on my knee. "Look, honey, as your and Sarah's mother I wanted to see you getting along again, and I pushed that too far. As someone who loves you deeply, I'm not saying you should forgive Sarah or Logan. Or that you should forget it ever happened. You have every right to be very upset, believe me, the rest of us were furious. We couldn't talk to either of them for months. But, slowly it all came around. What they did was selfish and wrong. I still feel sick for you when I think of what you had to see that night. But, I am the first to tell you that love doesn't understand what's right or wrong. Sometimes love has no boundaries, and I think they found that out in an instant. Logan and Sarah look at each other like they're the only two people on Earth. It's the same way Finn looks at you, like you are the only one in the room."

I paused. "Wait, what?"

Mom rolled her eyes. "Do I have to repeat the whole thing?"

I shook my head. "No, what was that last part...about Finn."

She tilted her head. "I said he looks at you like you're the only one in the room."

I was hit with the memory of Finn and me at the cafe.

"Oh, come on there's got to be somebody. What does it take to be qualified as Olive Moore's boyfriend?"

"I don't know. I want someone who will look at me like I'm the only person in the room."

I choked up again for what felt like the hundredth time tonight. When my head dipped and I sniffed, Mom pet my hair.

"Oh, honey. He'll be back, and you two will be fine I promise."

I almost told her then. That Finn was a stranger twelve days ago, and we simply played a game with each other for as long as I was in town. Instead, I put my head on her chest like I did when I was a little girl, and my shoulders shook with sobs as she patted my back.

***

After a rough night of sleep, I finally got the courage to text Finn.

Me: Can we talk?

Hottie from seat 15B: I get off at 2.

I anxiously waited around all day for two to come around. I worked as much as I could, read on my Kindle, helped Mom cook breakfast, anything to make time go faster. When one rolled around, I went straight to the lodge and waited in the lobby for him, right where we sat last time. I prayed he would get off early because I was so anxious.

After my talk with Mom last night, I figured I had two options:

> 1. Confess my love to Finn, even if I come across as psychotic.

> 2. Head back to Florida and pretend this never happened.

I considered both, my mind wrestling with them all night until I fell into an exhausted slumber. But, when I woke up, my mind was clear. I needed to talk to Finn. He told me only a few days ago that I was his favorite person, and I hoped he still meant it. I screwed up by not telling him about Logan, but maybe I had time to recover from this. Maybe we could sort this out.

When I saw Finn's tall, fit body making his way to where I sat, everything rushed into me all at once. He wore all black ski gear, and his hair looked slightly damp. When he reached me, I stood up.

"Hi," I whispered as I searched his face.

"Hi." He nodded to the seat behind me. We sat, and his eyebrows drew in. "So, what did you want to talk about?"

I could tell he was still upset with me. He wasn't his usual excited, cheerful self, but he didn't look furious like he had last night either. "I just wanted to say I'm sorry I didn't tell you about Logan. I know I should have, but I was just so scared. Finn, I have had the best time with you, and the thing is I'm not scared anymore. I've been heartbroken before and I know—"

"Olive." He stopped my rant, and I looked up to see his eyes were on me, but they were empty. "I think we should stop this."

I paused. "What?" The question came out shaky and weak.

"I mean it had to end at some point, and you go back home in three days. It's just easier, you know?"

No, I didn't know. Because I was desperately in love with a boy who just told me he wanted to stop seeing me. His nonchalant attitude felt like a stone landing on my chest. As if this was nothing to him.

"Oh." I tried my best to not sound disappointed. "Um, yeah. I totally get it."

I forced the bitterness down my throat and blinked away any tears. "I got to go. I'll see you around."

He stood over me and reached into his backpack, pulling out a small box messily wrapped in red and white paper. "I got you this a while ago. I was waiting to give it to you for Christmas, but you know..."

I shakily grabbed the present and nodded. "Oh, thanks. I didn't bring yours."

He shook his head and waved a hand. "Nah, don't worry about it."

I stood next to him and fumbled with my keys. "Well, thank you for...everything. I guess I'll just go."

He took a step back and let me go. "Bye, Olive."

That was it? After everything? Not even a hug goodbye. I mean it made sense; it was a barely two-week-long trip. It's not like we had the connection of a lifetime. But I thought...my throat clogged, and Finn disappeared without even a glance back.

So maybe there was no such thing as fate. Maybe this was another lesson.

I left the lodge holding it all in until I got to my car. I was strong-willed enough to keep the tears at bay until I was alone. Then I settled behind the wheel and turned on the heat. As the windows defrosted, I opened the gift he handed me.

Inside was a stuffed "Max the Dog" toy with a card attached. I smiled through my tears. I opened the small card on it and saw Finn's handwriting.

So you can count him to sleep at night, my little Grinch.
- **Love, Finn**

So, I curled back inside myself and drove home with blurry eyes. I should have known better than to let this happen again.

THIRTY-SEVEN
FINN

I used to think doing a misty flip on the snow was the hardest thing I ever had to do. I was terribly wrong. Letting Olive go, watching her choke back tears, and seeing the resignation on her face was ten times harder. I knew it would be difficult, but she would eventually see this was for the best. It took me hours last night to come to terms with this decision. Asking her to stay with me—to stay here, in Aspen? It was ridiculous. And it would be better if we both accepted our inevitable fate that this was never going to last. Like the shortest winter love there ever was, we were combustible. And we only had so much time with a passion like that.

I stayed up all night before wondering what to do. I loved Olive, no doubt about it. But I knew deep down this had to end at some point, and it was better for it to end now instead of dragging it out. The thing was, Olive didn't deserve the weight she carried by being back in Aspen. She deserved to be in the comfort of her own home and not feel like she had to tiptoe around anyone.

I knew she was going to be down about it, but she would get over me and go back to Florida, to men that worshiped at her feet. It broke me to think about, but it was for the best. And maybe one day she would think of me when she pictured Aspen at night. Or when she heard a Christmas song on the radio. Or even when her stupid tan, pretty-boy-surfer husband couldn't give her a proper orgasm. Either way, I'd hoped our short time together was enough to be planted in her mind forever.

"Come on, guys, pick it up," I instructed the kids, wanting them to quicken their speeds down the slope. I was being harsher than usual, and I reminded myself to reel it in.

"Mr. Finn, I'm tired," Little Lyla, as we called her, whined when she slowed her space.

"Then go all the way down and rest, alright?" I snapped, gruffer than I intended. She gave me sad puppy eyes and slid past me. Guilt hit me right in the face, but it didn't fix my poor attitude.

"What is your problem?" I heard Alea shout from the back of the group.

"Nothing, Alea. Finish your drills so we can be done."

She looked taken aback because even when she was at her worst, I never snapped at Alea. She knew she was my favorite.

When drills were done, I briefly told the kids bye and went to tear down flags and finish packing up for the day.

"Did your girlfriend break up with you?" Alea crossed her arms and lowered her eyebrows with a curled lip.

"No, Alea. I just have to go."

She shrugged. "It's a shame. I liked her."

That caught my attention, and I paused. "What? No, you didn't. You hated Olive."

She shook her head. "No, I really did like her, I just thought she took up too much of your time. Time you should've spent training me."

I let out a small laugh, the first since letting Olive go. "Well, you've got all my attention now, kid. I'll see you after the holidays, alright? Maybe we'll work on those jumps." Alea nodded excitedly and took off toward her mom, who waved my way.

I got home that afternoon, exhausted from lack of sleep and running kids around all day. I collapsed on my couch and reached for the remote, but when I turned the TV on the first thing that popped up was *It's a Wonderful Life*. I rolled my eyes and hit next.

Christmas Vacation.

Elf.

How The Grinch Stole Christmas.

Ugh. Fine. I turned the TV off and instead turned my gaze to my large windows and the cityscape below. Families walked by with their kids and couples held hands. It was sickening. I couldn't help but wonder if Olive was looking down from their house too.

A knock at the door had me jolting upright. I yelled, "Come in!" because I was too tired to get up. I put my trust in my recent luck that it wasn't an ax murderer.

"It's Coop!" He yelled from the front door, and I made no effort to get up.

"In the living room!" I shouted back. The door shut, and his loud boots smacked against my hardwood floors as he made his way to me.

He paused when he saw my sad, pathetic body on the couch. "I brought pizza and booze." He lifted a six pack of craft beer and a brown pizza box.

We turned on the Avalanche game and gorged ourselves on greasy pizza and beer.

"So, you broke up with Olive then," he said without looking up at me.

"How did you know?"

Coop shrugged and tilted his head. "Word travels fast at the lodge."

I lowered my eyebrows in confusion. "Alea told you?"

He shamelessly nodded. "Maybe."

Of course she did. "It's not really a break up if you never actually dated in the first place."

Coop set down his beer and looked me straight in the eyes. "Don't do that."

"Do what?"

He pointed at me. "Make it seem like it was nothing. It's not like you guys just slept around."

No, but maybe we should've. It would've been easier than this. This was why I was the fun guy, the guy you had one wild night with and told your friends about the next morning. I wasn't the relationship guy or the one you did long distance with. And I should've made that clear to Olive from day one. Instead, I stuck my nose where it didn't belong and broke both of our hearts.

"It's not like we were serious. We just met," I said bitterly.

Coop sighed. "You know, just 'cause you guys just met doesn't mean it wasn't serious."

I leaned back and studied him. "You sure are a love expert for someone with no girlfriend."

Cooper was the most single guy I knew; he was the definition of a bachelor. Since the day I met him, I watched as he left a long trail of broken hearts behind him.

"I don't have a girlfriend because I don't want one. And one day if I ever do, she is gonna be so damn lucky. I'd be the perfect boyfriend. But it would be a crime against the world for me to settle down. And I can't give all of this away just yet." He leaned back into my couch with his arms crossed behind his head.

"Well, either way, Olive and I are done. She is more complicated than I thought, and I don't want to do long distance. She's better off just going back to Florida."

Coop scoffed and took a sip of his beer.

"What?" I asked.

"I just didn't take you for a quitter."

I shot up from my seat. "I am *not* a quitter."

He shrugged. "Okayyy, but you seem awfully lazy for letting a girl you love go just 'cause she's *complicated*."

"I am not lazy, I'm smart. I'm making the right decision by letting her go back. She'll realize it when she gets back home."

Without moving his eyes off the game, he said, "Whatever you say, man."

I leaned back into my seat and furrowed my brows. I *was* doing the right thing. Right?

THIRTY-EIGHT
OLIVE

Taylor and I had been binging true crime documentaries and scarfing down pastries since I got home from the lodge. I hadn't told her Finn and I broke up. I didn't even say a word to her when I got here. I simply walked to my room, left the door cracked and sat on my bed in hopes that she would know that meant I needed her help.

Thankfully, Taylor was my true soulmate, and she followed me in. Without speaking, she simply put on my favorite show and handed me a cream cheese croissant. After we sat like that for an entire episode, until she turned to me. "Do you want to talk about it?"

I picked at the edges of my pastry. "No. Yes. Maybe?"

"Are you guys still together?"

Were we *ever* together? Probably not, at least not in his mind. I was simply another tourist and considering how often women fawned over him with their sultry voices and exposed cleavage, he would have no trouble finding a replacement. The thought of him quickly bouncing to the next girl made me shiver.

But then I thought back to our nights alone together. How he whispered sweet things to me and made me feel so beautiful in my own skin. How all my insecurities flew out the window when I was with him. Like he'd found an off switch to the part of my brain that told me I didn't look good in white pants or that I ate too many sweets.

"Nope."

"I'm sorry, Olive. I know you really liked him." Her sincerity almost made me burst. I shrugged like it was a casual break-up. Another one bites the dust. There's plenty of fish in the sea. No biggie. I'm fine.

"Maybe you should get everything off your chest before you leave. It's going to hurt more the longer you hold it in."

Her suggestion made sense. I desperately wanted to scream at them, but I probably should've at least heard Sarah out since Logan gave me his side.

But I was far more upset with Sarah than Logan.

Both had betrayed me. I knew that well, but it had been a deeper treachery from Sarah. She was my best friend, my *sister*, and I never thought she'd hurt me. Boyfriends came and went, and I certainly hadn't thought I was going to marry Logan. I was upset with Logan, don't get me wrong, but he had betrayed a girl he'd known for less than a year. You expected your boyfriend to hurt you, but never the girl who'd been by your side your entire life.

But when I saw them together, I had been far more furious with Sarah than Logan. I could be in a room with Logan and pretend he never existed, but I would never forget the sister I once loved so dearly.

"I don't know if I can. The last twenty-four hours have been too much."

Taylor nodded and took a bite of her muffin. "I get it, maybe just take it into consideration before you go."

When she left to go home, I gave her a brief hug and thanked her for being there for me. I sunk further into my mattress once she'd gone. My mind ran like a computer with twenty tabs open: replaying the memories I once had with Sarah, wondering about what Finn was doing, thinking of flying home early, trying to finish up work—it all gave me a headache.

I went to the kitchen for a glass of water, pausing in the hallway and turning to the gallery of pictures on the wall. My gaze snagged on the different pictures of Sarah and me. When we were toddlers, chasing Matt around the backyard. When we were in middle school with home-cut bangs and too much eyeliner. Her high school graduation, where I was squeezing the life out of her.

I dragged my eyes to my favorite one. It was Sarah in my arms on Christmas morning, hugging after I had given her a Ron Weasley poster. She was smiling and had her eyes closed, while I was laughing at her obsession over the red-headed wizard.

I sucked in a breath and dipped my head as tears filled my eyes. It was all too much. I hadn't had enough time to process the last three years, much less the last two weeks. I still loved Sarah deeply, and that love wouldn't go away no matter what she did to me. But I wasn't sure if we could ever go back to normal, if I could look at her as my sister, my best friend instead of the girl who'd hurt me so badly.

I went back to bed without my water and pulled open my laptop. I searched for plane tickets and began packing.

She might be considered the prettier sister, but I was the best at running.

THIRTY-NINE
FINN

"What the hell are *you* doing here?"

I'd just finished my last class for the year, and I went to the lobby to grab lunch before packing up my locker for the next few days, when I saw a familiar face come into my view.

Logan.

Also known as the shithead I wanted to knock out. My hand flexed around my backpack strap. Realistically, he was smart for coming here because I couldn't kill him on work property.

"Please don't hit me." He eyed my white-knuckled fist. "I just wanted to talk to you for just a minute, and I swear I'll leave you both alone after."

You both. Meaning he had talked to Olive too. Curiosity piqued, I nodded my head to the busy cafe behind us. I needed witnesses around to stop me from smacking this idiot around.

We sat down without ordering; the sooner we were done, the better.

"Get it out already," I practically growled.

"Look, I don't expect you to understand, but I want you to know this isn't Olive's fault—"

"Oh, I *know* it isn't Olive's fault." I raised my voice enough for the lady beside us to look me up and down before turning back to her limp salad.

"I mean it isn't her fault for not telling you. You didn't know her before everything went down. She used to be so...lively. She smiled at everything and everyone. She never met a stranger. Everyone was her friend even if they only spoke twice. Olive was spirited, like she could never be stopped."

I wanted to punch him for acting like he knew her better than me. So, what if he knew her back then? He didn't know her *now*, not like I did.

"When we were together, she really was an amazing friend, and I did love her. Or I thought I did. But I fell in love with Sarah the moment I saw her, and it was something entirely different than I had with Olive."

"Or you fell in lust with her," I accused.

"Maybe that too. I'm not saying it makes it okay, but Sarah and I had a connection the second we met. And Olive was clueless to that connection. We went through dinner and hung out with everyone, and I went to bed and realized that what I felt with Sarah in mere hours, I had never felt with Olive."

"What's your point?"

"My point is that sometimes we don't get to choose who we fall in love with or how it happens. I don't expect you to understand, but you don't have to know someone for a long time to know you love them."

"So, that made it okay to cheat on her?" I hated to admit it, but he made sense. I hated that I knew *exactly* what he was saying because I felt all of that with Olive.

"Absolutely not. I will always regret what I did to Olive. I did love her, but as a friend more than anything. She never deserved that, and I have tried so many times to find a way to get her to forgive me—"

"She shouldn't," I mumbled. She deserved better than both of us.

"I'm telling you to not make the same mistake as me. I know you broke up with her, and I'm letting you know, don't let what you guys have go just because of a guy in her past. Yeah, she didn't tell you, but can you blame her?"

The thing was, I couldn't. I was the type to always say what was on my mind, but if two people I was close with betrayed me like that, I probably wouldn't have said anything either. I'd be too hurt and embarrassed as well.

"So why are you here?" I needed this conversation to be over. Hearing Olive's name, and thinking about her, made me miss her more.

"I'm here to say don't let a girl like Olive go just 'cause she didn't tell you what some idiot did to her three years ago."

I shrugged like this conversation was nothing. Like my heart didn't feel torn at the thought of Olive holding back from me. I thought we were something more, something *real*. Our time together had been brief, but there were enough moments for her to tell me—and part of me was so hung up on that.

I was vulnerable with her, sharing parts of me that I hadn't exposed to anyone in years. I was foolish to think she would have done the same for me. Olive was the type of woman to have a line of drooling men in front of her, and I had no doubts she'd do fine in a week when she was back to her usual schedule.

"Well, thanks for the advice and conversation, but I think I'm good. Olive will be back in Florida in a few days, and when she gets there she'll do just fine."

I grabbed my bag to stand up, but he shook his head and reached up to stop me. "You know Olive is leaving today, right?"

I stopped in my tracks. "What?"

Logan looked at me confused. "Olive bought a ticket to leave early. I figured she told you already?"

She was leaving? I knew she was going soon. I was prepared for that. But I thought I had a few days. I thought I had time before she left. The fact that Logan knew this before I did was even more upsetting.

"When does she leave?"

He checked the time on his phone that had a Colorado Avalanche case on it, which made me even more mad that I wanted to appreciate his merch. If things were different, Logan and I could be good friends. Instead, he was the idiot that cheated on the most incredible person I'd ever met. Then again, I was the idiot that let her go. Maybe we were meant to be friends after all. Two dumb guys with similar taste in women and commonly known to make relationship mistakes.

"Her flight's in an hour."

Of course it was. I was thirty minutes from the airport, and traffic was ridiculous. "Why didn't you lead with that?" I shouted, grabbing my keys and bag, ignoring his smug face as I raced out the door.

Maybe I was an idiot for thinking I didn't need Olive, but I wasn't going to be an even bigger one for letting her go without a fight.

FORTY
OLIVE

Did you know that the day before Christmas Eve is the busiest day in any airport? Me neither.

I discovered that the hard way.

I was stuck in the line for security that stretched across the airport. After an hour or more of waiting, I made it to my gate only to discover my flight was delayed. So I sat at an airport bar, a virgin margarita in my hand because apparently when I drank on planes, I ended up with a stranger as my fake boyfriend.

I checked my phone and refreshed my notifications for the hundredth time to see if I had any messages from Finn yet, but there was nothing. The ice in my drink clinked against the chilled glass as I stirred it. Conversations of holiday plans, upcoming weddings, babies being born, and deaths being mourned filled the air around me—but I felt empty. I missed Finn deeply after only one day, and I wasn't sure I could ever go back to my numb state of mind now that I had all those memories of our time together.

I would keep those moments close and save them for a rainy day. For now, they were all I had.

My phone buzzed against the wooden bar, and I snatched it up, hoping it was Finn. Disappointment fell when I saw it was only Matt. I sighed and answered. "Miss me already?" I wondered if my voice sounded as down as I felt.

He chuckled deeply, and it gave me a small slice of comfort. "You wish, kid." Even though I was only a few years younger than him, he would always treat me like the baby of the family. "Mom's kinda pissed that you didn't say goodbye to any of us."

I knew she would be. But saying goodbye made it all too real.

"I figured. She'll forgive me when I ship her that saltwater taffy she loves."

"So that's it then? You're just gone?" I heard Taylor in the background, and I smiled at the thought of her telling Matt what to say.

"Yup. Got everything ready to go, should be boarding in..." I checked the clock behind the bartender, "...about ten minutes."

I paid my tab and grabbed my carry-on, dreading the walk to my gate.

Matt sighed. "Do you think you'll ever come back over here?"

No. "Maybe."

"Now you know I can't just fly down there every time I want to see you. Those plane seats kill my back."

I laughed at his stubbornness. "Okay, Grandpa. Maybe we can meet halfway." A tear hit my cheek, surprising me. Why did it feel like I was saying goodbye to more than Finn and Aspen?

"Seriously, Olive. We know this was a hard trip, but don't let it make you feel like you can't come back. I think Mom was the happiest she has been in years. Seeing you here? Man, she lit up." He paused. "Even though I'm still the favorite."

I laughed through my tears. "Well, I'm boarding now, so I have to go, but I'll talk to you later, right?" I sniffled and hoped it was quiet enough for him to not notice.

"Text us when you land. We love you, kid."

I nodded and said a quiet, "love you," trying to hold it together enough to board. I walked down the bridge, my ticket clutched in one hand, and my bag on my shoulder. I prayed I could get back home without second-guessing my last-minute flight.

Even if I hopped off this plane right now and ran into Finn's arms screaming that I loved him and I was so sorry for deceiving him, would he care? Would he want me back? Would he eventually grow to love me the way I loved him?

I knew the answers. And they weren't the ones I wanted. So I boarded my flight, shuffling along the narrow aisle until I reached my row. When I did, I shoved my bag in the overhead compartment. An overwhelming sense of déjà vu hit me, and I pictured the last flight I was on—pushing too-big luggage into a too-small compartment. The memory almost made me laugh. Almost.

I took my seat and looked out the window at the snow that fell. It was a picture-perfect Christmas in Aspen, like a snow globe came to life, full of lights and cheer. I knew one thing was true: Finn taught me to love Christmas again. And although I may be leaving almost as broken as I'd arrived, I would cherish the fact that he helped this Grinch's heart grow three sizes.

I sunk into my seat and leaned back. A child across from me screamed, and the passenger behind me repeatedly kicked my seat. I sighed and reached down for my headphones and the eye mask that the airplane provided, but when I went to grab them, I noticed they were both gone. It was the straw that broke the camel's back. I'm unsure if it was the overstimulation of babies screaming, crammed seats, kicking in my back, and the throbbing pulse in my throat, but something in that moment broke me. I tilted my head down, my blonde hair falling to cover my face. Tears viciously fell down my freckled cheeks and onto my yoga pants, soaking my lap. I sniffled and didn't care if anyone was staring at me. They were probably all going home to family while I was leaving mine.

Everything I had was crumbling, and in that moment with tear-soaked pants and tangled hair, I had never felt so alone.

It wasn't until I heard a voice I knew well that I lifted my head. My favorite person sat next to me, my favorite smirk lighting his face. My mouth gaped, but no words escaped it.

"Anxious flier?"

FORTY-ONE
FINN

When I found Olive, her blonde hair a curtain around her face, shoulders shaking with sobs, I nearly broke. The fact that she was as torn up over our break up as I was nearly made me smile. The shock on her face made sprinting like Forrest Gump through the airport completely worth it.

"What are you—"

"I love you." There I said it. Now I knew if I didn't have another moment with her, at least she knew the truth. Olive's expression remained shocked, so I continued. "I don't care that it's only been a couple of weeks. Truth is I am utterly, insanely in love with you, and," I huffed out a small laugh, "I don't care. I know that it's crazy. But the thing is, Olive, I don't want easy, or simple. I want absolutely crazy, and I want it all with you."

Olive opened her mouth. "Finn."

I held a hand up to stop her. "Just listen. I should be upset that you lied to me. That you hid all your baggage from me. But truthfully, it means nothing. That moment of pain I felt was miniscule compared to the love I have for you. And I swear I will be that old man at the dinner table telling our story to our great-grandkids for the hundredth time because I want them to know I found the love of my life in a matter of two weeks. So, I would gladly claim all your baggage if it meant you would be mine."

I took a breath after my rant, light-headed from my sprint through the airport and my confessions.

She smiled. "Are you done?"

Immediately I said, "No." Then, "Wait, yes."

Olive's chuckle blessed my ears, a sound I wondered if I'd ever hear again. "I love you, Finn." She placed a warm hand over mine. "I am so glad you're here. I can't believe how much I missed you already." She shook her head, her smile brightening her round, wet cheeks. I instinctively wiped her tears with my sleeve.

"So, we're doing this then?" She asked quietly.

I grinned. "You've always been mine in my mind."

We sat there like love-sick idiots, and I leaned down to plant a kiss on her perfect lips. Lips that I would gladly spend the rest of my life mesmerized by.

I nodded my head to the plane exit. "Come on, let's go before they—"

A familiar ding came from the speaker. "Please fasten your seat belts as we prepare for takeoff."

Olive let out a small laugh and leaned closer. "Just more time we get to spend together. Time to fall more in love."

I let out a deep breath and leaned into my seat. "I couldn't love you more if I tried, you know," I said.

She was everything. I took her hand in mine, and I leaned into our joint seats, not caring in the slightest bit that they were incredibly small. She was here, with me, and that's all I cared about.

FORTY-TWO
OLIVE

Thankfully, Finn and I easily scheduled a flight back to Aspen right when we landed in West Palm. He claimed it was due to his good luck, and I didn't disagree. We happily spent almost nine hours on planes together, not paying any attention to our surroundings. We spent the time talking about anything and everything. We joked about what it would be like when we got back home, how excited Mom and Taylor would be. I cried when Finn and I opened up about our truths in our pasts. We talked about me being able to let loose on my eating habits and knowing that sometimes an extra slice of pie is alright. Finn made plans for us to work on it together, trying to find healthy and well-balanced diets that supported my weight loss journey in a way that wasn't toxic. Finn held my hand as he spoke about his parents, telling me what it was like to be an only child and the vacations they went on together. I admired how he smiled through his stories, like he couldn't hold in the excitement.

It was the best Christmas Eve morning ever.

And when we *finally* got back to Aspen, after Finn showered and changed clothes, we went straight to my house. It was early morning, barely nine. Between the two flights, we'd stayed up all night, and although we were exhausted, neither of us cared one bit.

I poured us both a cup of coffee, and we sat in the living room waiting for my parents to get up. I knew Mom planned to have everyone over for lunch like usual, so we cuddled under a blanket on the couch and put on *Rudolph the Red-Nosed Reindeer*. The last two weeks hardly seemed real, like I would wake up back in my small apartment in Florida and that Finn would be a fictional being that my mind conjured in a fever dream. But I was cuddled next to him, my head happily laid on his chest with our arms wrapped around each other as he whispered sweet nothings in my ear and trailed a light hand down my back. My hair was a knotted mess on my head, and my makeup was completely gone. But Finn didn't care, simply looked at me like I was the most beautiful girl in the world.

I was reminded of something he'd said before.

"If you were mine, you'd never wonder how perfect you are."

The memory had me smiling, and I leaned further into his hold.

After getting no sleep in almost twenty-four hours, we fell asleep in a nest of fuzzy comforters, and I felt like I was on cloud nine.

***

"I knew he would bring her back to me."

"Shh. Be still, you'll wake them up."

"It's almost noon, Denise. It's time they get up anyway."

"Do you guys think I should grow a mullet?"

"Hush, Matt."

The familiar loud whispers woke me from my dreams, which featured backpacking across Europe with Finn. I blinked open my eyes and rubbed them, finding Mom, Dad, Matt, and Taylor standing over me and Finn. Mom's phone faced us, obviously taking pictures of us cuddled together and passed out.

"Mmm. What?" Finn sat up next to me, and I was sure we looked like a pair of sleepy toddlers woken up for snack time.

"Get up, love birds. It's noon, and you're taking up the whole couch."

I shrugged the warm blankets off of us and stretched my arms up. Taylor grinned so wide her cheeks had to hurt, and she glanced suggestively between Finn and me.

I retreated to my room to get ready for our Christmas Eve lunch while I left Finn in the living room with my family, like a sheep in a room full of wolves. They would no doubt ask him a million questions about how he got me back here. I'd be willing to bet he would say something like, "I guess she just couldn't deal without me."

I snorted to myself at the thought. After a much-needed shower, Finn's voice intertwined with laughter from down the hall as I got ready, and I sighed in comfort. It was funny how different things were from the last time Finn was here, from when he threatened Logan and stormed out, to now laughing and joking with my family again.

A knock came at my door, and assuming it was Taylor or Finn, I shouted, "Come in!"

With a curling iron in my hand and humming to the tune of *I'll Be Home for Christmas*, I looked at the reflection of my mirror to find Sarah standing shyly at the door. I knew it would be awkward when I had to face Logan and Sarah eventually, but I wasn't sure how uncomfortable it would be.

I quieted my hums when she stepped further into my bathroom. I sat on a small stool, the same stool I used to sit on with her when we got ready for events together.

"Hey, Liv," she said quietly.

"Hey," I whispered, not meeting her eyes.

"Um. Your hair is burning." She pointed to the smoking iron.

"Crap," I whispered and quickly freed my hair from the wand.

"Here, let me do it." I dropped my tense shoulders and let her take over my hair. It was like high school all over again. Getting ready for double dates or trips to the mall to buy too many Bath & Body Works candles.

We sat in silence while she worked. I flickered my gaze up to her face, and for the first time since I'd been back, I noticed the changes since I saw her that day three years ago. Her hair was longer and her face a little brighter. She had small dark circles under her eyes, and her lips sat in a natural pout. She was as beautiful as everyone claimed her to be; she truly looked like an angel. And no amount of backstabbing would change that.

"Hold this." She handed me a piece of my own long hair, and I rolled my eyes and grabbed it.

"Last time I did this your hair was a lot shorter," she mumbled, and my lips twitched.

"That's 'cause last time you did this you were helping me get ready to go to orientation, and I thought getting a bob would make me look more mature."

We snickered at the memory, and I felt lighter than I had in years. It wasn't much, simply a sister curling another sister's hair, but it was us. It made me feel like maybe one day she would be my old Sarah again.

She sighed with a smile and let down another curl. "How did we get here, Olive?"

I answered as honestly and abruptly as I could. "You slept with my boyfriend." It felt good to say it out loud.

She winced. "Well, I know that...I guess it was a rhetorical question."

She refocused on her task as she spoke. "I wish you knew how many times I tried to tell you what happened that night."

It was my turn to wince. "I don't want to know."

"No, I don't mean like what happened during it, I meant before. How I couldn't stop looking at Logan all night at dinner, how every time our eyes met I felt shaken to my core." She sighed. "I didn't *want* to like him, Olive. I would never purposefully do that to you, you know that. I simply couldn't stop. I don't know how to explain it. It was like he was a magnet to me, and I felt our pull instantly. I told myself all night long that I was just imagining it, and I had got up to go drive around when I ran into him in the kitchen. We talked for almost an hour before you came in there, and I don't know, Liv. It was like love at first sight. I know you don't understand because you've never had something like that happen to you but when it does…you just know."

The recollection of that night filled me with sorrow, but the worst part was she was wrong. I *did* know what that was like. I *did* understand, because I found myself falling for a man in a matter of days and forming a connection with him over such a small period of time.

I sighed and slumped. "I'm not saying it's okay, but I get it. I'm still pissed at you both, but not because you hooked up. But because you both knew me well enough to know I would've stepped aside. I would've never picked a man above you, Sarah."

She nodded and tilted her chin down. "I know that now. And Olive, I'm so unbelievably sorry. It was not okay, and it never will be. But I can't say I wish I never met him because he is everything to me. He is so funny and smart, and when he smiles his dimple—"

"You know I dated him too, right? I know all of that." I smirked up at her.

She let out a puff of air. "Right."

"He was my friend first, my truest friend. I guess we went into dating because it felt right, but I never had that with Logan. That passion and fire. It was more like friends with benefits than actually dating."

Which is why I couldn't understand why neither of them had simply talked to me and told me what was happening. That was what had me caught up for years.

Sarah nodded and finished up my hair. She pinned it in place, stood back, and smiled at her masterpiece; my hair looked better than it had in years. I gave her a small smile. We weren't back to normal, but it was something, and I would gladly take it.

I stood up and wrapped my sister in a hug. "I don't forgive you. I'm just not there yet. But I will one day. I know you made a mistake, but you're still my sister."

Sarah didn't answer, instead let her arms drape around me as her shoulders and chest shook. I held her through her sobs, and she eventually hugged me back.

"Alright, now let's go make sure Finn isn't killing your husband."

She laughed and wiped her tears. It was one small step forward. A step I would gladly take with her.

FORTY-THREE
FINN

Three months later

It was a big day.

I had officially got Olive to agree to go skiing with me again.

For almost three months straight, I had begged her to meet me at work and to let me teach her proper techniques, but she brushed it off or faked an illness—as if I didn't know that trick already. But today was my birthday, and when I pulled that card out, how could she refuse me? I guess my good luck continued.

She'd brought her own equipment and was clearly anxious while she got ready. She had moved in with me almost immediately after I caught up with her on the plane three months ago. I told her we could try long distance if she wanted to stay in the warm weather and work there. I would gladly fly back and forth for her. But immediately after I offered, she said she wouldn't want to be anywhere other than Aspen with me. The Moore men and I flew to Florida to help her move out of her apartment and get back where she belonged: in the mountains with me.

Watching her get ready in the mornings was my favorite. The bathroom was adjacent to my bedroom, and I could lie back on my mountain of pillows and watch her apply makeup and do her hair while she moved her hips to whatever music she was playing. It was one of my favorite pastimes. But this morning, she spent that time anxiously posing what-if questions while she pulled her hair back into two thick braids.

What if I get stuck on the lift thingy and we get separated?
What if I fall and break my neck?
What if we get lost in the woods?

I happily answered each and smiled as she nervously picked the ends of her braids. I loved when she was a little scared. When she was nervous, she clung to me like a spider monkey, and I *lived* for it. I'd flex my bicep and stroke her hair while she wrapped her small body around me.

Don't worry, babe. Finn would protect you.

It stroked my ego a little too much, but she never seemed to mind.

Alea caught us in the lobby and offered to show Olive how it was done. She actually said, "Since you probably won't do it right, I better come along." So, she hopped on the lift behind us along with Coop, and I could only imagine the torture she was subjecting him to.

Olive kept looking down at the snow and back up to the cables.

"You remember the last time we were up here?" I asked to distract her from the steep drop to the snow, nearly fifty feet below.

She chuckled and looked at me. "Oh, yeah. *Here, Olive, let me fix your goggles.*" She imitated my deep voice and gestured her hands to my face.

I laughed loudly and threw back my head. "It felt smooth at the time." I shrugged.

"I guess it worked a little bit." She leaned into my hold, and I smirked at her.

I had to give it to Coop—his moves worked out pretty well.

"What else could I have done? I had the most beautiful woman in the world on a bench with me, and I wasn't supposed to not make a move?"

Olive's cheeks pinkened and chuckled. I loved that I could still make her blush every time I spoke about how beautiful she was to me. My awe-striking Olive. My Grinch. She still hated when I called her that, but I couldn't help it. Although, I think Olive liked Christmas more than me these days.

I turned around to see Cooper mouthing, "help," as Alea actively ran her mouth—presumably about how much she knew about skiing. I laughed and turned my attention back to the girl I loved.

We were approaching the peak of where we had to hop off, and Olive tensed next to me.

"Hey," I said quietly, and she lifted her head and looked up at me. "Just follow me?" I grabbed her hands, and she nodded.

We jumped off the lift and slowly glided down the hill, exactly as I had done thousands of times. Olive looked down at her skis, and I turned so she could see me. "Eyes up, sweetheart." She raised those perfect green eyes up to me, and I could've melted in the snow. "Just relax," I spoke over the wind.

Olive nodded, and I let go of her as she released the tension in her body.

I smiled and jerked my head to the bottom of the hill. Alea and Coop passed us, and Coop waved. Alea matched my speed and said to Olive, "Straighten your feet!"

Little show off.

Olive breathed deeply and pointed her skis as Alea said. She grinned ever so slightly at me and loosened up her grip on the skis, letting herself naturally slide down the snowy hill. She was doing it. And I couldn't remember a time I had ever been so proud of anyone.

"That's it, babe! Keep coming." I sped up to get her coming down faster. She followed my lead, laughing loudly as she went faster.

"I'm doing it!" She shouted at me, and I couldn't help but laugh.

We were on a children's hill, people flying by us left and right. The ten-year-old girl beside me had done this a hundred times, but my Olive was effortlessly gliding down like a natural. We laughed and smiled until we reached the bottom. I stopped and lifted her in the air, her hips over my shoulder and her skis almost hitting me, shouting as I did.

"My girlfriend can ski!" I pointed to her sitting on my shoulder. Tourists stared at us like we were crazy, but I didn't care.

She laughed against me and said, "Put me down, Finland." I approved her request and plopped her into the snow with a kiss on her tiny red nose.

Alea rolled her eyes, "Remind me to never date when I'm older," I heard her groan to Coop, and I laughed.

We convinced Olive to go again and again until we were sore and exhausted from climbing and skiing. I was ecstatic. Nothing compared to this moment. Me with my little Grinch.

EPILOGUE
OLIVE

One month later

" Come on!"

"Get the puck, watch the puck!"
"Use the wall!"

Finn, Matt, and my dad were on their feet beside us, screaming at the men on the ice. My Christmas gift to Finn was tickets to an Avalanche game. He'd never admit it, but he cried when he opened them.

I bought three tickets, but when he realized I hadn't included myself, he immediately purchased one more for me. He said, "Not worth going if you're not there," which absolutely enchanted me.

The game was full of fights and shouting, which made the twenty-three percent of enneagram type two in me violently uncomfortable. They also played a celebrity look-alike game at breaks. It was hilarious to all of us until Matt popped up next to a picture of Miles Teller with his identical mustache. Matt's smile fell, and he said, "Pssh. I don't even look like him." He pouted in the next seat over. He *wished* he looked like Miles Teller.

The game was shorter than expected, so when we all left to head our separate ways, I felt as though the night was still so young. I looked over at Finn, who was talking to my dad about one of the players. They were spewing stats and laughing as they made fun of one of the coaches. I sighed in comfort watching the two of them.

"It's about time you get what you deserve." I heard Matt quietly mumble next to me.

I turned to my brother and smiled. "I think so, too."

A small, miniscule twinge of guilt raced through me at not inviting the only other male in our family to the game. Truth be told, I still don't think I could leave Finn in a room alone with him without someone ending up with a black eye, so it probably was for the best.

As far as Sarah went, things with her still weren't back to normal, and I wasn't sure when or if they ever would be. But I could be in a room with my whole family and not feel out of place, and I thought that was enough for now. All of it was thanks to Finn, the hot, albeit slightly irritating, stranger I met on a red-eye. If it weren't for him, I would still be in Florida, wasting away my days alone.

Finn shook Dad's hand and gave Matt a quick bro hug before putting a strong arm around my shoulders. We walked toward his car, and I smiled up at him.

"Where to now?"

"Anywhere you want, Grinchy. I'm there."

I knew then, fate was always on my side.

THE END.

Looking for more Finn and Olive? I have an extended epilogue where you can see what Finn planned for their twelve days of Christmas one year later! Sign-up for this is available in the link in my bio on my Instagram, @author.juliana.smith.

Also by Juliana Smith:

I Can Fix That

THANK YOU!

I have so many people I want to thank for their help through my second book but first I want to say a big thanks to all of you! I have been absolutely blown away by all of the love and support that my debut novel received. I have learned so much from the time I released I Can Fix That in comparison to releasing Baggage Claim, and I believe that shows in the comparison of these two books.

My biggest thank you goes to my girls- the burnt pancakes. Madison, Kelsey, and Amanda, you guys are INCREDIBLE. I am so blessed to be surrounded by such talented authors and I love our friendship dearly. Here's to poorly made friendship bracelets and good Mexican food.

Emma, thank you for every late-night answer to my stupid questions. You are such an incredible friend and I am so so blessed to know you!

Sam, thank you for making my cover dreams come to life! You never cease to blow my mind. Can't wait to work with you again and again!

All my ARC and beta readers, thank you so much for taking the time to read this book and giving back incredible reviews and feedback. I love you all dearly,

Justin, thank you for loving me since I was 17 and for being my rock. You are such an incredible dad and husband and I could never do this without you.

And as always: to all my El Le Juan girls, I don't say it enough but I love each of you more than you will ever know. Thank you for always being there.

ABOUT THE AUTHOR

Juliana Smith is an author in a small town in Alabama. She is a full-time realtor, and part-time author, but she spends a lot of her time with her husband and daughter. Juliana writes heartfelt romance filled with laughter and some warm fuzzies. She can usually be found in a Chic-fil-a drive-thru or listening to Star Wars theory podcasts, often at the same time.

To subscribe to her super amazing newsletter and receive VIP behind the scenes, special offers, and exclusives go to her Instagram @author.juliana.smith .

Made in the USA
Las Vegas, NV
13 December 2022